THE CRANBURY PAPERMAKER

MAUREEN LANG

Check out the latest from Maureen Lang at www.maureenlang.com

The Cranbury Papermaker

Book One in the ***Cranbury Chronicles***

Copyright © Maureen Lang, 2015 All Rights Reserved

eBook ISBN: 978-1-943210-01-5

Print ISBN: 978-1-943210-00-8

591 Press P.O. Box 23 Belvidere, IL 61008

591 Press Logo Image courtesy of the Early Office Museum (officemuseum.com)

Edited by Rachelle Rea

❀ Created with Vellum

PROLOGUE

Cranbury, Pennsylvania
1886

"Tell me again, Papa. Tell me how we came to be papermakers."

Arianne Casterton lay back on her pillow, knowing if she offered a smile Papa was more apt to tell the tale she most loved to hear. The story of those who came before her told Arianne where she must go, and having just reached her seventh birthday she wanted to know what her future held.

"A long, long time ago, in the old country across the ocean," began her father in the tranquil, English voice so often a pathway to Arianne's best dreams, "a young man told his father he had no wish to be a farmer, even though every generation as long as either could remember had been just that. To his surprise, his father said he never wanted to be a farmer, either, but hadn't learned to do anything else. So the man told his son to set out for adventure, and learn a trade he could enjoy for the rest of his life.

"Kissed by his mother, respected by his father, the boy marched off proudly as so few other young men did in those days. He traveled far from home, to places those from his hamlet never knew existed. Wherever he went, he learned something new. He learned to worship God in languages he'd never heard before. He grew in compassion for those who suffer because he saw sorrow in every land. He grew in courage to defend righteousness because unrighteousness was everywhere, too. But what could he learn to make his way in life? What should he be? He couldn't be a wanderer forever.

"After many prayers for guidance, he came across a man who was doing a most peculiar thing. With a long, wide paddle he was beating plants to a pulp! Why should this man do such a thing? Did he mash it because he had no teeth to bite into such leafage? Did he crush the plants to be rid of them from his land, a scourge that threatened his crop? Curious, he asked the man why he treated the plants so harshly. The man laughed with the joy of one who knows his purpose. 'I am a papermaker!' he proclaimed. He shared his craft and even before he'd finished, the boy knew the work he would bring home. He became the first Casterton papermaker.

"Since then, Castertons have made sacred paper for Bibles—only the finest quality to be worthy of the Word of God. And we've made practical paper for schools and important paper of many colors for everything from birth announcements to death cards. We've made paper strong and durable for the armies of our homelands and their war plans. Some of our paper has been made from secret recipes for bank notes so no one can copy them. Our paper is even beautiful enough to carry love letters and sketches, part of God's gift of art in words or pictures. We've made paper in Europe and now here in America, too, since I brought our trade here. I learned from my father, just as he learned from his."

"And now I'm learning, too!"

"You're learning well, little one. And with your drawings and strong fingers, you will be a watermark artisan, too. I've seen your talent already, the same I saw in your grandmother-God-rest-her-soul." He always called Arianne's grandmother that, as if it were one long name. Then he raised a palm and let his gaze catch hers, a gaze so blue it stood out after a day's work had darkened his skin. "You are a papermaker."

CHAPTER ONE

Cranbury, Pennsylvania
Twelve Years Later

Arianne held her father's purest white paper up to the light just as Cranbury's church bell clanged. The sound startled her because a little after ten o'clock in the morning was no time for bells, but the noise stopped after just two rings.

"Probably the wind," said Phoebe Turner, who worked with Arianne in her father's stationery shop.

Dismissing whatever meager warning the bell could have been, Arianne held up the paper again. The light revealed her watermark, created as a special order for the closest thing to Pennsylvanian aristocracy Cranbury had ever seen: Eliot Wardman.

She smiled at the imprint, a smile she offered more easily to the image than to the man. It was Eliot Wardman . . . and yet it wasn't. Having worked with enough wealthy customers to know they wanted less a mirror image than a subtly improved version, she was satisfied she'd found the right balance. His chin was slightly more chiseled, the eyes not quite so small as in real life, the brows—while thoroughly Wardman, so thick—did not take over the likeness yet balanced one brow against the other. The nose was sharp and true to the man, minus the bump that so handily offered a place for the spectacles he sometimes wore, at least when examining a bill of sale. Mrs. Wardman had not allowed spectacles to be included in the watermark.

In the lowest corner was another watermark: a tiny Casterton dove identifying where the paper had been made. Not in Philadelphia or New York or Boston but right here in Cranbury, Pennsylvania, with the extraordinary pulp of Egyptian rags, processed slowly and gently for strength and durability. Her father ran the single vat factory by himself, except for the occasional help of Leo Levick, the young carpenter. They produced two hundred fifty pounds of paper every day, unless her father made special paper that took more time, for the Wardmans or other rich Williamsport families. Those who could afford it were attracted by the whiteness achieved from those Egyptian rags or the purest cotton from the American south. Occasionally they wanted colors from her father's Turkish dyes, or sometimes customers sought their paper simply because of the unique and detailed Casterton watermarks.

Satisfied with the product, Arianne added the page back to the stack of two hundred forty-nine others just like it before turning to Phoebe. Though not a Casterton, Phoebe possessed nearly the same love for paper and its related products as Arianne herself. Even now, she carefully dusted the one- and two-ounce clear flint glass bottles of perfumed boudoir ink in the three colors they offered: lilac, green or black. Above the ink shelf hung an inscription of Lord Byron's: A Drop Of Ink May Make A Million Think.

"This must go to the printer, Phoebe." Arianne placed her hand on the stack of watermarked stationery ready for its final touch. "Mr. Pillifant said he would get straight to the inscription. Of course, Mrs. Wardman will want to see it before she presents it to her husband, so wrap it only with a loose ribbon."

With her last word came another ring of the church bell. Curious, she exchanged glances with Phoebe who approached the end of the polished walnut counter, offering a lifted brow of amusement. "You don't suppose Gideon snuck into the church again to ring those bells and cause a stir?"

"He's getting a bit too old for pranks, I think." Arianne straightened a row of stacked papers along the countertop, samples of everything from onionskin to Bristol board. She refused to be alarmed by the sound in case it stopped as quickly as last time.

The stationery shop was quiet this morning, not surprising so early in the day. But when the church bell rang a third time, it lasted too long for someone not to have caught any errant boy.

Arianne had walked only half the length of the shop toward the door before it opened from the outside, the excited jingle of the shop's own bell now competing with the louder ringing down the lane.

"Miss Arianne! Come quick!" Gideon Greene, errand boy for nearly every shopkeeper in Cranbury, hung on to the door without stepping inside. "There's a disaster! I heard ol' Tummers say so."

Arianne's heart picked up a beat. Tummers had taken her father and Charlotte to the train station in Williamsport early that morning, and mustn't have been back for long. What kind of disaster?

She drew up her skirts and chased after Gideon, leaving Phoebe, who was a dozen years older, behind, not caring in the least that ladies of their standing in town should never run.

"Train wreck!"

The two words echoed in all directions once Arianne reached the end of the street. Rather than immediate panic, the words numbed her, as if to forestall her worst possible fears.

But that numbness was only a moment's postponement of the terror that settled on her chest. Which train had crashed? Had Tummers heard about it when he'd first dropped off her father and Charlotte? Or . . . after he'd left the station? Her eager gaze swept past Tummers, thinking her travelers had returned with him, their trip unavoidably delayed.

But the Herdic carriage everyone called the Canary because of its bright yellow paint was alarmingly empty. Her father and Charlotte weren't there.

"Tummers!" she shouted, but he hadn't seen her. Arianne shouldered her way through her friends and neighbors, beyond the reach of Phoebe who'd caught up, not heeding the call of Binny, her maid who must have followed from the kitchen. Each step took her closer to Tummers, yet he never turned her way.

"Tummers!" she called again.

At last Tummers saw her, and Arianne's heart, so battered already by fear, sunk to impossible depths. His face held the horror of fearsome news. She stopped cold, stiffening as if to prepare for a strike.

"You'd best come back to Williamsport with me, miss," Tummers said, in a voice far too calm. "They're sayin' that's where the . . . the . . . victims will be brought to the hospital."

Arianne didn't trust her own voice. She simply followed Tummers to his carriage, barely trusting her legs.

"I'll ride ahead," called Phipps, the town's only newspaperman and photographer. He stuffed his cartridge Kodak in his saddlebag then kicked his horse into a gallop. He was gone before Arianne climbed through the back door entry of the Canary.

The concerned stares of the entire town penetrated the cab windows. Everyone knew her father had taken Charlotte with him, his bride of only a few months, even though it was a business trip. They were to be gone only a few days. Just a quick trip to Philadelphia—then back.

Leta Perkins, who ran the Cranbury dress shop near Arianne's stationery store, called out.

"Wait! Wait for me!"

Tummers slowed the horse that had already begun pulling the Canary on its way. Without waiting for assistance, Leta boarded the cab and plopped herself beside Arianne.

"But the shop—" Arianne's protest was as empty as her wish to leave Leta behind.

"Ingrid can take care of things on her own," Leta said, grabbing one of Arianne's hands and clutching it tight.

Arianne cast herself into Leta's waiting arms. "Now, now, Ari," Leta whispered. "We don't know what we're worrying about yet, do we? They could be perfectly fine."

But even Leta didn't sound hopeful.

———

Jonas Prestwich rubbed his thumb across the corner of the stationery. The words so flawlessly written had haunted him ever since arriving from a little place called Cranbury. But for the first time in two days, his skin registered the softness of the paper. Inviting to the touch, yet durable enough to withstand his near constant fingering. He'd even crumpled it in a moment of anger not long after receiving it, but the paper defied his attack by gently opening again, as if to restore itself to an original unsullied state.

She would arrive in Philadelphia that afternoon. And this evening, if he wished, she would come to see him at his home. She hadn't called it her home, though that's what it had once been. She'd then added, as if the suggestion had horrified her as much as it should have, perhaps he might prefer coming to the Hotel Walton where they would be staying.

It was the "they" that grated on Jonas, even now. Mother and *her husband*, the man for whom she'd left Jonas's father.

Something in him still rushed to her defense, resisting the accusation. That was likely why she wanted to see him, to ease her guilty conscience. Or defend herself against what she must think he believed. What everyone she left behind in Philadelphia believed.

Either way, he wasn't at all sure he wanted to see her. Not yet.

Besides, he was expected to dine at the Kitteridge home tonight. He might easily miss the dinner, except Kitteridge's daughter Julia, more than anyone else, had made sure Jonas hadn't drowned in the scandal his mother created. He hated to disappoint her.

Jonas placed the paper on his desk, smoothing it once again. He'd been sitting here for hours. The clock in the hall outside his father's library—his library now—chimed eleven. He had until this evening to make up his mind, and time wouldn't slow despite his indecision.

This evening. Which parent would he betray? His mother, or the memory of his father?

CHAPTER TWO

An uproar surrounded the Williamsport train station. Confused passengers and curious spectators got in the way of townsfolk rescuers who shouted orders right and left. A wagon waited to transport victims, and another had just pulled away.

Before the Canary came to a stop, Arianne jumped from its back. A man in a railroad uniform stood near the track as if looking for something. Arianne ran to him, but her gaze caught on people emerging from the woods alongside the tracks. Searchers? Survivors?

She scrutinized the harrowed faces, some lined with tears, with clothing askew. None were her father or Charlotte.

Arianne turned to the man in a stationmaster's cap. She wasted no time with niceties. "Was it the Express?"

He spared her little more than an annoyed glance and a nod. "Step out of the way, miss."

"My father was aboard!"

He pointed to a young man in a suit, waiting beside the wagon alongside the station house. "Wounded are being brought back on the pushcart and taken to the hospital. You can ask him if they've come up yet."

Leta and Tummers were already at her side, and kept up with

her dash to the man near the wagon. A quick description of her father and Charlotte brought nothing but a shake of the head.

"That's good news, then," Leta said, squeezing Arianne's hand. "They're probably on their way back right now."

She wanted to taste that first hint of hope, telling herself they might have purposefully chosen to stay at the wreck. Her father would consider it his duty to help others, and Charlotte wasn't likely to leave his side. How could they know she was here, frantically waiting for them?

If the accident had happened where they said, at the horseshoe, she knew it snaked through forest and hill. It was usually the most thrilling part of any ride southeast from Williamsport. But it was probably quite a bit farther on foot.

She'd no sooner started out anyway before spotting what the stationmaster must have been waiting for. A two-man handcart came into view, the men laboring over each end of a see-saw handle, while on the wide platform around their feet were people wrapped in blankets. Her breath caught at the sight of bloodstains blossoming on the striped wool.

Movement from behind Arianne quickened. The man tending the wagon yelled for help, and others she hadn't even noticed rushed to and fro, some toward the pushcart to transport the wounded and others to board the emptying cart with more folded blankets and buckets. In moments, the wounded were taken away, and no sooner was the platform empty than it was filled again.

In one leap Arianne forced her way aboard, grabbing the arm of a sturdy but stunned man in workman's clothing. When the cart lurched forward her instinct proved true: he had no choice but to keep hold of her if he didn't want to see her hurt, too.

"Hey, there!" cried the stationmaster, but the pushcart operators took no time to wait. They sailed along the rails so fast she would have been afraid had her fear not been swallowed up in terror for her father and Charlotte.

Arianne dared not even look at anyone else aboard. They were all strong men, worthy of their space aboard this cramped little vehicle. She didn't even look back at Leta or Tummers.

She just closed her eyes and prayed.

It wasn't long before the pushcart slowed. Over the squeaking brakes she heard the noise of more men, and banging in the distance. Some of those aboard jumped free of the cart before it stopped altogether, freeing the view before her.

Whatever fire had erupted was already out, leaving in its wake the charred ruin of the back end of an engine. Her first genuine spurt of hope sprang up at the sight. If the fire had been contained to the engine, surely no passengers had been burned!

The man whose arm she'd clung to all the way from the station took the time to help her alight, but that was the only courtesy he offered. He chased the others with an armful of blankets and buckets without looking back at her, headed in the same direction as everyone else.

The eager hope Arianne had allowed herself vanished as she neared the rails. Two cars, one atop the other, lay like giant toys down the embankment. More victims were being brought up on blankets, while others hovered nearby to lend assistance.

She searched for her father or someone to ask about him, but no one appeared in charge. So she went to the huddled group nearest the edge of the forest—survivors, likely, from the dazed looks on their faces, the unkempt hair and clothing. For whatever reason they seemed unwilling to leave the scene, looking past Arianne as if they couldn't take their eyes from what they'd just escaped.

"Is there . . . are there any dead?" She hadn't meant to ask that, she'd only wanted to know if anyone saw her father. But it was the one question she most dreaded to voice, and even more dreaded to have answered.

But no one addressed her question, as if all, collectively, had lost any ability to speak.

"Answer me! Are there any dead?"

One man nodded, then like a ghoul impervious to death

himself, he pointed, this time behind them, nearer the trees and bushes razed by the falling cars to the floor of the wooded hill.

Arianne set out to move, but someone gripped her arm, stalling her. It was the man who had pointed. "You'd best wait here, along with us."

She wrenched her arm free. "I'm looking for my father."

Then she walked toward the spot he'd indicated, and saw the covered mounds of two bodies. No one tended them, watched over them, acknowledged them. And why should they? It was only the living who needed any help.

Arianne's footsteps slowed. Not since her own mother had died had Arianne seen any deceased body outside of a church burial service. And that, more than ten years since. Her mother had died in her parents' bed, after a sickness that had shrunken her to skin and bones.

Surely the first body couldn't be her father; it was too slight. Nor could it be Charlotte, or the puffed sleeves of her lovely traveling suit would have drawn a different shape for the blanket to outline.

Perhaps it was that, knowing it could be neither, that allowed her the courage to pull back the blanket.

"Oh . . ." What little courage she had drained away at the sight of a young man, barely any older than herself, his eyes peacefully closed.

Gently, she covered him again, almost apologizing for disturbing him as if he were merely asleep.

She didn't want to look at the second body. Her father was a tall man, broad of shoulders, lean from years of working over the vat. Power from the river might have turned the wheels to mash the pulp and polish the pages, but his own constant movement playing all parts in the process—vatman, coucher, layman, presser —hadn't allowed anything but muscle to build upon his bones.

Still, she couldn't *not* look. The first body had been neither charred nor singed, showing no trace of damage from the fire. It couldn't be so very hard to pull back this second blanket, just to assure herself it was not him.

Her hand shook as it hadn't done the first time. There was something about the contour, the square shoulders, the length of the legs. She knew it wasn't a woman beneath that cover.

Slowly, she tugged on the blanket, but stopped just as the shoulder was revealed. How could she not recognize it? Her father's Sunday best. He never traveled in anything less.

Arianne fell to her knees beside him on the wet and prickly ground. "Papa! It's me, Arianne! You're—you're really all right, aren't you?" She pulled the covering completely away, refusing to believe it had been put there correctly. Surely someone had made a terrible mistake.

He lay so peacefully silent but for a small stream of blood pooled in the corner of his mouth. His skin was as weathered as ever and somehow still soft, his hands as strong as they'd always been while running his Hollander to pound rags into pulp, to assist the river in working the press to squeeze away every trace of water from the paper. Able hands, artisan hands.

"Papa?"

Cold hands.

Arianne didn't know how long she sat there. Everything else, from the noise of those working to free the trapped to the clamor and shouts of survivors, faded away. She cried on her father's unmoving chest, and only when she heard someone pass by did she move.

As she did, her fingertips grazed the ring her father had worn these last few months. His wedding ring. The one Charlotte had put on his hand.

She sprang to her feet. Charlotte! Where must she be? Thank God she wasn't with Papa . . . and yet . . . why wasn't she, if only to watch over him?

There were strangers nearby, as if they'd observed her but didn't want to interfere. The three were from the group of survivors that she'd first approached. None looked curious; rather they looked at her helplessly.

"I—I have another loved one aboard. A woman."

"A woman was seen with him just before the wreck," said a man in a common tweed suit. "They'd been enjoying the view at the back of the car. It tumbled on the end, right where they stood."

"But . . . she could be all right . . . Couldn't she?"

The man offered little hope. "They's searching to see if anyone was thrown. Over there."

She started to move closer to the wreck, but another voice followed.

"You could ask the doctor they fetched from town." It was the man who'd first pointed her toward the bodies. "He would know."

"Where is he?"

They all looked around, and in a moment another man raised a hand. "He's there—over there. See?"

Arianne followed the gaze and saw a man with a stethoscope hung round his neck. Hiking that way, she nearly tripped on the rough ground and lost precious time, her gaze wavering from the doctor only long enough to glance at the three patients laying on blankets at his feet.

One, the very one the doctor hovered over, was Charlotte.

Crying her name, Arianne reached her in moments. They must be readying her for transport onto the pushcart.

"Charlotte!"

The physician looked at Arianne, crouched on Charlotte's other side. Arianne didn't want to look away from Charlotte, not when she saw the flicker of her lids flutter open—but the doctor's face was too grim to ignore.

"Do you know this woman?" the doctor asked.

Arianne nodded. "She's my father's wife. Charlotte. Charlotte Casterton."

"She's been badly hurt, I'm afraid."

"Arianne . . ."

"Yes! Charlotte, I'm here. Right here."

Charlotte's breath seemed sucked from her, coming in short, painful rasps.

"You mustn't talk, madam," warned the doctor. He looked at Arianne, but only briefly before writing something on a pad of paper. "She'll need surgery immediately if she has any hope to live. As soon as the pushcart returns, be sure to tell them she's next to go, without any delay. Here." He shoved the paper into Arianne's trembling hands. "See these instructions go with her. There won't be a place for you on the pushcart, you'll have to leave room for other patients. Make sure this is secure on her person, on her clothes. Tell the pushcart operator she's the first to be tended."

Then the doctor turned away, with a call to another man nearby to tell him, too, that Charlotte was the next to go.

"Oh, Charlotte," whispered Arianne, seeing the woman in such desperate pain. But upon hearing her own horror she spoke with forced cheer. "Charlotte, Charlotte, you'll be all right! The doctor is seeing that you get the help you need, and right away, as soon as possible. You'll be all right!"

The woman, her pretty face nearly unrecognizable in pallor, looked again at Arianne. "Is . . . Samuel . . . Is he . . . dead?"

"I . . ." How could she tell her? It would only add to her misery.

"I was thrown. But I—I know . . . I saw . . ." She gasped again, and her face contorted. Then she looked at Arianne. "You must tell them he lived longer than me, Ari."

"But . . . what difference does it make? You're living, and you'll be all right. Do you understand? You'll be all right."

Even as she repeated the phrase, Arianne's fear grew that her words wouldn't be allowed to come true. But Charlotte was already talking again, with such weakness Arianne could barely hear anything, even as she leaned closer.

"Witnesses. Two."

"But there are many witnesses, Charlotte. Why worry . . ."

She stopped, frantic to understand what Charlotte was trying to say. Something about a will? How could she speak of such things? Except that she'd heard Charlotte and her father speak of another will, the one left by Charlotte's first husband.

"I bequeath to you, Arianne Casterton . . ." Her colorless face twisted in pain and she stopped speaking for a moment. " . . . all I would rightfully inherit. Oh . . ."

"Please, Charlotte," Arianne pleaded. "Please don't speak of such things. You'll live, you've got to. I can't . . . I can't lose my father and you, too!"

She whispered something—a sigh? Or was it a name? Jones? Joan? Arianne could not tell; the sound made no sense, yet breathed so tenderly in a last moment that seemed to carry no pain at all.

Shouts came from the direction of the track. The handcart was back and being loaded for another return trip.

"Hurry!" Arianne shouted, so loud her throat protested with a jab. "Hurry here! She needs the hospital."

The doctor returned to Charlotte. He took up her wrist then a moment later pressed the stethoscope to her chest, past the buttons of her gown that had already been ripped aside just enough to access her heartbeat.

When he stood, he faced the handcart operators, directing them to take the other woman nearby.

"Wait!" Arianne protested, standing. "What are you doing? You said yourself Charlotte is next to go back!"

The doctor shook his head. "There's nothing to be done for her now. I'm sorry."

"No!" She rushed at the two men, standing between them and the wrong patient. But the doctor pulled her aside, only long enough to allow someone else, another stranger, to take hold of her and move her out of the way.

CHAPTER THREE

Jonas stepped onto the plush carpeting of the Walton Hotel lobby, passing a polished rosewood table laden with fresh flowers. He noticed little more than the fragrance of hyacinths as he went straight to the desk.

"I'd like you to ring Charlotte Prest—Casterton's room, please." He hoped not to find himself in too many circumstances where he must say his mother's new name.

"Yes, sir," the clerk said, reaching for the guest book. He studied the open page, flipped to the previous page with a "Hmm," then turned to another ledger for a quick examination before facing Jonas once more. "We do have a reservation for Casterton, a Mr. and Mrs. Samuel Casterton."

"That's right."

"Only I'm afraid they haven't arrived yet. Were they expecting you?"

He nodded, pulling out his pocket watch to check the time. Although his mother had said to come by in the evening—and it was just barely that, at six—he was sure her note said they would arrive this afternoon. He'd spent the entire day pretending to wrestle with the decision, but some small part of him knew all along that he would come.

"We have a fine dining room if you'd like to enjoy a meal while you wait."

Jonas shook his head. Maybe they hadn't come, after all. Maybe Casterton had changed his plans, or changed his mind about allowing Jonas's mother to see him. Or somehow changed his mother's mind about her seeing him. Maybe Casterton didn't want her to have any connection to her past. There was no doubt Jonas was now part of her past.

"I'll wait here in the lobby for a while."

"Very well, sir. If you'd like to place a telephone call, we have lines available in the booths, there."

"Thank you."

Place a call? He didn't even know if his mother's new home had a telephone. If she'd stayed in Williamsport she certainly would have had one, but he doubted any of those backward, wooded boroughs near there offered such a luxury.

A huff escaped his lips as he settled on a well-padded couch. If she'd changed her mind about coming, the least she could have done was find a way to let him know.

He noticed another man join the one already behind the counter. They chatted a moment, which wouldn't have stirred any interest in Jonas, except the new one kept looking his way, causing the first man to do the same.

Jonas would never get used to being the target of whispers—not about him directly, but because of his mother's extended stay in Williamsport and then her too-quick marriage to Casterton once his father died. Jonas turned away, reminded that he shouldn't have come. It was her fault he'd lost nearly every friend he had. If it hadn't been for Julia Kitteridge, his name would likely have been struck from every invitation list. Of course, Julia's father had been his own father's partner for years, and now Jonas's—at least until the sale of the textile mill was completed. Jonas knew his status as short-lived partner in the textile business wouldn't have been enough to stay in good standing within the Kitteridges' social circle without her help.

It might have been tempting to retreat into privacy until the whole affair blew over, but what would it have achieved except a postponement of the whispers and stares? The moment he emerged, all of that no doubt would have started again. So he'd persisted right through, but the whispers never got any easier.

The clerk evidently was not to be ignored. He approached, causing Jonas to look up at him with some annoyance.

"I understand the party you're waiting for was to have arrived via train, originated from the Catawissa line?"

Jonas was momentarily surprised that the inquiry wasn't of a more personal nature. *You aren't the son of that woman who married another man less than a month after her husband died, are you? We don't cater to that kind here, now off you go.*

Jonas nodded, standing. "The Catawissa line, yes . . . from Williamsport."

"The reservation for the Castertons instructed us to send a carriage round to the station when the train came in."

"Yes, that's right," he said. "Was there some kind of delay?"

The man, a good bit older than Jonas with hair just beginning to gray above his ears, offered what could only be called a sympathetic smile. "Please have a seat again, won't you? I'll have a porter fetch a beverage for you." With the flick of the man's wrist, a porter was at their side, but even though Jonas reclaimed his seat as the other man sat as well, he refused the offer of a drink.

"What sort of news do you have?"

"There was an accident along the line, I'm told," he said. "Quite a serious one, in fact."

"A train wreck?" Jonas asked the question without a trace of emotion. That train was to have left early that morning. Surely somehow he would have been notified if his mother had been involved. The train line had records of its passengers . . .

Yet how could the railroad possibly know they were connected? Now that her name was no longer Prestwich?

His pulse ticked up, and he stood again. "I'd like to call the Williamsport station, if you don't mind. Excuse me."

"But, sir," the man called after him, "I'm sure the evening newspaper will have some information, and it's due any moment."

"They aren't likely to have a full report so soon. Or names if any passengers are seriously injured." Nonetheless, Jonas stalled his trek toward the telephone booth. It was useless to call a station that was likely inundated with stranded travelers.

He had no choice. He must go there himself.

"It's time we went home," whispered Leta.

Arianne felt herself nod, although she made no attempt to move from the hard wooden bench in the hospital hall. This end of the hospital had a wide but plain door nearest the back street, where mortuary carriages came to pick up the dead.

"There's nothing left to do now," Leta added, her voice still low. She took one of Arianne's hands, which had been folded calmly in her lap. Arianne's eyes were dry; she thought she might, or should, fall into a fit of crying, but couldn't seem to muster the strength for it.

How could they be gone? Both her father and Charlotte? It was inconceivable that she would never see either again.

"Oh, Leta, how can I go home?" A tear, so hot it seemed to have been brewing inside, slipped from her eye and rolled down one cheek. "There's no one there."

Leta placed an arm around Arianne's shoulder, which she welcomed as fortification against caving in to more tears. "Look at it this way, Ari. They wouldn't have been home tonight anyway. Or tomorrow. I know this will take some getting used to. There's no instant cure for grief. But you're not alone, not really. You'll have all of Cranbury grieving with you. And, Ari . . .?"

She looked up at her friend's uncertain tone.

"When I lost my father, and then my mother, I thought God had deserted me. You might feel that way, too. But in time . . ." She paused as if waiting for a protest, some resistance to the reminder of a God who could let such an awful thing happen. But Arianne had no protest. Maybe she would shake a fist at God over this someday, but today was not that day. For now, she clung to the hope that both Charlotte and her father were in God's hands. "You'll come to see that we can't be spared from the pain of this world, if faith is to mean anything. God may not seem good right now, but He is. It's His nature. And He knows your sadness."

Arianne nodded, but it wasn't heartfelt agreement. It was obedient.

Leta withdrew her arm, patted Arianne's hands, then attempted a smile. "You've done everything you needed to do. You've spoken to all of the authorities, you've let them know where the burial is to take place after transportation can be arranged and how to contact you with any questions. There's nothing more we can do here. We'll need to speak to Mr. McIntosh back in Cranbury. And Tummers is waiting to take us back."

Yes, Mr. McIntosh. She needed to talk to him. The undertaker; the one man in their little town no family wanted to do business with, but every family did, sooner or later.

Arianne let Leta take her like a child in tow. Back home.

But home would never be the same.

————

Jonas reached Williamsport after midnight. He thought it unlikely to find anyone at the station at such an hour, but went there anyway. Surprisingly there was an attendant on duty, as well as a couple of stranded passengers asleep on benches inside the station house.

"I have a relative who might have been involved in the wreck that happened earlier today—er, yesterday," he amended. "Do you know where I can learn the names of those who might have been injured in the Catawissa train accident?"

All the way here he'd wondered if coming was the right thing to do. Was he making a fool of himself, being so worried if it just turned out his mother hadn't bothered to telephone him to say she was delayed? Or that her plans had changed and she hadn't even been aboard? Maybe she thought it wouldn't have mattered to him. Maybe she thought he wouldn't even have met her in Philadelphia. He hadn't told her he would. Or perhaps she'd tried telephoning and couldn't reach him at home, since he'd left the hotel directly. If someone on his household staff had come after him, they would have gone to the hotel, but he hadn't been there long, either.

She would have returned to Cranbury after the accident, at least until other arrangements for transportation could be made. He had no idea where she was living, except the name of the town. While he had no intention of showing up at her door, this accident had proven one thing: despite everything, he'd been looking forward to seeing her, even after the turmoil she'd caused. And although he had no real reason to believe the accident had done anything more than inconvenience her, he wanted to be sure.

The solution was easy. He would stay in their Williamsport home, which now belonged to him, and invite her for a visit. Why hadn't he done so before this, anyway?

He knew why. Neither one was ready to face the embarrassment her actions had caused. Meeting in Philadelphia might have been more comfortable for Jonas; it was his home, after all. But this accident had tipped the scale. He was ready to see his mother now, even on territory that could only remind them that in Jonas's heart she'd deserted both his father and himself by marrying before the flowers had wilted on Father's grave.

The station attendant eyed him. "If you're another reporter, you're too late. I've told our own *Grit* writers everything I know, so you can read about it in the papers in the morning."

"As I told you, I have a *relative* who was to have been aboard."

His brows drew together as if believing Jonas for the first time. "Beg your pardon, then. We've had all kinds of reporters and story seekers here all day. Relatives were notified through the railroad if any loved ones were injured or killed."

"Killed?" The word nearly choked his throat closed. "There were fatalities?"

"Four altogether." He continued to eye Jonas closely. "You'd probably have been told by now if one of them was yours. Bad news has a way of traveling twice as fast as good, you know." His voice was considerably softer than before. "Likely anyone you know set out back home or planned to find a way to get to the station south of the wreck, at Kimbletown or Milton. Southeast line between here and Kimbletown's closed until debris is taken away. Workin' on it through the night and things will be getting through real soon now. You tell your relatives we're workin' hard as we can to get it ready again."

"I was told the accident wasn't far from here. Were the injured brought back here, then? Here to Williamsport?"

"That's right. To the hospital over in Old Oaks Park. You know where that is?"

Having spent a fair number of summers here, he knew the town well enough. Jonas thanked the man, then re-boarded the carriage he'd instructed to wait, giving the man directions to the Williamsport Hospital.

The brown brick hospital was modest in comparison to some of the other buildings in town—the post office, the courthouse, even some of the tall and sprawling homes along Millionaire's Row on West Fourth Street where the lumber magnates lived. Inside the hospital, the halls were dark and quiet at this pre-dawn hour, but it didn't take long to discover a lighted desk. Behind it sat an older woman in a black dress covered by a starched white apron, her dark hair piled beneath a white cap.

She looked startled, and not a little concerned, at the sight of him. Standing, she stood as stiff as her apron and pointed back in the direction he'd come. "Oh, sir, visiting hours don't start until afternoon time. You'll have to leave."

"I came to inquire about those who were brought here after the train accident yesterday."

"The hospital isn't open for visitors of any kind at this hour.

You'll have to leave and come back in the morning and make your inquiries to the proper people."

Jonas had learned young to be a rule-follower. He hadn't wanted to disappoint either parent, for fear of causing more tension between them. So he knew he was anything but an imposing figure right now. Clutching the hat he'd removed upon entry into the building, he offered a smile. "I'm sorry. I know this is out of the ordinary. It's just that I've been traveling since last evening, and the time spent getting here somehow allowed worries to materialize where likely there shouldn't be any." Then, seeing a crack of compassion form in the woman's eye—she was, after all, old enough to be his mother, and a nurse at that—he continued. "I was expecting my mother in Philadelphia yesterday afternoon, and when she didn't arrive I grew concerned. I wouldn't have been notified if anything happened to her, you see. She's recently remarried, so her name is different from my own. We . . . we haven't seen each other in some time, and it's doubtful anyone connected to her would have thought to contact me."

"Well, now, young man, I wish I could help you, but I'm not sure that I can. Are you quite sure she didn't simply go back home? Is there no way for you to contact her directly?"

"She doesn't live here in Williamsport any more. She's been living in Cranbury, but I don't have an address. She married a businessman from there, a papermaker."

The information created a new reaction; he saw it even in the dim electric light. Through her professional control, he saw a flash of something in her eyes—concern, even fear—he was sure of it. One of her hands fluttered like an uncertain schoolgirl's, smoothing her already smooth apron.

"Rumors have been bouncing around the hospital since the accident," she said, not looking at him, "and I've learned not to trust many. So I beg you, young man, go home and wait for your mother there. I'm sure she'll be in touch soon."

He shook his head. "If she thought of doing that, she would be calling my home in Philadelphia. I suppose, in retrospect, I should have waited there, but I was a little anxious. She won't know to contact me here."

"The hospital will open in just two hours. There will be more staff available then to answer your questions, if we can be of any help. I simply don't know enough to tell you anything for certain, and I'd rather not let rumors give you any undue concern."

"What rumors?" He couldn't keep the exasperation out of his tone. "Surely you know which patients you have here? My mother's name is Charlotte Prestwich—Charlotte Casterton, I should say, that's what she goes by now. Is there a patient here by that name?"

"No, I'm quite sure there isn't."

Jonas wanted to believe her, even take comfort in the words, but there was no denying he'd been far more assured of his mother's wellbeing before coming here.

"I don't mean to be difficult." He kept his voice quiet, pulling out his calling card. "My mother grew up here in Williamsport. Banfield is her maiden name. As I said, she married a man named Casterton. Samuel Casterton, of Cranbury. I can send someone to Cranbury in the morning, I suppose, to let her know I'm here in Williamsport. But if she's already made alternate travel arrangements, a message might not reach her very quickly." He ran a hand through his hair, suddenly aware he was rambling. "I don't know why I'm telling you all of this. I . . . suppose I shouldn't be here at all."

The nurse stood again, coming around her desk and taking one of Jonas's hands as if she were an aunt or old friend. She led him to a bench along the wall, where patients no doubt usually waited to be seen by a doctor. Poor patients, those who couldn't afford to have a doctor come to them.

She sat, and since she didn't let go of his hand he sat, too. There was a noise down the hall, someone mopping a floor. Jonas watched the washerwoman for a moment, sensing somehow that whatever news this nurse had, it was something he would rather not hear. So he watched the other woman doing such a normal, mundane task as washing the floor.

"News spread quickly yesterday about folks from Cranbury, the papermaker and his wife, a woman who used to live right here in Williamsport. I know I'm not the proper person to be telling you this, but it doesn't seem right to keep it from you, or send you on your way only to come back to the news later. You see, young man, there were several fatalities in the accident, and among those who died were this papermaker . . . and his wife."

Jonas's head filled up with blood or air or a combination of both, creating something like cotton that muffled his ears and slowed his brain. He heard the nurse go on about witness reports that the husband and wife had been in the exact wrong spot the moment the accident occurred, in the back enjoying the view. They'd been holding hands just before the explosion that rocked the train cars loose, sending them tumbling down an embankment. That end of the train car took most of the impact, sealing their doom. The papermaker had died right away, and his wife soon followed.

"You—you're certain? There's no mistake? Charlotte Casterton is the name of one of the dead?"

The nurse nodded, her face full of compassion and tenderness. "I'm so very sorry, Mr. Prestwich."

"Is she here?" He suddenly looked around again, wanting to see her. He wasn't sure he would believe she was gone otherwise. "I'd like to see her. To make sure."

"Oh, no, son, I'm sorry I couldn't take you there. For that you really will have to return when someone in authority is on duty." He started to protest, but she went on. "I would lose my job if I did such a thing, and I'm sure you don't want to be responsible for that."

Jonas took in a deep breath, a gulp that made his head light again. He should go, but his body felt leaden. He would wait. He had no choice.

"If you don't mind, then, I'd like to wait. Right here."

"Perhaps you have a place to stay here in Williamsport? You might be more comfortable there."

The home his mother would have inherited from her parents had been mortgaged, something Jonas's father had taken care of upon their marriage. But that brought her family home into his ownership, and he'd successfully bypassed letting Jonas's mother inherit it through his will. Jonas hadn't visited there since she had vacated the place in favor of Cranbury.

"I'd rather wait right here, if I may." Truth was, he didn't think he could move. His father had died only a few months ago. It was impossible that he should lose his mother as well. They had their faults and they may not have loved one another as a mother and father ought, but they'd both loved him.

It had been one thing to lose his mother to a new life, especially so quickly after his father's death. But to lose her like this—permanently? Surely it was impossible that she was really and truly gone, the rift that had separated them unmended.

Until he saw her, he refused to believe it.

CHAPTER FOUR

For so early in the day, Arianne's table was already full, both with food and people surrounding it. Between generous visitors and Arianne's hardworking maid Binny, there would be more than enough to offer the inevitable callers likely to come and go throughout the day. Plenty, too, to follow the services at the church tomorrow, after the bodies were retrieved from Williamsport today.

The bodies.

Arianne had welcomed the company last night. She'd needed to know the house wasn't empty. People came with favorite memories of her father, and she knew such memories were to be all she had with no more to come, so she wanted to hear what they had to say.

But now the tales came slower, as if the loss was becoming more real to everyone. Arianne slipped outside, seeing the wagon from Mr. McIntosh the undertaker leave for his grim errand. How could it be that her father would come home again only one last time, in Mr. McIntosh's wagon?

There were two flagstone paths near her stationery shop, one from the village and another at the back of her garden. Like the rest of Cranbury, the paths had been cut through a dense forest, a patch of wood that hadn't been touched by the lumber industry.

The trees parted naturally only for the Susquehanna, the river that supplied both water and power for the paper mill. It was a good walk down the trail from the town's high ground, a way she knew well. One of her only memories of her mother was on this path, how they'd planted Corsican mint to enjoy the scent to and from the mill.

That grief, long since scarred over, jabbed anew and made her aloneness that much more complete.

Her father's papermaking factory wasn't large but was certainly well maintained. How many hours of her father's life had been spent over his single vat, filled with water and linens and rags and cotton, to be macerated into the pulp that would become his paper? Plunge the moulds, shake the moulds, right to left, back to front. Strong forearms were needed to manipulate the moulds just right, to cross and matt the fibers so they would be equally strong in both directions. Durable yet elegant. That was how her father's paper always turned out under his artistic touch.

Even now the Hollander turned, driven by the power of the river below, as if waiting for her father. *Where are the plants and cottons for me to mash today?* it must wonder.

Arianne walked through the mill, going up to the drying loft where an order still waited for her attention, something she'd promised her father she would do yesterday. She scanned the hanging paper, savoring the moment, checking, as she always did, for that one sort of sheet that somehow stood out from the rest. The ones about which she would ask her father if they were suitable for *the project*.

There was no hurry to complete this private, special order. A sheet here, a sheet there, and only from orders of the same kind. Purest white; watermarked only with their dove in the lower left corner; a matched weight; a consistently deckled edge.

It was nearly complete, that special project. It was as if her father had kept it purposefully going, waiting for her to come to him and let him know the date of her wedding was near. That was the day he'd planned, from when Arianne was born perhaps, to give her the fruits of this special project.

A thousand pages of identical whiteness and, nearly impossible, of close to identical weight, to be handed over to the town printer who would send it to his brother, the printer of Bibles. Such paper, Mr. Pillifant had once said upon his first glimpse of her father's growing collection, had never been seen in his own print shop. He was certain his brother would be honored to use it for their tender undertaking.

The Bible that Arianne's father would have presented to her upon her wedding day.

Arianne stood, arms folded tight against the heaviness in her soul, staring at the papers. Her father's hands would never again touch the papers in the drying loft. Never again would she hear his voice ask her to run the pages though the glazing rollers. Never again would she wrap in brown paper the batches her father's talent had created.

She wondered if she could simply leave them here unfinished, a connection to that last job she had done with him, the final fruits of his labor.

"You ought not to be workin' today, Ari." Leo Levick had stepped into the factory and climbed the steps to the loft without Arianne even knowing it. The young man had been her father's coucher, at least when Leo could afford to be away from his father's carpentry business. When he moved toward the hanging paper, as if to finish what Arianne had such mixed feelings about doing herself, she put a hand to his brawny forearm to stop him.

"No, Leo," she said. "Leave it."

He looked down at her, his vibrant blue eyes filled with concern. Leo was just a year older than Arianne. He'd worked so long in the mill that Arianne once believed he might become Cranbury's next papermaker. But Leo's father and brothers were carpenters, and though Leo claimed to love papermaking as much as he loved working with wood, he had yet to announce which vocation he wanted to follow.

"I don't mind doing it," he said. "I came today because your father would've wanted me here. And you have plenty of company waiting back at the house."

How could she explain? How could she tell him that once this task was finished, she would never again be doing something her father had asked her to do?

She said nothing, and Leo made no further attempt to do the job. But he didn't leave, either.

"I am sure going to miss your Papa."

"Yes, Leo. Me, too."

He folded powerful arms across his massive chest, a chest made strong from the hard labor he'd always known. "There's a line of orders settin' inside your Papa's workbox, Ari. I can take them on, beside my work at the wood shop. Might take me a bit longer than it would your Papa, and we both know the paper won't be near as perfect. But it'll be better than any other hand mill can give, that much I know. There weren't any better teacher than your Papa, and never will be." He was standing only a foot away, close enough to touch her shoulder, which he did now. "Except maybe you. So if you and me were to get those orders done together, they'd be sure to get done right."

Her lower lip trembled, there was nothing she could do to stop it, and she couldn't meet Leo's sympathetic gaze.

"We'll work well together, Ari," he whispered. "We always have."

It was true; Leo might not have the touch to weigh out the moulds that turned the pulp into the finest papers, but he was hardworking enough to keep at it until coming close. She should be grateful he was willing to help her carry on her father's work, even if with only part of his time.

But just now there was a familiar tone in his voice, a look in his eye she'd seen before. A hint he might be willing to devote more of his time here . . . to her. Would her loss give him the boldness he'd lacked so far? Or was he still waiting for the encouragement that she could not give?

Nearly before the thought was complete she found herself turning back toward the loft stairs. If she let him talk any longer, she knew he would ask something she didn't want him to ask. Not now.

"You're right that I should be with the others now, Leo. I'll see you . . . later."

Then she fled outside and back up the path she'd taken to flee the other way not many minutes before.

———

A gentle shake startled Jonas and he jerked his head back to an upright position. Disoriented, he glanced at his unfamiliar surroundings, wondering for a moment where he could be.

Then, seeing the face of the man who'd awakened him, it all came back. His mother was to have returned to Philadelphia yesterday . . . only she hadn't arrived, and he'd come looking for her.

"I'm Dr. Winchester," the man said. "I understand you're inquiring about the Castertons."

"Yes, that's right. Particularly Charlotte Casterton, my mother."

"Come along with me, won't you?"

The doctor led him down the wide, recently buffed floor, to a room evidently used for examinations. There was a table tucked against a wall, two solid wooden chairs at one end and a sink in the corner next to a cart filled with bottles and bandages.

"I tended to the train accident victims myself, at the site yesterday. It was a tragic scene, I'm sorry to say. Have a seat."

Jonas remained standing, knowing if the man had good news he'd not have brought him in here; he'd have brought him to his mother. Instead, the privacy felt like a warning, provision in case emotions got the best of him once this doctor told him what he didn't want to hear.

"Do you know what happened to my mother? Unless I

dreamed it, a nurse told me last night that a papermaker and his wife had died in the accident. Is that true?"

The man raised a sympathetic gaze, nodding. There was no longer any sense in denying it, or hoping for it to be otherwise. His mother was dead.

"Can I . . . see her?"

"Please, have a seat. Settle yourself for a moment."

"I'd rather not. Tell me what you saw."

"Very well." He leaned on the edge of the table, as if to invite Jonas to relax, which he couldn't do. "There was a woman there, quite a young woman, at the side of Charlotte Casterton when she died. The young woman was obviously greatly distressed, and I later learned she was the daughter of this woman's husband, who also perished in the accident. Was she your sister?"

Jonas shook his head. "My mother was married to Casterton a short time ago. I'd heard he had a daughter. That must be the person you saw."

He stood and placed a hand on Jonas's shoulder. "The two were obviously quite close, and 1 can assure you your mother was not alone."

Jonas shrugged off the man's touch. Someone who was a stranger to Jonas had been at his mother's side when she'd died. He didn't find that in the least bit comforting. If it hadn't been for Samuel Casterton, his mother wouldn't even have been on that train.

"She produced ample proof that the man was her father— witnesses, even, who attested to the necessary paperwork. She also brought witness that the woman, your mother, was his wife. So when she requested both of the bodies for burial together in Cranbury, we saw no reason not to agree."

"Do you mean to say she's already claimed the bodies?"

"They're being transported this morning."

"So . . . they're gone?"

"If not, they soon will be. Unless you wish to contest the action, in which case we need to contact the local authorities."

Now Jonas did sit. Why this came as such a shock, he did not know. What could be more natural, that his mother should be buried alongside the man she'd loved enough to marry just a few short months ago? Would she have preferred to be buried alongside Jonas's father, a man she couldn't even live with during the limited years he'd had on earth, let alone for eternity?

Still, the thought of his parents not being buried side by side dumfounded him. And, much to his selfish regret, he quickly realized this was one more thing the gossipmongers of Philadelphia would no doubt find amusing—an expense only he would pay.

Jonas wasn't sure which he would regret more. Protesting, or not protesting, his lack of involvement in his mother's burial. But he wanted to do one thing. He rose and faced the doctor.

"If it isn't too late, I'd at least like to see my mother. I have to . . . to really believe this is all true. Can you understand that?"

The doctor was silent a moment, but nodded at last. He led Jonas out the door and farther down the hallway, to a room marked with the ominous sign:

Morgue.

CHAPTER FIVE

"Yoo-hoo! Arianne!"

Arianne was in the storage room, where she kept paper for restocking shelves and packing material for orders ready to go out. She used only the sturdiest paper for wrapping orders, of pulp from the bottom of the vat. It was Leo's favorite kind of paper to make, being the easiest. No need for delicate handling since it was strong, thick, and durable. A little like Leo himself.

She recognized Leta's voice immediately and smiled. All the inhabitants of Cranbury had been faithful in their support during these last few weeks, offering her regular invitations to lunch or dinner, and weekly Sunday afternoon visits from nearly everyone she knew at church. But of them all, Leta had been the most frequent, and most welcome, visitor.

To Arianne's surprise, Leta wasn't alone. At her side was an older gentleman carrying a gleaming leather satchel in one gloved hand and was just removing his hat with the other.

"Mr. Hargrove was passing by my shop," Leta said, "and I came right out to see if I could be of assistance."

Arianne smiled, knowing the true meaning behind the words. Everyone was curious when a stranger came to town. But knowing this stranger had been looking for her didn't inspire the easy curiosity it might have had she not been the recipient of the last set of visitors to town. Not long after the train accident, two men came to assess the value of everything her father had owned. Had this man come to collect the inheritance tax the other two warned her about? She had so little money in savings and such an uncertain future, the thought ignited renewed concerns. Something she'd been successfully dodging in recent weeks.

Why hadn't they at least sent her something in writing, to let her know how much she would owe? Give her time to gather what she needed?

"Mr. Hargrove," Leta said, "this is our Miss Casterton, one of Cranbury's finest. There isn't a better stationer anywhere." She slipped a smile Mr. Hargrove's way, as if charming the man might insure he'd bring only good news.

"Yes, yes," he said, barely looking at Leta. "Thank you for escorting me, though I'm sure I could have found it on my own."

Arianne set aside the package she'd just brought from the storage room, knowing too few other orders were ready to go. She must give in and ask Leo if he could spend more time at the mill; her father's inventory was dwindling faster than she'd expected or could possibly replace on her own.

"How do you do, Miss Casterton?" He didn't extend his hand. Instead, he reached into his leather bag then pulled out a long envelope, the thicker, heavier kind they sold to businesses rather than more elegant weights for personal use. "I came to put this into your hands, for legal purposes, you understand. If you have any questions about the contents, please don't hesitate to telephone me at my office. Instructions to reach me are enclosed."

The moment the envelope was fully in her possession, he dipped his chin as if in salute, then turned on his heel, returned his top hat to his head and went back out the door that had barely closed since letting him in.

Leta watched him go through the oval glass in the door. "Well, what do you suppose that was all about?"

Arianne lifted her shoulders. "I thought he was here to collect taxes."

Phoebe, Arianne's clerk, joined them from where she'd stood behind the counter. "Perhaps that's what's in the envelope."

Arianne tested the weight of the contents, which promised either heavy paper or many sheets. Maybe both. "I hope it isn't the tax bill. Such a big file couldn't be good news in so large a packet."

"Open it!" Leta said, as if she couldn't tolerate another moment's delay.

Arianne slid her finger under the flap, which easily gave way to her invasion. The small stack of paper was indeed impressive, judging by the combination of typewritten text, handwritten calligraphy and large, flowing signatures at the bottom. Official seals and legal marks dotted nearly every page.

It wasn't easy to read, due in part to the often fancy script. Behind the top sheet was a listing of some detail, one item after another. She recognized papermaking equipment first. Sorting bins for rags; cylinder washers; copper-lined Hollander beater with beater-knives and bed-plates of bronze; stuff-chest; vat; knotter, and on and on. The last sheets contained some surprisingly familiar items as well. Two parlor chairs and one sofa; cast iron cookware; kitchen table with five chairs. What dining set but her own would boast an odd number of chairs? She returned to the top page, where one portion from the middle caught and held Arianne's attention.

As subject to the laws of Descendents' Estate and appointed under authority of the act of the General Assembly of the state of Pennsylvania, notice is hereby given that one-third of all property belonging to the deceased, Samuel Richard Casterton, both personal and real estate, passed into the estate of his widow Charlotte Casterton, formerly known as Charlotte Prestwich nee Banfield. Upon her death the estate of Charlotte Casterton hereby legally passed to her son and sole heir, Jonas Prestwich.

Therefore, the value of one-third of the following property shall be assumed by Jonas Prestwich:

Casterton Paper Mill

Cranbury Stationery Shop

Land and Home and all it contains in the name of:

Samuel Richard Casterton

Co-heirs to this estate may share ownership and all profits heretofore, or purchase outstanding shares within one year of the date of this document. If purchase is denied or not afforded, all properties will be sold and profits distributed under the terms of inheritance codes of Pennsylvania, 1898.

She read it again, then again. It simply made no sense.

"Does that really mean what it says?" Phoebe whispered.

"What else could it mean?" Leta said.

Binny, having wandered in from the kitchen as she often did, didn't even try to read the paperwork held between the three other women. She asked what the fuss was about, but neither Arianne nor the others spared a moment's attention from the paper. Binny moaned, wringing her hands. "I can tell by yer faces it's not any good news. What is it? What's on them papers?"

Arianne raised her gaze to Binny, too bemused to believe the document in her hand. "It says one-third of everything I inherited from my father is going to Charlotte's son." She glanced at the page again, having already forgotten the name. "A Jonas Prestwich."

"What! All yer Papa worked for and built is going to some stranger? I didn't even know Mrs. Charlotte had such a boy!"

"One-third—of everything!" Leta's voice took on a shrill, angry tone. "Even Mr. Casterton's personal belongings!"

"There must be some mistake," Phoebe said. "Surely if a judge —a sensible judge—knew the circumstances . . . yes, Mr. Casterton was married to—to this person's mother, but that ought not give him the right to any part of what Mr. Casterton wanted for *you*, Ari! What have you to do with him, or he to you? He's a stranger, with no right to anything at all."

Arianne turned the rest of the pages more slowly now, the

inventory of what the assessors must have submitted, those two men who'd visited days after the accident. The lawfulness behind the document revealed itself: the moment her father died, all of his property went into legal consideration. As his wife, Charlotte was due to inherit one-third of all his possessions, unless a will stated otherwise. Arianne knew the claim was correct; her father had no will registered with the state. Why should he? A man not even fifty years old, and in the best of health.

A conversation she'd overheard between Charlotte and her father came to mind, one evening not all that long ago, when they'd left their bedroom door open to a breeze. She'd heard them easily, as if that breeze carried the words straight to Arianne's ears.

"You ought to make a proper will, Sam," Charlotte had said. "Don't put it off."

"I've no intention of putting you through widowhood again, my dear. At least not for many more years to come."

"Still, this sort of thing is better left up to you and not some stranger in the capitol deciding where your assets should go. Ari will allow me to stay living right here with her, should anything happen to you. We all know that. But you ought to put in writing that *everything* will go to her, just as it should. She's young, unmarried, and with a long future ahead. I don't want anything to be uncertain, least of all money matters."

"Yes, yes, I'll get to it."

"It must be in writing, darling. Life can be unfair to women, and I don't want to be responsible for any unfairness in her regard. I love you both too well to be the cause of any unpleasant surprises."

"I know. I agree."

"Sam." Her tone had said she saw his lack of urgency, and how right she'd been.

How had Charlotte known the potential of such unfairness? Arianne had thought the real discovery of the overheard conversation was her assumption that something unfair must have happened to Charlotte, something Charlotte hadn't told Arianne.

Although she often spoke of Williamsport, she rarely spoke of the life she once had away from her home town—back in Philadelphia. Arianne wondered, after hearing that, what some deceased parent or perhaps her first husband must have done to teach her such a lesson.

Until this moment, Arianne hadn't even known she had a son. One who now owned a third of everything that rightfully belonged to her.

———

Jonas looked at the packet of paper, confused. This was the second time in a matter of months that he'd received an inheritance. Both had been unexpected in their own way—the first, having received *in entirety* his father's belongings. And now this: realizing his mother had left him anything was a shock indeed.

Yet here it was, spoils of his mother's second marriage. As her sole heir, he had inherited one-third of what she would have enjoyed from her new husband, had she lived longer than a few hours after he'd died.

Incredible as it sounded, everything seemed to be in order. He'd even been provided a list of exactly what this inheritance entailed.

A paper mill in Cranbury was hardly something he'd be interested in. Paper made the ancient way in some dark little town in the woods. By hand! It was ludicrous.

Still, he studied the list of his impending belongings and remembered again having met the man long ago at his father's textile mill. He'd arranged for the purchase and delivery of clean rags for his papermaking business. Before knowing the truth about him, Jonas had recalled Casterton to be a pleasant man. He carried an easy, comfortable smile, as if life hadn't yet taught him it was supposed to be hard. Soft-spoken, in stark contrast to his father's booming voice. In fact, that was one of the reasons Jonas remembered him. The difference between him and Jonas's father was as vivid as morning to midnight.

It was a difference his mother must have welcomed.

Among the belongings listed were an unprecedented number of books. Perhaps this wasn't unusual for a papermaker, one who might have provided the paper for such products. And yet those specifically listed, apart from a Bible, were mainly various books of sermons from both American and British pastors.

Jonas couldn't help but smirk. Speaking of contrast, what had a man who quite likely attended church been doing carrying on with Jonas's mother, a married woman?

This inheritance might be a surprise; it might even be unwanted. But it was his nonetheless. Maybe it was the correct price to be paid from a man who had sullied the reputation of Jonas's mother, and nearly destroyed Jonas's reputation as well.

At the very least, it was worth an investigation before converting it all to cash. It might come in handy since he was about to sell his portion of his father's business to the partners who wanted to move south. He would need all the new investment capital he could get to pave the way to his new future here in Philadelphia.

Because, like it or not, he couldn't spend the rest of his life at parties or the racecourse. In short, he needed to take charge as the next generation representing his father's name.

CHAPTER SIX

Two Days Later

Arianne followed the footpath that ran parallel to the road between Cranbury and Williamsport. A carriage passed her quite easily, but she didn't even look to see if it was one she recognized. She knew only that it wasn't Tummer's yellow Canary. This one was a deep burnished brown, one that would likely bypass Cranbury when the road forked up ahead.

She blinked away a rush of fresh tears, forcing mundane thoughts instead, like the number of ruts in both the footpath and the road after a long winter. Such thoughts were far better than those really demanding her attention. She'd come from the kitchen at Wardman House, where Ivy Grenville was the housekeeper. Born in Cranbury, Ivy never turned away a neighbor in need of a telephone. Electricity and telephone wires went as far afield of Williamsport as Wardman House, and no farther.

It had been two days since Arianne had received the awful news of the split inheritance. Two days of hand-wringing and worrying, with few moments of hope. She wanted to let herself think this person, this Jonas Prestwich, must have enough of his mother in him to see reason. Perhaps that was why he hadn't already hurried out to Cranbury. Perhaps he was at this very moment composing a letter of refusal, to see that the entire inheritance went where it rightfully belonged. To her.

But Arianne refused to build false hopes, and she'd wanted to be prepared for the possibility the man might prove troublesome. The news she'd learned through today's phone call to Mr. Hargrove, however, offered little hope of contesting the inheritance laws. He'd said it would likely cost almost as much to fight this in court as it would to simply buy back the one-third fortune she'd lost—and with no assurance of winning it could be twice as costly to resist.

The sad fact was that if her father had intended his entire estate to go to Arianne, he should have made sure to put his affairs in order. After all, no one knew when one's time would come.

Cranbury was just around the hill, but Arianne slowed her step as she came upon a familiar fallen log at the edge of a clearing. The spot overlooked a view she loved, valleys and trees and the river in the distance. In the fall, when God set the leaves ablaze with color, she often came here just to enjoy the many gifts of creation. The shades of spring green after this last gray winter could take her breath away just as the reds and yellows and golds of fall could.

But today she could barely see any beauty.

She let a tear roll down her cheek, not bothering to catch it or curtail those so eager to follow. In town where a neighbor might see her grief, or even at home with just Binny, she'd hidden such evidence. But here, with confusion added to that grief, she saw no reason to pretend control.

Why did God allow this, on top of her grief? Didn't He know this would be too much for her, to deal with so many decisions without her father's guidance? How could she run the mill, work the shop, and tend to legal problems while still so filled with grief? Work did make the hours pass quickly, but knowing she was unable to do it all by herself only made her grief harder to bear.

When her mother died, both she and Papa had turned to the mill for solace. He'd made more paper that year than he had in any year prior. And Arianne had worked so steadfastly on her water-marking skills that she'd surpassed even her father's hopes. A talent she had no time for anymore, and that wasn't likely to change.

The truth was, as she sat there crying, she found herself wishing her own time had come. Tales of heaven sounded so far superior to what her life was turning out to be that it would be far easier to just give up than to go on.

No sooner had she told herself such a thought dishonored God than a breeze fluttered the cape that had once belonged to her mother, as if tugging at her to consider something beyond herself. A noise from the wood below drew her attention. The chirps and warbles of birds, bold enough to reveal themselves after the noise of her arrival abated, brought a song of spring to her. A moment later three flashes of yellow streaked from branch to branch, tree to tree. Another pair of birds accompanied the goldfinches, the redpoll with their red-dashed chests and heads.

A smile pulled at her lips, but she was reluctant to let it take shape. She wanted to wallow a bit longer in her grief, perhaps let some resentment join in. God could have prevented all of this, after all.

And yet in that moment, she was reminded of His glory. What kind of God provided the loveliness of such a vista, populated with colors not only of seasons but of creatures within? None but a loving one.

Arianne sat still, enjoying the concert of song, the flutter of color. Before long a chipmunk scurried past, taking a moment to stare at her from a safe distance, flick his tail and run along a path he must have followed more than once from the trail carved in last year's fallen leaves.

She'd meant only to allow herself this moment to cave in to her grief, to count her fears, to acknowledge her aloneness. And yet

God had reminded her He was with her. Never alone, never without His gifts, never without His love.

She stood, more refreshed than she'd been since that awful day when she lost her father.

———

Jonas Prestwich instructed the driver to follow Cranbury's single, main road through town so he could get a look at first one side then the other along the unpaved street. A church had been the first structure to greet him, its steeple tall and white, complete with a bell.

The cemetery nestled next to it drew his eye, and he nearly called for the driver to halt. She was there, buried somewhere. He leaned closer to the window, searching for a recent grave, evidence of new residents, but saw nothing.

Sitting back in the carriage, for a moment he stared straight ahead instead of outside. He hadn't come here to grieve, yet realizing his mother had spent the final days of her life here hadn't escaped his attention. His lips tightened. Perhaps he should be grateful she wasn't buried in Philadelphia, where gossipmongers would be reminded of her pitiful marriage to his father. She was out here, where no Philadelphians would ever happen to see her final resting place.

Here. In a shabby if quaint little town in the middle of nowhere. He looked out the window again, prepared to do what he'd come to do. Assess this new inheritance.

The center of town offered a few modest but neat homes between a butcher shop, bakery, a greengrocer and post office, along with a hotel. Why such a small town would require an inn was unfathomable, but at least he knew where he could stay until this inheritance affair was settled. No need to waste time going back and forth from his house in Williamsport.

On the return up the street he saw more homes and a hat and dress shop, a photographer's shop, café and, at last, the store he was looking for: Casterton's Stationery. But he let the driver he'd hired in Williamsport continue on, coming to a halt in front of the Cranbury Inn. He might as well see about a room now rather than later.

The building was fashioned after a home, two stories high, wood framed and painted an inviting shade of forest green with darker trim. The stairs and porch were clean, although he wondered how it would fare under a rainy day with little more than packed dirt for a road leading to it.

Stepping from the carriage, Jonas directed the driver to return to the Williamsport house to ask his servant Olice to pack enough clothes and personal items to last him a few days.

"Be glad to bring a suitcase back, sir," the driver said, "but there's a train due in at Williamsport that I depend on for my regular fees. Won't be able to come back 'til this evening, if that's all right."

Jonas nodded; he wouldn't need his belongings until bedtime anyway.

Inside the hotel, a tidy foyer stood empty but for padded chairs and a sofa before an unlit fireplace. But the bell on the door had jingled, and it wasn't long before a woman appeared from a nearby corridor, greeting him with an outstretched hand.

"Good afternoon!" she said. "Welcome to Cranbury. How can I help you?"

"I'd like a room, please."

"Will you be staying with us long? Visiting a friend . . . or relative? Or here just to enjoy our lovely spring?"

As if spring came only to this little town? "I'll be here a couple of days, at least."

"All by yourself, Mr. . . . .?"

"Prestwich."

"Prestwich," she repeated. Then, as if the name on her lips had curdled her tongue, her shoulders stiffened. "Is that Jonas Prestwich, by any chance?"

Startled, he nodded. "Yes, that's right. But I didn't make a reservation, so how did you . . ."

She folded her hands at her waist, making the plumes of her generous upper sleeves appear more like wings than clothing. "I'm afraid we don't have any rooms available, Mr. Prestwich. Good-day to you."

She walked past him toward the door, holding it open as if to hasten his departure.

The quiet inn gave no evidence of a full house, especially given her initial welcome. He stood his ground. "You're certain you have no rooms?"

"That's right." She offered him only her profile.

He eyed her suspiciously but saw no purpose in arguing the truth out of her. So he retraced his steps outside, regretting that he'd sent the carriage back to Williamsport so quickly. He doubted he could catch it on foot.

He might as well get right to business, then see about finding another way back to civilization.

The train ride from Philadelphia had allowed Jonas plenty of time for reflection. He realized the portion of his inheritance might have come as a surprise to the Casterton daughter. Unless Casterton had specifically explained his plans to leave the standard third to his wife, Jonas's mother, it was probably unexpected that Casterton's primary heir now had a partner, albeit the lesser one.

But a business, especially one that no doubt demanded physical labor, was likely more burden than blessing to a woman. What was she to do with such an albatross? He was quite sure he could find a buyer if the business wasn't too archaic. Considering it was housed in the middle of a place resembling a glen from a fairy tale forest, he could use all of the business sense his father had taught him to improve the paper mill until it was fit for sale. He'd even remembered an old school mate whose father was in the papermaking business. No doubt Jonas could count on them for advice on improvement, and with any luck perhaps an outright purchase. They were practically neighbors back in the city.

The Casterton daughter may very well be grateful he'd been foisted upon her through this sudden inheritance. He was just the person to remove such a burden.

The stationery shop was only a short walk down the street. Though the road itself wasn't paved, a wide boardwalk gave access to the shops and homes. The boards weren't entirely level, but the wood was likely an improvement over mud whenever it rained.

Jonas stopped in front of the stationers and assessed the two-story building with a quick glance, guessing by the lacy curtains swaying gently at an open upper window that floor was private. The shop itself boasted bay windows, displaying a variety of items for sale. A leather portfolio first caught his eye, right next to a banker's case complete with strap and leather. He'd seen plenty of men in the business world carrying such cases, and even he knew the quality of a man's case was evidence of his wealth—or lack thereof when carrying something inferior. There were two types displayed here: both were leather and looked of surprisingly high quality. Why would someone in such a remote town have need of such an item? Surely Williamsport folk didn't come all the way out here to shop.

There was a typewriter and ribbons on display, an assortment of desk accessories like writing utensils and pencil sharpeners, a hand blotter and inkstands. The other window displayed a variety of books: blank books, ledger books, reading books, even a small ivory-covered pocket tablet with a fancy little sign next to it iden-tifying it as a "Ladies shopping memo tablet."

And he owned one third of it all, at least until it could be sold.

Like the hotel, a little bell sounded when he opened the door. The shop itself was amply sized, immediately pleasing to the eye with symmetry in the design. Neatly stacked shelving graced all three presenting sides, with narrow tables attractively displaying goods while leaving plenty of room to navigate. More books lined an entire wall, while various writing instruments dominated another, along with miscellaneous paper, envelopes, even postcards of color or sentiment.

"May I . . . help you?"

The question had started out friendly enough, but the catch in the woman's voice came with a look he would call more suspicious than interested. Did she greet all potential customers in such a way? The woman emerged from behind a long, dust-free counter, someone he would call average by any standard: average height for a woman, neither chubby nor thin but somewhere in between. Her hair was neither light nor dark but a dull hue of ash-brown. As she neared he saw any welcome in her too-small eyes disappear entirely, hardly the reception anyone would hope to see from a store owner.

This was his newest partner? She was older than he would have expected, but Casterton might have been older than he looked to have fathered a daughter such as this.

"I'm Jonas Prestwich, and I believe you were expecting me. My mother—"

She folded her arms as if he'd brought with him a chill, though the day was pleasantly warm. "I guessed who you are, Mr. Prestwich, and if you're any kind of gentleman, any kind of man worthy to be called the son of Mrs. Charlotte Casterton, you'll go right back out that door and never return."

The words, and the hardness behind them, made it all too clear he'd been judged against his mother and found deficient—quite the reverse of what he'd left behind in Philadelphia.

Just as clear was that he'd been a fool to think this woman would welcome his help in the disposal of her inheritance.

The tone of her voice must have echoed beyond the storeroom, because from a doorway at the back another woman emerged, this one dressed in a maid's garb but with an identical look of dislike already on her face. She hurried forward as if to form a line of ready defense.

Very well. The shop might have been more impressive than he expected, but the venom these women aimed at him made evident the one thought he'd purposely ignored: this inheritance was obviously unfair, and this Casterton woman wasn't about to let him overlook such a detail.

Still, that didn't make it any less legal. Blast it all, this woman's father had nearly ruined Jonas's life by stealing his mother from his father. Hadn't Jonas a right to some recompense for that?

"I take it the terms of the inheritance came as some surprise," he said, in no way ready to retreat.

The maid stepped around her employer as if she were going to rush at him, and the other moved forward, too, as if they were a unified force.

"Surprise?" said the Casterton woman. "How about shock, Mr. Prestwich? This business has always belonged to the Casterton name—since the beginning. This town was nothing but a pleasant view before the paper mill came here."

He lifted a brow. "The paper mill has employees? I was told it was run single-handedly."

"So it is." The maid's voice was as high-strung as the rest of her, judging by the near dance she did, shifting her meager weight from one foot to the other, clenching and unclenching her little hands. "But not all that long ago there wasn't nothing but a couple of houses and a church and grocer 'round here."

"The stationery shop was the first attraction in Cranbury." The older woman leaned closer as if to intimidate him. "This shop brings folks all the way from Williamsport so they can choose the *best* items on the market. Can you blame other businesses for taking advantage of those visits from wealthy Williamsporters? A hat and dress shop, a wood working business, the finest bakery in all of Pennsylvania offering a pastry or even a mid-day meal. We specialize in excellence, from our strawberries to dresses and right here with the books on our shelves. Our town has a reputation that goes far beyond Williamsport, and it started over twenty years ago with the Casterton Paper Mill. So you can just leave us alone and let the inheritance stay where it belongs."

"We don't need no stranger," added the maid, who had bobbed over to the door and now took up an umbrella from the stand at the threshold. She was slight, even bony, but for a moment he wondered if she would actually use the instrument the way she appeared willing to do. As a weapon.

The Casterton woman grabbed his arm, pulling him back toward the door. And although he allowed her to move him, he had no intention of leaving.

He held up a palm, offering a smile because he knew he could easily disarm the one while staving off the other. This Casterton might be sturdy, and the other wiry, but he towered over them both. It would be like withstanding the attack of children. "I concede there is an unforeseen element in all of this, but Mr. Hargrove made it clear this distribution is not only legal, it's binding. The courts will see this through unless we come to some agreement."

"No need for a courtroom if you refuse to accept what isn't yours anyway!" The maid lifted the umbrella higher above their heads. It was long and black with a carved wooden handle, and even with the wire and canvas to soften any blow, the tip might do some damage if used effectively.

"You've no right to a single stick of furniture," said the Casterton, wagging a stout finger in his face, "or to a single piece of paper, or a single penny of profit."

Before Jonas could issue a response—one he wasn't quite sure would be heeded anyway—the bell on the door chimed. But the umbrella-wielding maid was in the way of it opening, demanding her attention long enough for Jonas to remove the would-be club from her clutches.

"Oh, Miss Ari!" the maid said, offering no objection to having the umbrella taken away. "He's here! That awful man who's stealing what's rightfully yours."

A third woman entered, and although the open door let in more light from the sunshine she brought with her, even that seemed to pale in comparison. He saw immediately she was lovely. Taller than the other two, yet still delicate, with a trim waist accentuated by the cut of her skirt and shirtwaist beneath the shortest of unnecessary capes for such a fine day. Her hair, dark golden like the sun on ripe corn silks, was piled loosely, a few curling tendrils drawing attention to the size of her contrastingly dark eyes.

Eyes that just now looked between the other two and him with growing alarm.

"What's going on here?"

"You—you're Arianne Casterton?"

"That's right." She took the umbrella from his slackening hold, replacing it in the holder behind her. "And I assume from the way my friends have greeted you that you're Jonas Prestwich."

He held out a gloved hand. "At your service. Your new partner."

Although she glanced at his extended hand, she lifted only an icy gaze, letting his friendly gesture go unaccepted.

CHAPTER SEVEN

Partner?

Had he truly just used such an amicable word for this outrageous predicament?

"You're mistaken, Mr. Prestwich," she said, glad her voice was far calmer than her insides, "if you think I welcome any partnership."

Then she strode past him, crossing the room and taking a stand behind the counter. The fixture offered a bulwark for her, its warm, smooth wood something to latch on to, hide behind, even lean against if need be. She removed her cape, pretending busyness by putting it where it did not belong, on one of the shelves underneath. She must do something to spend her energy, and at the moment such inane movement was all she could think of.

He followed with a confident smile on what she must reluctantly admit was a handsome face. She wanted to search his appearance for some resemblance to Charlotte, some glimmer of hope that a part of that dear woman—her kindness, generosity, humor, grace or intelligence, but most of all some hint of her faith—resided in him. But Arianne refused to let her gaze do any more than sweep over him.

"It's true I know nothing of you or the business your father built here," he told her. "But I also know that one young woman such as yourself," he spared a glance at Phoebe and Binny, "even with a staff as obviously *loyal* as yours, might find it difficult to run a business on her own. I can assure you I'm not only well-educated but experienced in the machinations of businesses far bigger than this. I could be of great assistance, having a vested interest in its greatest value."

She narrowed her eyes at him. "And I can assure you we don't need any assistance. We're already quite successful, and credit for that goes to my father and to him alone. He taught me well how to carry on."

Mr. Prestwich's brows rose. "And you alone plan to continue?" A grin betrayed his lack of confidence in her claim. "Forgive me for saying so, Miss Casterton—it is Miss, isn't it? But as I understand it your father worked the mill by himself. You plan to take his place? In the mill itself, actually making paper?"

"That's right." Her heart thrummed hard against her chest, as if denouncing her own words. She *could* run the mill . . . at half the speed of her father, if she ignored every other aspect of the business. Phoebe was already carrying on alone in the shop without a raise in pay, and Leo helped when he could. But besides working over the vat, it had been her father who did everything from procure the best fibers to finding new customers—in Cranbury, Williamsport, Philadelphia and even New York. Finding buyers outside the shop was one portion of the business she'd never done before.

"You know, Miss Casterton," Mr. Prestwich's voice took on a softer tone, almost intimate. "I met your father on more than one occasion. Though he obviously had his faults, he struck me as having some discernment, at least as far as choosing what he purchased from us. How is it, I wonder, that you are so unlike him?"

The words pierced her, particularly since the man had the audacity to refer to her father as if he had faults as obvious as his discernment. "And how is it, Mr. Prestwich, that you are so entirely unlike your mother? She never would have allowed this inheritance to take place, had she the power to change it. She knew the difference between fair and unfair."

He did not even blink at her matching insult. She saw, in spite of her words, that he had inherited something from his mother after all: the color of her eyes. They were light brown, nearly gold.

"Fair or not, you shouldn't be so quick to refuse my help." He leaned closer. "A partner may be just what you need."

She lifted one skeptical brow. "I doubt you could even identify the difference between factory and handmade paper. The last thing I need is an ignorant partner."

"Ignorant, perhaps, but that is a temporary condition. You're proud of your father's accomplishments, and as it happens I have something of a legacy from my *own* father." The eyes that bore the color of Charlotte's now hinted at something Arianne had never seen in Charlotte, something dark like anger or frustration or resentment. But it was gone before she could tell for sure what she'd seen. "My mother may have failed to share with you the business talents of my father. He taught me well how to succeed, and as a partner I would be willing to help you in that regard."

"I don't see how you could be of any help, Mr. Prestwich, knowing so little of papermaking."

"Is that all there is to this business, then? Only production? What about sales and reputation, nurturing demand through advertising and innovation? The fundamentals of business are similar nearly everywhere. And there are other things to consider." He let his gaze fall from her face, as if taking in the size of her. He didn't need to say another word for her to guess he found her insufficient. "Your knowledge of papermaking may be as vast as my ignorance of it, but I can't help wondering how a woman, even one hearty and hale, can truly work a job that likely demands the measure of strength I saw in your father."

Her heart pounded anew against what felt very much like an accusation of disbelief. "Do you doubt I'm telling the truth? You don't believe I can work the mill?"

One of his shoulders—not so broad as her father's had been, but masculine nonetheless—lifted as skeptically as she'd lifted her brow a moment ago.

Without a word, she turned on her heel.

"Come with me, Mr. Prestwich."

———

Jonas followed Miss Casterton, going around the counter and noticing she was confident enough not to look back to see if he'd obeyed. He was glad the other two didn't follow, even though he'd sensed they'd listened attentively to every word just exchanged and likely wanted to come along, at least to witness a show.

She led him through a cluttered kitchen then outside to a far corner of the yard. There, he spotted the entryway to a narrow path that wound beneath a canopy of trees, with ferns and ivy lining its edges. Moss releasing the aroma of mint softened the stones with each step he took.

Descending some distance, he heard the steady flow of water just as he spotted the tin rooflines of a line of stout, frame buildings, all attached in a neat row leading from the riverfront. A small garden was planted at the foot of the path, the only spot sunlight had any hope of touching.

"Flowers?" he asked as they passed the recently worked ground. She wouldn't have time for something as frivolous as gardening if she planned to work this business by herself.

"We sometimes use flowers and seeds, and other plants, for certain colors or textures with special orders. It's just as easy to grow our own as to buy them at a market." She pointed to the river. "We use cattails, too."

He tried not to reveal his surprise that the garden was anything but sentimental, realizing his absolute dearth of knowledge regarding papermaking. She could tell him little fairies came and made paper during the wee hours of the night, and he might not believe her but wouldn't have any evidence to disprove her, either.

Two steps led into the nearest end of building, but she walked through the first room all the way to the other end. It was warmer there, even though they were nearly on top of the river. "The water in the dipping vat is heated, which is why it's always a bit warmer in here than outside." Had she read his mind? Was he so easy to read? She crossed to the farthest side of the room, which he guessed from the multi-paned window was directly over the Susquehanna below. A cylindrical machine was running under the pressure of water power.

"This is the Hollander, where we mash the rags and fibers into pulp—which then transfers to the dipping vat." She pointed to the column overhead, connecting one to the other with the vat along the outside wall. "As you can see, the river does the hard work. Our equipment is placed deep enough to run beneath the ice in winter, so we can produce paper year round."

Her tone was laced with an I-told-you-so, and as much as he wanted to listen to the method she went on to describe, about deckles and moulds and the right kind of felt for the paper to rest upon during the drying process, he couldn't help but try spotting a portion of the process plainly beyond the strength of a woman.

When he guessed water must be squeezed out of the piles of felt-laced stacks of paper, he wondered if the combination of water, felts and paper was too heavy for a woman to maneuver. But a water-powered hydraulic press crushed Jonas's brief hope as efficiently as it must remove water from the paper. Perhaps, as she claimed, she really could work this small factory all by herself.

One thing was clear as she went through a rudimentary explanation of how the product was made: she not only knew the business, she loved it. She finished the tour in an upstairs room she called the drying loft, where window slats on all four sides would catch a breeze from any direction. At the moment they were open only north to south, with a few papers hung width-wise to catch any air without twisting the sheets.

"My father ran this business in a methodical, sensible manner," she said proudly, "built upon knowledge from generations before him. In short, Mr. Prestwich, he knew what he was doing and taught me well how to carry on."

"Your father must have been quite the model of papermaking virtue." Jonas hadn't intended to be snide, but the meticulous care Casterton took to run his business only contrasted how shoddily he'd treated the bonds of marriage between Jonas's parents.

It was too late to recant the words now, though, especially seeing Arianne Casterton's eyes momentarily widen as she interpreted the comment in exactly the manner he'd too hastily intended: with disrespect for her father.

She turned away a little more quickly than she might have had he kept his mouth shut. Possibly the woman was as ignorant of their parents' illicit relationship as Jonas was of the papermaking business. Or worse, she'd condoned what their parents had done. If that was so, he had every right to take full advantage of this inheritance. It might take some time to sell such a specialized business, but there was likely a market for such a thing.

Downstairs again, there was a door to another room off to the side that she appeared ready to bypass.

"And what's in that room? Storage?"

She shook her head, but if he could presume to read the expression on a face he'd only just met, he would guess at sadness when she glanced toward that room.

"We store paper in the annex, farther from the river, as well as up in the shop. This room is for watermarking."

"But you don't want to show the room to me? Perhaps a family secret is in there, known only to Casterton papermakers?" From the vague instructions she'd shared so far, he guessed she'd guarded quite a few trade secrets.

"It's a small room, for one worker only, and dark. I need to control the light when I'm working with the wax and wires."

"So you do the watermarking? That isn't something your father did?"

She shook her head, and attempted to leave the small factory altogether, not even allowing a peek into the little room. Without thinking, he took a gentle hold of one of her wrists as she passed. He instantly regretted his boldness when she wrenched herself free. Men never touch women; he'd been taught that from the earliest age. But somehow, out here in the middle of a Pennsylvania forest he'd forgotten the rules of fashionable society. Or maybe it was the battle inside of him, pulling him in two different directions when it came to this woman and her inheritance.

"I'm sorry." He took back his hand, palm up. "It's just—I have to ask. If you concentrated on watermarking while your father made the paper, will you have time to do both, even if you're fully capable of doing both?"

She lifted her chin. "Casterton paper is watermarked with a dove, and that design is already made, reusable and quickly repaired whenever necessary."

"Among the lists I received, I noticed there was a recent influx of money from an order marked only 'special watermark.' Will you be able to fill those kinds of orders in the future, since they seem to be the most profitable?"

"I'll manage."

He didn't believe her. "I've seen the books, the orders, the bank accounts, everything, Miss Casterton. You've proven you can make paper, but I haven't seen anything to convince me you can produce the same quantity as your father. Even if I didn't require you to buy my one-third—"

She flashed a look at him so fierce he knew a gentleman would assure her he would demand no such thing. But he held back. One thing he'd learned in business was never to let emotion rule his decisions.

All he said was, "I suggest, Miss Casterton, that you get used to me, at least until we can figure out a mutually beneficial solution."

CHAPTER EIGHT

The moment they stepped back inside the shop, Arianne knew Phoebe and Binny had not only been plotting further tactics against Mr. Prestwich, they'd sent for reinforcements. Leta didn't even pretend to be a customer. She approached Mr. Prestwich and looked him over as if he were one of the displays.

"So this is the man who would steal one-third of everything your father worked for?"

Arianne had no way to tell what Mr. Prestwich must be thinking, having to face yet another of her allies. But he didn't look rattled.

"I assure you, everything is as legal as it is binding." Dismissing Leta and her righteous anger without another word or glance, Mr. Prestwich turned back to Arianne. "I was told at the Cranbury Inn there are no available rooms," —he glanced at the unfriendly hosts beside her— "since I made the mistake of introducing myself before procuring the room. I further assume from the lack of a single pole there are no telephones in this town. I intend to stay in Williamsport, then, until we work out our situation. I made arrangements for someone to come for me, but he isn't available until this evening. I'd like to return to town sooner than that, but

I'll need transportation. How do you arrange for that sort of thing here?"

When no one, not even Arianne herself, hastened to answer, he had the insolence to offer her a wink along with his ever-present and all too confident smile. "Surely you're eager to be rid of me, Miss Casterton? Enough to provide information on the best way out of town?"

"Only if you *stay* away."

As much as Arianne wished she could echo Binny's sentiment, two realizations came to mind. First, she knew this was only the beginning of his company; being rude wouldn't help their *situation*, as he'd called it. Secondly, ever since she'd returned to find him here she'd been ignoring the conscience God gave her. How quickly she'd forgotten the comforting presence of her Creator after having spent so enjoyable a time in His company only a short time ago. Even if this man's behavior was entirely objectionable, God not only loved him, but wanted her to love him, too.

Or at least not hate him. Still, the man had made such strange comments about her father—rude at worst, impolite at best—that she couldn't shake her eager ill will, even when she reminded herself he was Charlotte's son. Knowing Charlotte never spoke of him only heightened Arianne's resentment of him. There must have been a reason for him to have been estranged from someone as sweet as Charlotte.

"You can find Mr. Tummers at the post office," she said at last, "just down the street. He runs the Canary for hire, a yellow Herdic." Glancing at her watch pin, she added, "If you hurry you can catch the afternoon mail run. He's due to leave at five."

Breathing came a little easier when he put a hand on the door handle, but she caught her breath back when he turned once again to face her.

"Thank you for the tour of the business, Miss Casterton. I can see you'll need some time to adjust to me, so I'll leave you to ponder what kind of help you might welcome from me until we can work something out." He pulled open the door just as Arianne's neighbor Mrs. Crane stepped inside. Evidently she'd only just heard about their visitor. Mr. Prestwich bowed courteously and stepped aside so she could enter, placed his hat on his head, then, at the threshold, he looked once again at Arianne. "Until . . . tomorrow."

Tomorrow. Arianne wasn't sure she'd ever so dreaded the coming of another day.

————

If the large sign over a modest post office wasn't enough to let Jonas know he'd come to the right place, the yellow carriage nearby confirmed it. Two men struggled to load a crate on to the brightly colored coach, each on ladders and hoisting the bundle onto its flat, solid roof. One of the men lost his hold but the crate did nothing more than land on top with a thud. The noise startled the horse and, if Jonas hadn't been close enough to grab the bridle, the animal likely would have taken off down the street.

The older man, grasping the decorative edge of the yellow cab's roofline as if without it he'd lose the ladder beneath him, caught his breath then looked Jonas's way.

"How do, young man." The greeting came with a salute carried out with an unsteady hand. "I'm obliged for your help."

The other man, much younger, had sprung from his own ladder shortly after the crate's crash. He'd likely been headed for the horse, but stopped when he caught sight of Jonas.

"Thanks, mister." Turning to the old man, his youthful face turned to a scowl. "I told you to let me and Chester do this, Tummers." He grabbed the man's arm when he nearly missed the bottom rung of the ladder, assisting Tummers to the boardwalk.

"No harm done, Leo. Now climb back up there and tether that thing or it'll land right back here on the step when I get going."

Jonas stood by while the younger man went back up the ladder. "I'd like a ride to Williamsport, if you have the room for a passenger."

Mr. Tummers glanced through the glass at the number of smaller mail packages taking up much of the carriage space.

"Sure, we can scoot some of them boxes out of the way, can't we, Leo?"

The man grunted as he pulled on a leather strap affixing the crate to the carriage, but nodded just the same.

Mr. Tummers grinned, adding a wink. "He don't like to take orders from me, but most of them boxes are from his family anyways. Wood carvings, going to market in Williamsport."

"It's a good thing they're not glass," Jonas said.

The younger man hopped down from the ladder, looking at Jonas curiously. "Don't think I'd send 'em with Tummers if they were. He depends on the springs a little too much, if you know what I mean."

"Ha! I can catch an insult when I hear it. I know how to avoid the ruts same as any other driver."

Leo patted the man's shoulder. "Sure, sure you do," he said, at the same time shaking his head at Jonas. Jonas sensed affection behind their comfortable sparring, a camaraderie of close neighbors he guessed might be the only good thing about living in such a small town.

"What brings you out from Williamsport?"

Jonas was hesitant to answer, at least until they were on their way—and even then, the driver might desert him on the side of the road if he had a smidgeon of the loyalty to the Castertons he'd seen so far. "Just a little business. Do I pay you for the ride, or is there a ticket office inside the post office?"

"Might as well pay me, unless you got other business in there."

"No, nothing today." Jonas pulled out his billfold, asking the price even while he felt a curiously intense gaze from the younger man.

"Just passing through, then?" He glanced at Jonas's empty hands. "Carrying no samples, I see."

"No, not selling." Jonas replaced the billfold in his inside pocket, looking again at Mr. Tummers. "How soon do you think we'll be on our way?"

The man pulled a pocket watch from his vest. "'Bout two minutes or so. Can't leave before five, in case anyone else shows up last minute, you see."

"Well then, maybe I can help this woodworker shift some of his boxes a little?"

The one called Leo looked momentarily startled, as if he'd forgotten he'd been assigned another task. He turned to the rear of the carriage and its door, but there wasn't room for more than one to work in such a small space. Jonas watched, hoping the final two minutes would pass quickly enough to avoid any further chance for questions. The older man disappeared inside the post office, giving Jonas a bit less to worry about.

"Room enough for one, then," said Leo as he stepped back down to the road.

Jonas moved forward, taking hold of the open door, but Leo didn't move out of the way.

"I noticed you came out of the stationer's."

Jonas eyed the other man. Facing down a couple of spinsters was one thing, but a robust man this size was another thing altogether.

Still, there was nothing to do but admit the truth. "Yes, that's right."

"You have business at the stationery shop, then?"

Jonas nodded, keeping his gaze steady.

"You wouldn't happen to be the so-called heir to a part of the Casterton property, would you?"

"Afraid so."

He snorted. "Better not tell Tummers, or he's liable to make you walk all the way to Williamsport."

Jonas kept his gaze level with the other man's. "Yes, I sensed I wasn't altogether welcome here. Evidently Miss Casterton is well liked."

"What's fair is fair, mister, and this sure ain't. Your own mother woulda' seen that. So unless you came here to refuse that inheritance, I don't see how anybody in town would welcome the sight of you."

"You should have learned by now that life isn't fair."

"So you're gonna take it? What's rightfully Ari's? Just steal it right away from her?"

Jonas would have liked to end the conversation, partly because some infinitesimal part of him wanted to agree it was stealing, but more importantly because even if it was, it was a valid price for her to pay. Ari, as this young man so fondly called the woman, might be the only one in town who could guess why this inheritance wasn't entirely unfair. If she knew her father had lured his mother out of a legal and binding marriage . . . then she deserved to pay what her father should have before his death.

And if she didn't know, Jonas might as well enlighten her.

"I can see that you, right along with the rest of the town, feel a sense of loyalty to her. I understand that—applaud it, even. But have you considered the possibility that a partnership with me might secure the business? Do you honestly think she'll be able to carry on alone?" At least until they could sell it for a decent profit, but he didn't want to bare his hand.

"As far as I can tell that's none of your concern."

Hearing Mr. Tummers emerge from the post office, Jonas pushed past the younger man toward the seat in the back of the Herdic. "I don't see how this town's loyalty will help her keep up production of paper or secure future sales. As I see it," he said, jumping into the carriage, "Miss Casterton needs me. Only she doesn't yet know it."

Rather than closing it, Leo held open the door. The carriage jostled when Mr. Tummers took the driver's seat up ahead, and Jonas saw Leo's grip on the door handle whiten his knuckles. The look on the man's face went from unfriendly to downright hostile.

"She's got a partner right here already, one who knows how to make paper. Me."

"So you're a woodworker and a papermaker, too?" Jonas asked skeptically.

"That's right. And we don't need you."

Leo slammed the door shut just as Tummers urged the horses forward.

The only thing Jonas welcomed was that the final interchange allowed no time for Leo to share with Tummers the nature of the business that had brought him to town.

Tomorrow, just to be on the safe side, Jonas would hire his own buggy from Williamsport.

CHAPTER NINE

Arianne rubbed at an ache that had arrived with the morning, residue of working in the mill from the moment Jonas Prestwich had departed until well into the night. She'd slept later than usual, and finished her breakfast barely in time to open the shop.

"He's a handsome devil, I'll give him that," said Leta, leaning to look out the front window. She'd arrived ten minutes ago, and had been watching for the return of Jonas Prestwich ever since.

"Handsome is as handsome does," chimed Phoebe, taking a feather duster to the bookshelves nearby.

"I just hope I don't have to feed him," said Binny, who'd followed Arianne from the kitchen instead of cleaning up the dishes left behind. "I'm afraid I might do something awful to his food."

Arianne laughed. "There is only one way to be rid of this particular scourge, and that's to convince him to see reason. He's Charlotte's son, after all. Surely she always modeled goodness. He must know the difference between right and wrong."

"Hmph," said Leta. "There must be a reason she never spoke of him."

"But she did," Arianne said, her eyes filling with unwanted tears. "I'd forgotten until last night, when . . . I remembered the last word Charlotte spoke to me, before she died. She said his name. I didn't understand it at the time, because of the way she said it. So tenderly. But now I know that's what she said. Jonas."

Leta must have seen her struggle against tears, because she left the window for Arianne's side, putting an arm around her shoulder.

"I don't see what good that says about Mr. Prestwich," said Phoebe. "It only means his mother loved him no matter what he did. And that proves what we already knew, how wonderful Charlotte was."

"Who knows why they never spoke this past year or more?" Leta asked. "He must have done *something* to cause the rift."

"Musta been really terrible to make someone as nice as Mrs. Charlotte ban him from her life," Binny said.

Surely Binny was right. While drifting off to sleep last night, Arianne tried imagining why someone as affable as Charlotte suffered strife with anyone, let alone with her very own offspring. The fault must be with her son; there was no other explanation. "He didn't even ask about her grave," she whispered. "His own mother is buried here in Cranbury, and he didn't think about paying her the respect of a visit."

"What more proof do we need of his lack of character?" Leta asked.

"Speak of the devil, there he is!" Binny hissed, her gaze on the glass door.

Arianne really ought to caution her friends about so easily linking Mr. Prestwich with the devil, even if he was doing the devil's bidding by stealing her inheritance. She'd hoped yesterday's visit had changed his mind, but his reappearance today proved just how naïve such hopes had been.

———

"Never without a customer, I see," greeted Jonas as he stepped inside. He added, "Too bad they don't seem to actually purchase anything."

The one he could tell didn't work here lifted her chin at the pronouncement, stepped away from Arianne Casterton's side then left the shop without another word.

As she did yesterday, Miss Casterton retreated behind the shop's countertop. She lifted what appeared to be a weary hand to her forehead. Perhaps she, like him, had been awake well into the night, wondering how they would work this out. Was it fair that he demand she sell, even if her hopes of running it on her own were unrealistic? He knew what it was like to have a partner demand a sale; he'd just been through that with his father's textile mill. His father's old partners, Julia's father and Mr. Watson, had decided to relocate the mill to Atlanta, closer to the source of cotton. Jonas had welcomed the fair market value of his share that fattened his bank account, but he privately questioned if his father would have wanted the business he built to disappear from his home town.

Jonas didn't fool himself into thinking Miss Casterton would welcome a sale here. Even during his limited tour, he could tell she cared more about papermaking than the realities of the business world.

Still, he had a right to be here now and couldn't help wondering if thoughts of him and their new partnership had kept her awake during the same late hours he'd been thinking of her.

"Mr. Prestwich," she said, "I really don't see what your visit achieves. I concede you have the law on your side. But since the mill isn't something that can be literally split, you'll have to settle for one-third of the profits going forth. That doesn't require you to be here."

"I believe you've misunderstood the terms then, Miss Casterton. While I do have a right to future earnings should the mill remain in our possession, I also have a right to one third of the property as it is. I understand you are unable to buy my third, so if this business is to remain intact, we'll need to cooperate with each other." He removed the old jacket he wore, one he'd found in the wardrobe at the Williamsport house. "As you can tell, I'm dressed for work. I intend to learn the trade myself, so we can keep the mill running at its expected speed. And maybe, by the time we receive any more special watermarking orders, since those seem to bring in the most profit, you can see to that while I work the mill."

He might have laughed at the way her mouth hung open, except even with such shock on her face she was still lovely. Did she really think him so incompetent? Surely papermaking couldn't be more challenging than he thought. The important thing was to find a buyer for this business; it behooved Jonas to know what he was selling, and keep sales up to attract prospective buyers.

"You?" she said at last. "Work? In the mill?"

"That's right." He offered her a palm to lead the way. "Shall we get to work then? If you can be spared here in the shop, that is?"

"I . . . I was just about to go," she said as if carefully choosing her words. "But frankly, Mr. Prestwich, you'll only be in the way."

"At first, perhaps. But the sooner we get to work, the less time it'll be before I'm of real help."

Jonas was more than a little surprised that was all it took for her to comply. He'd expected more of a fight, at least if she intended to show him the real workings of the mill. But without another word, she led him to the path through the forest.

All night he'd wrestled with his choices going forward. If accepting this inheritance really was retaliation for what Samuel Casterton had done to sour his parents' marriage, then forcing the sale of the mill was the best, most immediate answer. He knew she couldn't afford to buy him out, especially with an inheritance tax still to be paid. Seeing how much she loved the place had convinced him yesterday that was the way to strike the deepest retaliatory wound.

And yet he couldn't deny a few other, more surprising thoughts that kept him up last night. He'd actually pondered ways to expand the mill, to widen its market, to capitalize on the sound founda-tion Mr. Casterton had created. Perhaps it could be done, with hard work and the insight he could easily mine from his father's connections in the Philadelphia business world. If this mill could ever prove profitable, perhaps investing in it was a better choice than selling outright.

Greater success might do two things. One, it would give Jonas a new business opportunity, which he needed now. Two, it would prove, though Samuel Casterton might have been a competent papermaker, he fell short not only in romantic ethics but also in enterprise. Jonas would do what Casterton never had: make this business flourish.

While outshining Samuel Casterton in his own occupation did hold some appeal, Jonas knew he could improve this business or destroy it altogether; he'd be equally justified in doing either.

Until he knew what he wanted to do, whether he wanted to help or hurt this business of his father's enemy, he would involve himself just enough to remind Samuel Casterton's daughter of his legal right to one-third ownership.

Seeing her squirm beneath the uncertainty of what he might do was a modest, even shameful bonus, especially since he'd already questioned whether or not he harbored any true malice for her. It was her father, after all, whose actions had ruined his mother's reputation. Not this woman.

As they reached the mill, more thoughts from last night returned to him, ones he should probably forget. Somehow in the dark of night, well after midnight, Jonas had wondered what it would be like to see Arianne smile—at him. He'd learned how to trifle with a woman's affections. Julia Kitteridge had been an excellent tutor because that was what she'd done with him. Flirted, then act the coy maiden. None of it meant anything, and he was fairly certain he could win over Miss Casterton without involving any of his own emotions.

Seeing her face as somber as it had been the day before did make him wonder just how pretty she would look with a smile.

Rather than taking him to where he'd been told yesterday the papermaking process began—at the Hollander for mashing fibers

—Miss Casterton stayed in the first room, where the presses were housed. To his surprise they were filled, when less than twenty-four hours ago they'd been empty.

He eyed her, childishly disappointed. Not only must her fatigue be due to good, honest hard work and not to the rumination that kept him awake, he had a strong suspicion she intended to keep some of the details of papermaking a secret even to him, her new partner.

During the next several hours, Miss Casterton schooled him on everything from the nap of the felts separating each piece of paper to the importance of uniform weight in the press, from the center to the edges to keep the pages consistent. She instructed him on subsequent pressings and the rest of the drying process, followed by the intricacies of what she called polishing.

With so much care, it didn't take long for Jonas to wonder if this was a business or a hobby. It was only right to demand integrity in a product. But perfection? In the textile mill he'd learned there was room between acceptable and unacceptable, but he wasn't sure the Casterton mill would sell anything that didn't meet this woman's high standards.

Miss Casterton spoke only during training or answering Jonas's questions. The silence between those exchanges was anything except companionable, but after a while the tension did seem to drain away along with the water that was pressed from the newly formed pages. He worked steadily, without complaint even though he was unaccustomed to working so physically. If this woman, or any woman, could work this way, then certainly so could he.

Tomorrow, though, he would eat a bigger breakfast than just a cup of coffee. It wasn't long before he wondered how much more time would pass without stopping for a midday meal.

Perhaps she would never stop, just to spite him. He'd had the foresight to bring his own food from Williamsport, in case the Cranbury café or bakery refused him service as had the inn. The sack was tucked safely in the back of the carriage he'd hired to bring him here, a carriage he'd hired for the entire day just to wait for his call. He could leave the mill right now if he wanted, except the thought didn't sit well with him. To stop working before she did would be like blinking first in a staring contest; he wasn't about to give in to his hunger before Arianne Casterton did.

When a shadow passed the open door, drawing his attention, he hoped it might be that maid, the spindly one who'd brandished the umbrella against him. What were maids for, except to deliver meals? But at the door he saw instantly this shadow was too tall.

It was the woodworker he'd met yesterday. The *partner* Miss Casterton already had. If this late hour started the workday for him, there was no doubt Jonas could prove himself more valuable, once he learned this blasted business.

"Ari," the woodworker called, sparing a cool glance Jonas's way through the threshold between the pressing and vat room. She turned to the man immediately and Jonas watched her face closely, to see what kind of welcome he ignited. Jonas had already guessed the kind Leo wanted.

There was something there, all right. A smile. This being the first he'd witnessed, Jonas couldn't gauge the depth of its sincerity. Maybe it was just his own pride, but he was fairly certain that smile hadn't been quite as instantaneous as Leo might have liked.

"Binny said you haven't had lunch yet. Is something wrong?"

"No, not at all. We were just working. I lost track of the time."

Jonas wanted to claim his stomach had certainly remembered, but decided to let Leo think he'd been enjoying himself so much he hadn't given a thought to the hour, either. Since he wasn't sure Miss Casterton would offer the courtesy of an introduction, he approached the man without being invited.

"Leo," he said, the single greeting coming with an exchange of curt nods. No handshake, just an acknowledgement.

Miss Casterton's brows lifted. "You know each other?"

"We met yesterday at the post office."

"I was shipping an order to Williamsport."

"Quite a large order, too," Jonas said, folding his arms and leaning a thigh against the table nearby, as if settling in comfortably for a chat. "You must have a successful wood shop." *And therefore not be available to partner in any other business venture . . .*

"That's right," came the prideful answer, not from Leo but from Miss Casterton, who took another step closer to the man and entwined her arm with his. "Leo and his family have many customers, in both Cranbury and Williamsport. Their woodcarvings are becoming famous throughout the area."

Jonas wasn't sure which bothered him: her obvious effort to present herself as more than a little friendly with the man, or that Leo's business was a family endeavor. If it was a large enough family, the man could easily leave that business for another without harming its productivity. And Leo wasn't the kind of third partner Jonas had in mind.

Proud as a peacock, his hand possessively over the one on his arm, Leo was every bit as tall as Jonas but with Miss Casterton clinging to him he appeared even taller. Looking at her now, there was no doubt she saw the same thing Jonas did. Leo was in love with her.

CHAPTER TEN

Arianne felt worse than a false friend. She was practically throwing herself at dear Leo, displaying more affection than she felt in stark contrast to the mistrust she aimed at Mr. Prestwich. She wanted to be sure this stranger, this unwanted *partner*, noticed.

"I suppose you've eaten already, Leo?" she asked him, amazed with herself when she sounded downright pouty. Where and when had she learned to flirt? She'd never in her life behaved this way before.

He turned to face her, taking both of her hands in his, which she easily accepted. She refused to contemplate that it took so little encouragement for Leo to take advantage of Arianne's whim. Surely he would understand when she explained later. "I came to work with you this afternoon," he said, "but I'll make sure you eat first. Binny said she was holding lunch for you."

He started to lead her away, but Arianne hesitated. Even if he did own a third of everything in the kitchen, Arianne had no intention of inviting Mr. Prestwich to share the meal.

"There is a bakery in town that serves sandwiches," she said politely. "And a café for more substantial fare. Or the Cranbury Inn, if you prefer tablecloths."

He walked toward the door with that same confident smile

she'd seen on his face before. Evidently he didn't care whether she offered him a meal or not.

"I doubt the Inn would serve me," he said, far more amicably than such an admission should warrant, "which is why I brought my own meal. I'll be back in an hour, then?"

"Make it half."

He stood aside to let them go, but she stopped when he moved to follow. "Will there be three of us working this afternoon, then?"

Leo flashed him a smile. "That's right."

Arianne knew she ought to feel proper gratitude for her friend's offer. Though she'd worked as hard as ever that morning, training Mr. Prestwich hadn't allowed her to go at her own pace— one half that of her father's. Leo would certainly speed things along.

But somehow she wasn't as pleased with the notion as she should have been.

———

Leo was Jonas's afternoon tutor, allowing Arianne to work elsewhere.

It was easy to think of her as Arianne instead of Miss Casterton, hearing Leo refer to her as such. The name suited her. Graceful, even while working.

Jonas knew immediately that Leo wasn't as precise in his method as Arianne, but he still proved competent and careful. One more testimony to the business integrity of Samuel Casterton, even if he had been the worst cad when it came to personal matters.

The afternoon wasn't as long as the morning had been, for which Jonas was grateful. He could only imagine what kind of aches he might feel tomorrow, having exerted muscles he'd never demanded use of before.

Neither Arianne nor Leo invited him near the vat, which so far he'd seen only Arianne employ, dipping moulds and shaking away the excess, creating a first hint of the paper those fibers would become. After Arianne released the material from the mould to what he'd been told was an asp, a drainage-horn that let excess water drain back into the vat, Leo soon carefully transferred the paper to the felts before bringing it to the press. They let Jonas run the press that squeezed water from the pages, rotating stacks carefully after a specific amount of time. Evidently it was the only step in the process that didn't require meticulous care; by the time Jonas received the pages, they were sturdier than they'd been earlier. Although he watched first Arianne and then Leo carefully work with the individual sheets, they didn't trust him to actually touch the paper until it had been strengthened in what was called a sizing process that had been performed the day before on the inventory Arianne had already created.

His job was no more than a repetitive task any bright young boy could do. Before the day was out, his mind roamed to more challenging thoughts. There was opportunity here; that would be clear to anyone with half the business sense and training Jonas possessed. More than once he wondered what Clarence Fitzwater would say about all of this, Jonas's old school mate whose family was heavily invested in the paper industry.

Such thoughts seemed to guide his intentions whether he was ready for them or not. He didn't even mind when both Leo and Arianne barely said good-evening to him; he returned to his hired carriage with orders to return to Williamsport—but not to his home. He knew there were at least two stationers in Williamsport, and he wanted to know what they thought of Casterton's products.

———

Arianne pulled down the shade on the front door of her shop. Phoebe had already gone home, and Binny was in the kitchen, leaving her alone with Leo. She hoped he didn't plan to stay much longer; after the amount of time she'd spent in the mill today, all she wanted to do now was go to bed.

"My father will need me in the woodshop tomorrow," Leo said. He lingered by the door, even though she put a hand on the door-knob, ready to open it for him. "I'll try to come again in the after-noon, but—"

Arianne shook her head. "Your first responsibility is to your family, Leo. I appreciate any time you can spare, but you mustn't feel obligated to spend every free moment here."

"Obligated!" Leo scooped up her free hand, bringing it toward his mouth for a kiss, but she pulled gently away before he could complete his mission. He frowned, placing his hands on her shoul-ders. "Arianne, I thought . . . today, that is . . . we worked together like never before. Even with that thief in the way, it was like . . . like a dance! We made more paper in a few hours than we've ever done before. We were the kind of partners you've always told me you wanted. Two workers who could see what the other needed without saying a word. We did that today. Didn't we?"

"Yes, we did. We always work well together." She turned away, to the window she'd just hidden with the shade. She regretted that Leo was the one paying for her flirtatious actions today. Not Mr. Prestwich, not her. "My father taught you so well."

"He did, but there was something else special about today besides that." His voice was a whisper, and he leaned closer even though there was no one else in the shop. "There was something in you today I never seen before. I thought . . . I thought you looked at me different."

Another arrow of guilt pierced Arianne's heart. She *had* looked at him differently today, but not for any reason she cared to admit, even to herself. She couldn't let him leave with an impression she shouldn't have offered in the first place. "I'm sorry, Leo."

He rested one of his hands on her shoulder. Although he didn't pull her close, she knew he would if she gave him the slightest encouragement. She didn't even look at him.

"Sorry? Today was the best day I've had since the first day I followed you home from school." He turned her to face him again. "I guess having that fellow here must have given you the idea to make him feel like an outsider. 'Course, that's what he is. So maybe you acted a little more friendly than you're used to. But if we work together like that, like today, then it won't be long 'til you're lookin' at me that way all the time. I can wait, Ari. I can be patient 'til it's there for real and not just for show."

Then his lips were on hers, soft and quick, before she could stop him. The kiss ended before she could pull away, then he brushed aside the hand she still held on the doorknob, and let himself out.

———

The first stationer was closed by the time Jonas arrived, so he could do no more than study the goods displayed in the window. If anything, the Cranbury shop had better variety and more interesting items, although he conceded he might already be biased by his partial—if unwelcome—ownership.

He jumped back into the carriage, naming the other shop that the driver claimed was several blocks away. Closer to the center of town, it offered more convenience for customers. An expensively carved sign hung above a wide doorway, and a quick glance at the goods on display revealed better selection and more costly items than the previous business offered. He'd have to take a closer look to see if they were indeed worth the prices advertised on the displays, because by comparison Arianne's shop was far more reasonable.

Seeing the proprietor at the door just pulling down the shade, Jonas hopped from his carriage and waved, catching the man's attention. Despite pulling open the door, a ruffle of annoyance crossed the shopkeeper's brow.

"I'm sorry, sir, but we're closing," he said.

"I won't take more than a few moments, and I don't even need to come inside. I've just visited a little town not far from here called Cranbury. Do you know it?"

"Yes, of course."

"There is a stationer's shop there. Do you know about that, too?"

The man stiffened, nearly imperceptibly, but Jonas saw the man's impatience transform into something else. Intrigued by the topic? "Yes, I'm familiar with it. What do you want to know?"

"General information, as someone considering an investment."

"I assure you, a lesson in the stationer's business entails a bit more than a curbside conversation. I suggest you start out as a salesman to acquire knowledge of the goods. Now good-day to you."

He began pulling the door closed again but Jonas put a hand on the edge of the door as someone already in sales might do. Balancing the bold action with a smile, he said, "Tell me one thing, sir, as a man in the same circle of commerce. Does the Cranbury shop have a reputation? Among other store owners such as yourself?"

He looked at Jonas curiously, as if he, not the topic, stirred his interest now. "Everyone knows the original owner of the shop. Or I should say knew. Samuel Casterton was probably the best paper-maker in the entire eastern half of the country, maybe in the entire country. His daughter has been running the shop for years, and has an eye for carrying the right goods. Let's just say as a competitor I wouldn't mind if the shop closes altogether, though I'd be the first in line to offer that girl a job right here if she needed it. Now," he added, tugging on the door again, "I insist upon closing. Good-day."

Jonas tipped his hat. "Thank you for your time, sir."

Settling back into his carriage, Jonas mulled what he'd learned. He wasn't at all surprised to learn others respected the shop, though how it stayed in business so far from any town of real size was still a mystery.

He had one more stop to make, at the train station where he could send a telegram back to Philadelphia. He'd known his neighbor Clarence Fitzwater long before their days at Yale; they'd attended primary school together and lived not far apart. Although the man might be surprised to receive a lunch invitation from someone he'd rarely seen in the two years since their last graduation, curiosity alone might be enough to garner the positive answer Jonas expected.

Perhaps all anyone needed to capitalize on the Cranbury papermaker's business was to expand.

And to do that, Clarence was just the person Jonas suddenly needed to know.

CHAPTER ELEVEN

Arianne dressed early, ate a hearty breakfast of oatmeal and strong tea, then started her day in the shop's storage room that served to separate the business from kitchen and private quarters. She wanted to be sure she had enough of the most popular paper goods before starting on a new order she'd received earlier that week from Williamsport. The invitations would require a watermark of a lumber magnate's business insignia, but it was an emblem she'd created a few years ago and used for this customer's annual ball. It would be an easy order to fill once again. If she could keep Mr. Prestwich happy doing the simpler tasks involved in papermaking, she could work faster.

Inevitably, when she scanned the storeroom's shelves, her eye was drawn to a special canvas-covered box on the highest shelf. Even though both Phoebe and Binny knew the contents belonged to Arianne, never to be used to fill outside orders, the box spoke to Arianne as if it were a secret between her and her father. A happy secret, a loving gift from father to daughter. A special collection of paper he added to every so often, as he'd done ever since she'd been born.

She couldn't resist. Stepping on the stool she kept nearby for just such a purpose, she reached the highest shelf and took it down. Placing it on the ample counter space, she settled the box and drew off the lid.

Arianne didn't touch the paper resting within the tissue, although she knew each sheet was remarkably like the others, in color, weight, and texture. How could she touch it with fingertips damp from wiping away her tears?

"Thank you, Papa," she whispered. "Somehow, I'll finish this myself. Soon." She smiled at her own words, knowing she alone would determine when the project needed to be completed. If Leo had any say in the matter, she would need the project finished any day now. "Soon enough."

The pain of missing her father rushed through her again, as raw as if it had happened that morning instead of weeks ago. She'd learned from her mother's death that grief was repetitive; just when she thought she was adjusting, it reappeared as fresh and stinging as if she'd gone back in time to that worst, first moment of learning about her loss.

But her intimacy with grief had also shown her those moments wouldn't revisit as often as they had in the beginning.

Replacing the box, she sought peace once again. Her father waited for her in a place where she, too, would go someday. Such a reunion felt far off, but knowing it would come added all the comfort it could.

———

Jonas slowed the horse he'd rented as he neared the first welcoming building on the edge of Cranbury, the white church with its tall steeple. He had much on his mind today, eager plans that could change not only his life, but everyone's in Cranbury. After what he'd learned about the impeccable reputation of Cranbury's paper mill, it was clear a quick sale was premature to achieve the highest profit. Regardless of whether or not he manipulated a sale at the appropriate time, he would work toward changing it. Improving it. A paper manufactory would bring far more than just jobs to this remote little hamlet. An enlarged business would draw many workers, inevitably swelling the number of residents. Eventually such a business would bring telephones and electricity and every convenience this little village was currently lacking.

He was nowhere near ready to share his aspirations, even if he was certain the foundation already existed for sound profit. He realized he had much to learn about the paper industry, but he was already working on that. As soon as he heard from Fitzwater, Jonas would likely know more about manufactured paper than Arianne did. He had every reason to believe her knowledge was limited to handmade paper.

Jonas pulled on the reins. He'd chosen to take a horse on such a fine day, rather than subject a driver to a long day's wait in a town too eager to turn its back on anyone associated with him. He'd kept up a fast pace, arriving fifteen minutes earlier than he'd expected.

Dismounting, he tied the horse to a post outside the church, nearest the iron fence surrounding the graveyard tucked to the side. He'd made himself stay away on his previous visits, telling himself he'd said goodbye to his mother that awful day at the morgue. More than once, he'd wished he hadn't seen her. The doctor had shown him nothing more than her face, but the grayish pallor, uncoiffed hair and oddly set countenance had for a time blotted out every memory of the beautiful woman she once was. He'd hoped to see some evidence of peace on her face, some hint that she'd found the happiness she'd once claimed to have with Casterton. But the sad woman he'd known was all he could remember.

He walked through the yard, seeing headstones older than he expected carved with unfamiliar names. There weren't even any Castertons, which vaguely surprised him until he remembered the clipped, British way Casterton had spoken. He was likely the first of his family to be buried on this side of the Atlantic, but that didn't explain where his wife was buried. His first wife, Arianne's mother.

"Can I help you find someone, young man?"

Jonas looked up, startled at seeing someone who must have been there all along, judging by the rake in his grip. But this was no ordinary gardener; he wore a black jacket and minister's collar.

"Yes. I'm looking for—"

"Charlotte Casterton?"

Jonas wasn't sure he was pleased or annoyed that this man already knew him. It was only more evidence of how much the town whispered about him. He'd had enough of that in Philadelphia.

The minister was past middle-aged, the skin on his face and neck well lined. He balanced the rake against the nearest headstone then approached Jonas with the first friendly greeting he'd received in this town.

"I'm Reverend McNichols, and I've been expecting you, once I learned Charlotte had a son." He started walking along the path down the center of the graveyard, inviting Jonas alongside. "We didn't know about you here in Cranbury, so I hope you'll forgive us if we were a little surprised at the turn of events between you and our Arianne."

"Considering you're the first person to speak to me in a civil manner, I'd say surprise might not be quite the right word."

He smiled. "We tend to be a little protective of our own, I suppose. I'm sorry if anyone offended you. Now tell me, are you planning to stay involved in the Casterton business?"

Jonas eyed the man. Civil or not, he wasn't likely to welcome Jonas's plans unless he believed they were for the good of "their Arianne." It was best to keep his plans to himself, at least until he was convinced of the direction he wanted to take.

"I'm involved already, just by virtue of the . . . situation." He looked around, still not seeing any sign of a recent addition to this old, crowded graveyard .

The minister pointed beyond the parsonage nearby. "We have a new cemetery," he said, "up beyond my house. Can you see where the forest opens and it looks like the hill had a haircut?"

Indeed, the trees did part some distance up. But they must have been cleared some time ago, since the meadow showed no evidence of tree stumps and grew only lush green grass, cut to easily navigable height. In the center of the area was another iron fence, and inside were several stones here and there. Two fresh oblong plots, side by side, were near the center.

Another image struck him, visions of his father's gravesite which wasn't much older. He was buried in Philadelphia, without any evidence that he'd spent his entire adult life married to this woman who was now buried beside someone else.

"Thank you," Jonas whispered, then turned in the other direction without looking back at either the minister or his mother's grave.

CHAPTER TWELVE

Arianne planned to employ Mr. Prestwich at the glazing rolls today, skipping altogether the sizing process and its ingredients, the step just prior to the rolls. He might not have any intention of stealing the family secrets her father had brought with him from Europe, but there was no sense taking a risk. Jonas Prestwich had a right to only *one-third* of this business, including only one-third of how it was run.

He'd arrived by ten that morning, just when the shop opened, but she'd been working for nearly two hours already. "After the second drying, the paper is brought here to the saul," she said, as if introducing him to the room even though he'd been here on his first tour. "This is where we make sure the paper has a smooth, uniform surface, and where the pores are closed so it'll be ready to accept ink. This room is also where, after the paper has sat in the dry press for a few days, you'll ultimately package the product for shipping."

She stood before the pair of huge solid rollers her father had fashioned before Arianne was born. He'd meticulously searched Pennsylvania's forest until he found what he needed, first for strength and then for size. Then he'd carved and polished the wood straight and smooth, cut it in two identically matched pieces and placed them into service using the power of the water beneath them.

She demonstrated to Mr. Prestwich how the paper was fed and where it exited to be picked from the felt, piled and readied for the drying loft.

If he resented being given another task she'd learned to do when she was seven years old, having to stand on a stool because she'd been too short to see, he didn't reveal it.

It was fortunate she knew the task as well as she did, since her mind was not on the work. What was he really doing here, this city person who had the power to demand she sell everything if he wanted to be paid his legal portion? Why was he interested in working here, as if he intended to continue as its part owner, claiming personal interest in keeping it going? Hadn't he a life elsewhere, wherever he'd come from? She could tell by his clothing—his shoes alone were the finest she'd ever seen, and must have cost a fortune—he didn't need to depend on this mill for an income. What was he *doing* here?

"Is there something else?" he asked.

She tried ignoring her thoughts, afraid she might give voice to them. "No . . ."

He turned to the rollers, as if cheerfully ready to tackle any task before him, no matter how menial. She had plenty to do, so she should be off, back to the vat. Still, she had a hard time inspiring herself to move. Those thoughts refused to be ignored, after all.

"Why do you keep coming back, Mr. Prestwich? Why do you want to work here?"

He considered her the same way she'd been considering him: curiously. "Haven't I a right to work here, since I have a vested interest in seeing it succeed?"

"Surely you have other responsibilities. In the life you had before . . . this inheritance?"

"Let's just say the timing suited me."

"You aren't hiding away from something, are you?" What else could he be doing here, so far from the city?

He laughed. "No, Miss Casterton." He began placing the pages on the felt that would feed them through the sizing rolls, just as she'd taught him. "Not everyone who leaves the city is running away."

She studied him, wondering what he meant, but he didn't look at her any longer, already starting to work. The words—and their oddly disrespectful tone—raised a defensive chord in Arianne. This wasn't the first time his vague reference made her feel this way, that he referred to some specific person or incident that she should recognize. She wasn't entirely sure whether the man meant to be disrespectful or if he was just generally unpleasant.

Of one thing she was certain: he was nothing like his mother.

The day went quickly, and Arianne was pleased with the amount of paper she produced. Mr. Prestwich's presence might not be welcome but he nonetheless helped her feel more productive with the intricacies she managed. She'd always thought her father had the best touch with the moulds, instinctively knowing the weight of the captured fibers to form the most consistently admirable pages. Yet when she compared her paper to his, something she hadn't done since she was thirteen and making paper on her own for the first time, she began to see what he'd said of her in recent years: she was as fine a papermaker as he.

The realization was as sweet as it was bitter. If only they hadn't gone on that train, she would still be making paper at his side. She could only imagine his indulgent smile, telling her he was proud of her work.

"I won't be coming tomorrow."

Leaning over the felts nearest the vat, Arianne was startled at the pronouncement. Other than letting her know he was leaving, and then back at lunchtime, Mr. Prestwich hadn't spoken a word to Arianne all day.

"Yes, I wouldn't expect you tomorrow," she told him. "It's Sunday."

Hanging the leather apron he'd worn on a hook near the door —sturdy protection from the sizing material—he offered a grim smile. "Just another day to me. But as it turns out I hope to have a business appointment in Philadelphia. Depending on the trains being on time, I expect to return from the city to Williamsport some time tomorrow evening and will be here by Monday morning."

"There's no need to hurry back. Perhaps your business would be better handled on Monday than on a Sunday."

"As I said, Sunday is just another day to me."

"I'm sorry," she said softly, surprised at the depth of her sincerity. She didn't mean to tell him he ought not do business on a Sunday—his cool response revealed how little the day meant to him. But that did make her feel sorry for him, because God was the only source of comfort she'd found since the death of her father. How must this man handle the loss of his mother, if he believed he would never see her again?

He might have left without another word, but instead he hesitated, regarding her with the same sort of interested look he'd aimed at her earlier. "Why are you sorry?"

"I feel sorry for anyone who doesn't take a Sabbath rest, who misses an opportunity to think about the God who made us."

"This faith of yours," he said. "Did you learn that from your father, just as he taught you to make paper?"

She nodded.

"Then I suppose that explains why his success was so modest."

"I'd hardly call my father's success modest. You have only to ask anyone for the finest paper in Pennsylvania, and my father's name would come up. And even if his success is modest by your standard, what has his faith to do with it? Are you suggesting God doesn't want those who believe in Him to succeed?"

"On the contrary, Miss Casterton. I'm saying if your father had truly been as talented as you seem to believe, his business would have claimed a larger share of the market. It's clear to me he was as limited in his faith as he was in the workplace."

"What!" Arianne's heartbeat, already on an increase, burst into a pounding rush. She'd had enough of his references to her father, and this one wasn't nearly as vague as those that came before. "How dare you speak ill of my father! You didn't even know him."

He put his hand on the door as if ready to leave, and Arianne had no desire to hold him back—or she might say something she would regret.

"I may not have known him face-to-face, but let's just say knowing *of* your father was enough for me. Good day, Miss Caster-ton. Like it or not, I'll see you on Monday."

———

Jonas fairly stomped up the hill, around the Casterton home and stationery shop, down the street to the livery where his horse waited for him in the custody of yet another unfriendly Cranbury business owner. Jonas was as angry at himself and his loose tongue as he was at the memory of both her father and his mother. He shouldn't have spoken, shouldn't have revealed there was another layer to this simple, if unfair, inheritance. He was nearly certain Arianne Casterton knew nothing about the beginning of their parents' relationship.

It didn't help that everything he'd seen in these few days working at the mill had revealed a quality of life he could admire. They lived simply, that was true, but it was as if by choice rather than due to limitations on the quality or effort involved in his business.

But the fact was her father must have set aside whatever faith he had—just as his mother had, too—in favor of their own selfish desires. What did that say of their faith? That they followed it only when it was convenient to do so?

They were as false as those Jonas had left behind in Philadelphia, those who sat in church on Sunday and gossiped about his mother the rest of the week.

Arianne might be hardworking; she might even be fooling herself into believing she could carry on this business to honor her father; she might have a face that haunted his dreams. But she was still the daughter of a man who had nearly ruined Jonas's life . . . and may well have been the cause of the early demise of Jonas's father. Who knew?

Tomorrow he would see Fitzwater. He would learn all he could about forever changing the way Casterton Paper Mill made their product. He would improve and expand this business until what Casterton had worked for all his life was a quaint memory and nothing more.

Topping off that revenge, Jonas would not only line his own pockets with more money than he could ever hope to spend, he would make Arianne far more secure than she ever would have been under her father's care.

CHAPTER THIRTEEN

Clarence Fitzwater was so pleased to see Jonas that he wondered if the man had confused him with some other neighbor or another former classmate. They rarely saw one another as children. What Jonas remembered about him was Clarence's propensity for numbers, making him the ideal study partner for all levels of mathematics. Back in those days, still under the mistaken impression that Jonas could somehow please his parents into a happy marriage, he had been both the ideal student and the most faithful of churchgoers.

But the truth was, the moment Jonas had graduated, he hadn't given Clarence another thought. Part of that was a wish to escape further attention from Fitzwater's family—in particular his two chatterbox younger sisters. So when Jonas arrived at the Fitzwater home, he was surprised but glad to find the house uncommonly quiet. He hoped it stayed that way for the duration of his visit. Clarence would be easy to ply for information, and it would be all the quicker with no one interfering.

"I suppose I shouldn't be so helpful if you're going to invest in a mill other than my father's." Clarence spoke briskly on their way to the dining room, but his smile was too sincere to lend much concern to such worries. "Future competitor and all that."

Before Jonas could reply, his eye was drawn to the man already at the dining room table. Clarence's father.

"What's this?" Mr. Fitzwater said. "Not only a guest for lunch, but a competitor?"

Jonas's hopes of easy access to all the information he wanted plummeted. Mr. Fitzwater might be the deepest well of information, but that didn't mean he would be so easily tapped.

At least there were no talkative sisters to compete with—or Mrs. Fitzwater, either, whose memorable image included various forms of frowning.

"You remember Jonas Prestwich, Father," said Clarence. "Or perhaps you recall his father's business—Tailored Textiles, the company that's just announced it's moving."

"John Prestwich's son?" He reached across both his ample belly and the plate in front of him for a handshake as Jonas took a seat adjacent. "Too bad about the company moving, though. Put a number of people out of work around here. Now what's this about another mill? Another textile mill?"

"Oh, no, Father. Jonas is interested in investing in a paper mill. Like ours."

Mr. Fitzwater's gray brows rose. "Like ours? Not ours? You don't want to invest with us, eh?"

Jonas laughed, hoping he sounded more at ease than he felt. If Clarence and his father had heard rumors of his mother, he only hoped they hadn't heard details that included an obscure papermaker.

"So you want to convert from textile to paper? Your employees might not be much use for such a drastic change, if that's what you had in mind."

"No, I recently came to part ownership of a much smaller mill, up in a little town not far from Williamsport, called Cranbury. Right now it's a simple, one vat operation, but I'm wondering about the possibility of expanding. So I've come to ask the advice of the brightest school mate I ever knew, to see what he has to say about this particular business."

"And my son will give you sound advice, too. Handmade paper, then? Well, that's a bit different from what we do in our factory, of course." He filled his plate with a variety of luncheon items a servant offered from a long tray: chicken quenelles on mashed potatoes, string beans and a small side of lobster salad. "We're not likely to be of much help unless you'd like to convert to larger machinery, of course. Even the largest handmade factories can't compete with our manufacturing volume, or the consistency of the product. Now I'll admit factory-made paper hasn't withstood the test of durability yet—if we could produce the same pulp they used a thousand years ago, for example, we'd have a chance to compare durability. But who's to say ours won't last just as long?"

"I'm here to learn what I can about converting the factory altogether, away from handmade and entirely to manufactured," Jonas said. Despite what Clarence proclaimed, Jonas's modest plans wouldn't be much competition of such an established factory as Fitzwater's. At least not yet. "It's a small company but with a solid reputation that I think can be beneficial if we want it to grow."

"Ah, reputation! The secret of every business's success."

Jonas listened to the advice they were all too willing to give, soon suspecting that although Mr. Fitzwater's passion was for paper produced in a factory, his enthusiasm might match that of Arianne Casterton's. His fervor was hard to miss. Jonas had never possessed much interest in his father's textile products, despite it being easy to sell, and briefly envied such zealotry. But if Jonas lacked some portion of their excitement he reminded himself of his father's success. He'd only cared about profit, not textiles specifically, so Jonas saw no reason he couldn't follow the same pattern.

"Few people care about old-fashioned paper anymore," Mr. Fitzwater was saying. "The best orders are the largest, and no handmade paper mill can produce the same amount of paper a factory can. It's a simple matter of economy to modernize, without sacrificing quality. And what I said about factory paper proving its durability? To that I ask what need has anyone of a newspaper once it's a day old? It's hardly any good for pulp anymore."

Mr. Fitzwater proved far more talkative—and informative—than Clarence, although when his friend could get a word in between those of his father he proved knowledgeable about the business as well. Everything he learned only increased Jonas's appetite for a paper factory. He might even get the Fitzwaters to invest in the expansion, if not a sure sale when the time came.

Soon coffee was served and Jonas knew he ought to be on his way if he wanted to make any stops before catching a train back to Williamsport. He'd had a note from a couple of his old friends who'd missed him at the racecourse lately, and wanted to make at least one visit before it was too late. Jonas had worked too hard to remain in the Philadelphia social circles to let his spot slip away due to temporary absence.

On their way out of the dining room, Mr. Fitzwater waved away the servant who had shown up with Jonas's hat and gloves. Jonas ignored his impatience to leave, knowing the delay would be worthwhile to his business, if not personal, interest.

"Now just a minute, young man. It's only just occurred to me. Did you say earlier that this one vat mill you're planning to convert is up in Cranbury?"

"Yes, that's right."

He snapped his fingers as if something had clicked in his memory, and Jonas had only one hope: that the memory had nothing to do with rumors about his mother.

"Why, I've just recently received a fine example of paper from up that way."

As Jonas released an imaginary sigh of relief, they followed Mr. Fitzwater into another room nearby.

"Father is a collector of all the paper made along the east coast," Clarence said. "Don't tell anyone, but Father has spies everywhere, looking for unusual products even if it isn't direct competition."

Mr. Fitzwater pressed an electric switch that ignited a light overhead. It was an impressively plush library and office, with a massive desk in the center. The dark wood, book-lined walls and warm leather furniture presented an inviting mix of business, success and pleasure.

He pulled out a drawer in the center of the large desk and withdrew a long, yellow envelope similar to the kind Jonas had used for business contracts. It even closed with tabs and a string.

"Now this is something you don't often see." His voice was nearly reverent as he admired the paper he carefully extracted. "The paper itself is fine enough, excellent quality in fact. But it's the watermark that bears notice. Extraordinary. The best I've seen, in fact."

He walked a few steps to the window that illuminated the desk from behind. Holding up the page to the sunlight, he nodded and pointed to an image that came into view only as Jonas neared.

The lines letting light pass—while not marring the smooth surface of the page—presented the face of a man. Not exceptionally handsome, yet the detail was striking, as if the person were as real as those in the room. It was like an ethereal portrait, there only because of what wasn't there, those fibers thinned in just the right design making the rest of the page plain.

"May I?"

Jonas reached for the paper and held it in his hand, studying the work before him. He'd seen many examples of watermarked paper before. On business stationery and banknotes, on contracts and even social invitations. None compared to this. It might be the epitome of vanity on the part of the person whose image the paper bore, but it was also the epitome of talent for someone to create such a portrait on a page that was both subtle and superior.

And in the lower right corner was a tiny dove. The standard watermark of Casterton paper.

"I have some final advice for you, young man." Mr. Fitzwater called Jonas's attention from myriad thoughts filling his mind. "Some might say it would be a shame to lose this kind of paper quality if you do convert from handmade to manufactured. I don't agree, of course. There isn't enough of a market for handmade to be very profitable." His brows drew together, as if fortifying what he was about to say. "But if you do convert, don't lose this watermark artist. The truth is, when I saw this page I wanted to hire him myself—no matter the cost."

CHAPTER FOURTEEN

Arianne was in the mill shortly after dawn on Monday morning. There was plenty of work to do with regular orders continuing to come in, but it wasn't business that made her escape her bed. Ever since Mr. Prestwich had left on Saturday, she'd done little else but recall his words. He had no reason to insult her father. How dare he insinuate there was something less than honorable about him? What would make the man say such a thing? Surely Mr. Prestwich must have some goodness in him, being Charlotte's son, and yet so far he'd been nothing but trouble.

The only thing that had taken her mind off Mr. Prestwich, at least for a short time yesterday, had been church. And Leo. He'd sat beside her rather than with his family, closer on the pew than she'd expected. She'd scooted away, maintaining the same distance she always kept when he'd chosen to sit nearby. No sense having people wonder if something had changed, now that she was not only alone but under a shadow in the shape of Jonas Prestwich. Until she could look at Leo as anything but the affectionate brother he'd always been she wasn't willing to give him any more encouragement than she'd already mistakenly offered.

She carefully stripped a new sheet of paper from the asp over the vat, transferring it to the waiting felt. But even her work couldn't demand all of her attention, and once again her thoughts returned to Mr. Prestwich. How dare he invade her home, her shop, and her grief? Had he no grief of his own, though he'd lost a mother as wonderful as Charlotte? What a terrible son he must have been. He hadn't even visited her grave.

Dear Lord, there must be a way to be rid of him!

If only she could figure out how.

———

Jonas let the horse trot inside the Cranbury livery stable, offering no more than a salute to the surly man who ran the place. He took Jonas's money easily enough at the end of the day, but offered not a single word otherwise.

Walking briskly toward the mill, Jonas bypassed the stationery shop altogether. Beating her to the job this morning might help to reduce whatever ill feelings he'd so foolishly kindled on Saturday.

Yesterday had been an illuminating day. Between Clarence and Mr. Fitzwater, they'd easily convinced Jonas that paper could provide a living—a very good one at that—with some necessary improvements. What other way was there to communicate the written word, than through paper? Newspapers, catalogs, books, advertisements, letters—not to mention vast files of paperwork supporting every industry in the country.

The future was in factory paper, of course, not handmade. The Fitzwaters could probably be convinced to buy up the factory right now if Arianne could be convinced running the mill was too much for her. What could be easier than letting Fitzwater convert the factory himself?

Jonas had thought of little else all night. It might take some persuasion for Arianne to sell, or even allow an investor to update the Cranbury Paper Mill. But why shouldn't she want to make a fortune two-thirds larger than the one he was planning to make? Such success should ease whatever reason she had to cling to the way her father had always done things. Surely she would thank him in the end.

He easily took the steps up into the mill, grabbing the leather apron from its hook. Yesterday being the Sabbath, no work would have been done and so he knew exactly what to do next. Packaging paper left from the other day was the kind of work a clerk might perform, but he hoped it wouldn't be long before this place was a factory filled with employees to do every task from menial to meticulous.

He moved a bundle of paper from the press to the wrapping table and set to work. All he needed was a little time to convince Arianne of a brighter future.

———

Arianne was surprised to see the man this early, and saw no reason to put off asking what she wanted to know. Standing at the foot of the stairway from the drying loft where she'd been working, she folded her arms and watched him a full minute, knowing he hadn't yet seen her.

As much as she hated to admit it, as much as she wished otherwise, she was struck again by the man's appeal. He might not be handsome in the way of classical portraits she'd seen in a New York museum, but he had a certain heartiness with his sharply cut jaw, bold dark brows, and a nose that was straight and just the right size for his face.

His image would be more than pleasant to watermark—far more enjoyable than the one she'd created for Eliot Wardman. This wasn't the first time the thought had annoyed her, and did so again now. Was she so shallow to be influenced by evidence of this man's strength, by the cut of his chin or the attractiveness of his profile? Still, if ever she would enjoy making the watermark of a man, his at least would be beautiful.

None of this meant anything. Someone who maligned her

father's name deserved only contempt—and certainly not one-third of all her father had worked so hard to acquire!

When Mr. Prestwich turned and appeared surprised to find her standing there, she unfolded her arms and approached with her chin high. She refused to honor him with an apology for having startled him, a greeting or even the courtesy of eye contact.

"I'd like to discuss with you something before we start working today, Mr. Prestwich. Before you left here on Saturday, you spoke ill of my father, and I demand an explanation."

"I beg your pardon?"

She couldn't look at him, her cheeks suddenly burning with a flare of anger she'd tried suppressing since last seeing him. "I wish to know why every personal reference you've made to my father hints at something less than respectful."

"My apologies if you've misinterpreted some of the things I've said." His voice, usually cordial, was especially so now. So cordial she didn't believe his sincerity for a moment.

She stared at him, astonished. Was he trying to make light of his attitude, dismiss such insults as unimportant?

"So you're saying you never meant to insult my father with your vague innuendoes?"

Something on his face—some hint at honesty, perhaps—confirmed she hadn't misunderstood. But he replaced the brief, grim look with a smile. "As I believe you told me on Saturday, I didn't know the man. Did I?"

"Then why . . ." She stopped, sensing it was futile to continue. Folding her arms again, she decided on a new line of questioning. "Then tell me this: why in the world would such a wonderful person as your mother never speak of you?"

He turned away as if the topic was as inconsequential as the weather. There were two stacks of paper waiting to be counted into reams—the mill sold by count, never by weight, since it was impossible to make the pages entirely uniform—and he seemed calmly content to set about the mundane task.

"I'm not at all surprised my mother preferred not to talk about her life before knowing your father," he said at last. "Why are you?"

"Whatever can you mean? You make it seem as if she had something to hide."

"I'm saying only that she had ample reason to keep her lives separate."

"Past life—with you—and present life, with my father? But why?"

He was looking at her curiously now, as if trying to tell if her question was sincere. She had no trouble staring at him in return. He'd confused her beyond measure.

"Because her past life wasn't exactly past, was it? Her life with your father considerably overlapped her life with mine."

She frowned. What did he mean by such words? That word in particular . . . overlap . . . sounded as if . . . as if . . . he believed Charlotte had been less than free to be with Papa. As if her father would have been involved with a woman married to another—to Jonas's father!

She took a step closer to him, tempted for the first time in her life to slap another human being. Instead, she clenched her hands into fists. "What are you saying? Are you accusing my father and your mother of some kind of . . . of dalliance?"

His gaze filled with anger, the anger she'd only glimpsed before he'd hidden it with a smile. He made no such attempt now. "Yes." His tone was soft but savage. "Why should I be the only one to have suffered for it? If you didn't know, if this entire, blind little town never knew the truth, then count yourself lucky. Maybe now you know why I have a right to some kind of recompense for what your father did."

"What my father did? How dare you besmirch his name? Not to mention your own mother's! They were fine, decent, God-fearing people, both of them. How could you say such a thing? How could you believe it?"

"Because she lived in Williamsport—a distance from my father, and cozy enough to your father—for an entire year. My father died on New Year's Day, and less than one month later my mother married your father. You tell me if the timing isn't more than a little suspicious. At least," he added with a grim set to his mouth, "it was all very amusing to my mother's former friends in Philadelphia."

Arianne turned away, unable to look at his accusatory face. She gripped the edge of the table, struggling for an even, calming breath of air. Everything this man said was abhorrent. Papa was a good man, a God-fearing one. A man who took God's commandments to heart. It wasn't true; how could it be? Was it possible there were nasty-minded people in Philadelphia who whispered and snickered about her father? And Charlotte?

And yet . . . New Year's Day? Arianne had no idea Charlotte had still been married as recently as that.

Certainly this man had no proof of anything improper having happened!

She remembered her father's courtship of Charlotte, the woman who had begun as Arianne's favorite customer from Williamsport several summers ago. She'd been so kind to Arianne as they became friends. Charlotte would come all the way from Williamsport to browse their books or purchase a new pen or other such item, eventually staying to share tea, and then lunches with Arianne. It was true she rarely spoke of her own life, hinting only that she lived more than comfortably in the city. Instead she let Arianne, in her yearning for a mother, talk endlessly about herself. Charlotte had always seemed more than willing to be Arianne's surrogate mother, selflessly listening and rarely speaking.

Then when her father began joining them, she'd quickly guessed he enjoyed Charlotte's company, too. They were friends for so long. Only friends! They couldn't have spent time alone together before this year, could they? Papa was never gone from home except for business trips. And Charlotte often came to see Arianne when Papa was away, just to be sure she wasn't too lonely without him. The allegation was just too preposterous to be believed.

"I knew Charlotte had been married before, and that she married my father in what seemed a whirlwind," she said at last. "Charlotte faced some sort of financial crisis. Their marriage seemed the perfect solution."

"My father wrote my mother out of the will, because of abandonment."

She offered him one raised brow. "You needn't say another word, Mr. Prestwich. She was given nothing, while you were given everything. That was her financial crisis."

He nodded, although she took some meager comfort in seeing that at least he didn't look smug about it.

"It didn't occur to you that any financial trouble could have been avoided had you provided for her, in spite of the will?" The words came out brittle, the way her spine felt.

Mr. Prestwich leaned closer, a touch of that smugness showing up now. "I tried. I offered to take care of her, but she refused. She obviously knew your father would be taking care of her and she didn't need me."

He turned his face from hers but not soon enough to conceal that the derision was gone, replaced by pain . . . at his mother's rejection? In spite of herself, a spark of compassion rose in her. None of this could be true, but that Mr. Prestwich believed it was all too clear.

She sucked in the deep breath she'd struggled for a moment ago. "You have no proof they did anything improper. I knew them as friends for over two years now. Friends. Only friends. In fact, I was your mother's friend first."

"Are you so sure of that? When she must never have spoken of her husband or her life? Or me?"

"She spoke of her childhood years in Williamsport, of her parents. She hinted once that she had a child, but I assumed . . . I thought . . ." She couldn't say aloud that she thought whatever child Charlotte had mothered had died. How could she, when it seemed so harsh to this living son before her? "Her family, her husband . . . never came up."

"That's convenient."

Arianne would not be persuaded, yet this conversation had revealed more about Mr. Prestwich than she'd expected. He believed he deserved this inheritance, and now she saw why.

It also revealed something about Charlotte that she never knew: just how unhappy her life must have been before she'd married Papa. So unhappy she couldn't bring herself to speak of it.

"There is one person who might be able to rid you of your doubts about your mother," Arianne said. Perhaps, if she could convince Mr. Prestwich whatever rumors he'd heard had been untrue, he might refuse the inheritance. "Your mother was sometimes accompanied here by her maid, a personal maid who used to fix her hair so beautifully. She was let go when . . . the money ran out. She had no need of a maid here, other than Binny, of course. Surely if this personal maid from Williamsport was at her beck and call night and day, as I assumed she was, she would know if anything improper happened. Have you ever spoken to this maid?"

"Why should I have done so? I never doubted what happened."

Arianne frowned. "Why was it so easy for you to think ill of your mother? She was a faithful, kind-hearted woman."

"Faithful? To whom?"

"To God."

"But not, I'm afraid, to my father."

"You owe it to her memory, to yourself, to find out the truth. The maid was called Clauson, after the English way to call her by her last name. Do you know where Clauson is now?"

"I knew her, of course, for years. I assume she's working for some other wealthy family in Williamsport. My mother would have given her a reference."

Arianne could see he wasn't giving much credence to her hope that his mother and her father hadn't been more than friendly well before his father's death. That only made her more determined to prove him wrong.

CHAPTER FIFTEEN

Jonas set the horse at an easy pace, in no particular hurry to return to Williamsport despite being shooed away from the mill before finishing his first task of the day. Arianne refused to allow him to "waste time" working while he still believed what he did about their parents.

When she asked him to find his mother's maid as soon as possible, it was clear she meant just that—as *soon* as possible. And so, if only to take the first step toward some kind of amicable relationship, even if it meant destroying her obviously idyllic memories of her father, he'd offered to leave immediately.

Although he refused to allow himself to hope otherwise, it had never occurred to him the rumors might not be true. Recalling Arianne's question—why had it been so easy for him to believe the worst of his mother—Jonas asked himself that very question now.

He knew why. Because his father had believed it. Who would have more right to know the truth than his father? Besides that, Jonas had lived through much of their marriage. Whether his father was at home or away, his mother was nearly always sad. All that seemed obvious to him was that they were mismatched. Cordial at best, often cold, and sometimes, his mother seemed almost afraid of his father. Certainly he could be cruel with his words, comparing Jonas's mother to ice or a mouse or any number of less than flattering standards. But he'd never touched her— never, in all the years Jonas could remember. Which in itself suddenly condemned him. He'd never touched her in anger, but nor had he ever done so with affection, at least not that Jonas could recall.

Surely his father was solicitous, though. Always in public, but it seemed more than genuine. That was why Jonas had clung to the social set in Philadelphia. At dinners and concerts and lectures and picnics he knew his parents would get along, even if it was only for others to see.

His mother's Williamsport house was built in the Victorian manner, with pitched roof and ornate bric-a-brac. Smaller than their home in Philadelphia, it had certainly been large enough for the three of them and the staff during summers and a week at Christmastime. His mother's father had built the home and this was where his mother had been raised, so it came as little surprise when she'd expressed an interest last year in permanent residence. It was the one place he'd seen her smile more often than her frown. She'd made it clear both Jonas and his father were welcome to stay there as well, but that was out of the question due to business concerns.

Jonas had once wanted to believe his mother simply didn't know how much time it took to run a textile mill . . . or at least oversee those who did. Jonas's father had welcomed him back from the University years ago with an office of his own, so Jonas couldn't very well live in Williamsport, either.

"Olice!" Jonas called once he was inside the house. The caretaker had stayed on after the rest of the staff—a housekeeper, cook, gardener, maid of all work and Mother's ladies' maid—had all been dismissed. Olice Brown and his wife lived in a small room off the kitchen, taking care of the home and plot of ground as they had done ever since Jonas's grandparents had been alive.

The old man moved quicker than he probably should have for

someone his age, bustling down the hallway from the kitchen to the parlor and entryway.

"Here I am, Mr. Jonas." The greeting came while still pulling on the jacket he wore inside the house, more formal than the one he wore while working outside. Jonas had told Olice he didn't need to act the butler, but some habits evidently couldn't be abandoned.

"I'd like to ask you a few questions," Jonas said, and up until this moment he hadn't realized how awkward the investigation might be. He was, after all, about to bring up a delicate subject regarding his mother, whom this man had known since she was born. "Sit with me a moment, will you, Olice?" He led the way into the parlor, but although the man followed he still stood by, as if ready to follow any order except to sit.

"May I take your jacket, sir?" he asked.

Jonas pulled away the garment and would have laid it aside on a sofa, but Olice grabbed it first, draping it over his arm. Having Olice refuse to sit forced Jonas to remain standing, too. "I wonder," he began, wishing he'd given more forethought to phrasing his inquiry, "that is, I'm interested in learning a little about the way my mother lived here before she left. Can you tell me about that?"

Olice had a long, narrow face with overgrown eyebrows and skin that sagged with age, particularly at the jaw. But there was nothing wrong with his hearing, and even though he looked as if the question had confused him, he didn't ask for it to be repeated.

"She lived here the way she always spent her summers, Mr. Jonas. Filled her days reading or sewing blankets and hats for the little ones at the orphanage. She went for a walk after lunch every day. She watched over the garden. Had visitors sometimes, but not as often as when your father came."

Jonas put a hand on the back of his mother's old favorite chair, where he'd seen her sewing as Olice mentioned. "What about visitors when we weren't here, particularly within the last year? Were her visitors from here in Williamsport? Just neighbors?"

"Yes. Not many people came up here from Philadelphia, and

your mother never mixed as much with the upper crust of Williamsport the way your father did."

His father never left business unattended, even out here. "I wonder if any of my mother's visitors came from Cranbury? Do you recall?"

"Cranbury? Before she moved there, she went there to shop. Came home with books and paper and bakery goods for the staff. She preferred the dressmaker from there, too. We used to receive regular deliveries from the Cranbury dress shop."

Jonas was tempted to ask outright if a certain papermaker had visited her—alone—but wasn't sure he wanted to risk revealing what he knew. He wasn't sure anyone in Williamsport had heard the rumors or whispered about his parents' obvious estrangement, but if they had, like Cranbury, society here was a little more protective of its natives than the social circles Jonas had frequented in Philadelphia. City gossip was far from Williamsport, and he was hesitant to repeat it even if he did believe every word of it.

"I'm interested in finding Mother's maid. Clauson. Do you know where she's working now?"

Olice nodded, mentioning the name of a local Williamsport family Jonas had heard of but didn't know personally. The family was one of many lumber magnates, and if Clauson had landed a position with them it was likely a step up for her.

Jonas thanked Olice then reclaimed his jacket before preparing to leave the house again, knowing the older man likely had an equal number of unasked questions as to why Jonas had just brought up such things.

Or maybe he, like Jonas, wished the topic never existed.

————

Arianne worked that day as if fighting off the devil himself, forcing her thoughts to stay on tasks she knew well enough to do mechanically. She wouldn't let herself stop, not even for a rest. She ate only when Binny brought her a sandwich and refused to leave until she had an empty plate to take back to the kitchen.

And although Binny asked what had changed between that morning when she'd gone off to the mill and lunchtime, Arianne didn't answer. Arianne didn't return to the house until well after Phoebe had closed and left the shop, and, when Leta tapped on the kitchen door after a late dinner, Arianne asked Binny to let her know she was going straight to bed.

And she did.

But it wasn't long before she remembered her bed was no refuge from the thoughts that haunted her. She might have wondered about the source of Mr. Prestwich's animosity toward her father, but knowing what he believed was far worse. Telling herself over and again that he was wrong, misguided, and needlessly suspicious did little to help her sleep.

Never once had it occurred to Arianne to question the nature of her father's friendship and his budding, if quick, romance with Charlotte. It hadn't seemed so quick at the time, since Charlotte was already comfortable with them and they with her. Arianne had little knowledge of life outside of Cranbury or Williamsport, but their marriage had seemed so ordinary. So right. How glad Arianne had been for both of them, for her father to have someone to share his thoughts and cares with, knowing someday Arianne would likely get married herself and no longer share the same roof.

She recalled how they had been in church together once they'd married, singing hymns and praying. Surely they couldn't have sung to God with such open adoration if they'd broken one of His clearest commandments.

There must be some explanation, some proof that Mr. Prestwich was wrong. Why hadn't he returned today? It took less than an hour to ride to Williamsport even if he'd taken his time; he certainly had been gone long enough to interview Charlotte's former maid and return before the dinner hour.

Was it good news or bad that Mr. Prestwich had stayed away? Perhaps he was embarrassed to have found out he'd leapt to the wrong conclusion. She doubted he would be so hesitant to tell her if he'd verified what he already suspected.

After a fitful night, Arianne ate a scant breakfast just to please Binny, then returned to the mill. There was one good thing about this newest upheaval: she'd never produced as much paper all by herself as she had yesterday. She could do the same today.

When the door to the mill opened near midmorning, Arianne turned expectantly, disappointed to see Leo rather than Mr. Prestwich. If he recognized that disappointment he didn't say, although he did not stay long, citing more work at his father's wood shop. He seemed glad not to find Mr. Prestwich there, but he didn't ask about him and Arianne didn't offer any comment about the absence of her "partner."

It was just as well for Arianne to work alone. She didn't want to speak to anyone until Mr. Prestwich was as convinced as she was about the nature of her father's relationship with his mother. Not that she could speak of such a thing to anyone else, but for her own peace of mind she needed to keep to herself.

After Leo left, Arianne stopped working long enough to take a cool drink from the pitcher her father had always kept near the door. She was growing vexed by the time, nearly eleven. The other day Mr. Prestwich had arrived far earlier, proving he could make it here from as far away as Williamsport and put in a full day's work. He was late by any measure of a workday today. Where was he?

As if her thoughts conjured him, she saw him coming down the pathway through the trees. He carried the same tray Binny usually used when she brought lunch.

She met him near the garden, taking the tray from him and setting it on the rough-hewn table she'd shared many times with her father on lovely days such as this. Arianne didn't even look at what was under the towel; she merely faced Mr. Prestwich and waited for him to speak.

"Binny said I shouldn't bring that tray back—"

"Unless it's empty," she finished brusquely. "I know how Binny is about meals. Get to the point, Mr. Prestwich. Did you speak to your mother's maid, or not?"

"No, but not for lack of trying. The family she works for has closed their Williamsport home for the summer, which is why I didn't return yesterday. The caretaker wasn't even to be found until this morning. A neighbor said Clauson is working there, and likely traveling with the family to Europe for the summer. I wanted to make sure so I waited to speak to someone in the family's employ. They told me the same thing, that Clauson would be back, along with the family, in September."

"September!" More than a month away. She eyed him with unveiled annoyance. "I suppose you still believe the worst?"

"I see no reason to have changed my mind. But I wonder if you have?"

"Of course not!"

"Arianne," he said, in a tone far gentler than he'd ever used before. When had he begun calling her by her first name? Why hadn't she noticed before this? And why did it feel so natural? "I propose we call a truce. I'll make an attempt to believe the best, if you agree to understand why I've been less than charming about this whole inheritance. I'll admit, when I learned about it, I wanted to use it as some kind of retaliation against your father. But maybe I was wrong. In fact, I believe we're both wrong to worry about what went on between our parents. It's over now. What's done is done."

She shook her head. "Not for me. I want to know the truth."

"We may never know."

"I can wait until September, if I must."

He waved toward the tray waiting on the table. "Why don't you eat the meal Binny prepared? I've always found a good meal improves my disposition."

"There's nothing wrong with my disposition." She knew it

wasn't true. Her disposition had been mostly surly since the day
Mr. Prestwich had entered her life.

"Still, a smile might improve things."

She offered no such thing, although she did allow him to guide
her closer to the bench next to the table. He sat beside her and
uncovered the tray, where a bowl of fruit and a sandwich waited,
next to a small stack of mail. Binny always separated what looked
like business mail—orders, bills, payments—because Papa often
went through the mail after lunch and entered new orders in a
ledger kept handily nearby.

But the envelope on the bottom wasn't from anyone familiar. It
appeared to be from the United States government. Curious, she
pulled that one from the stack. Papa had made paper for various
banks, but their mill had never dealt with the government before.

"That's an official letter," Mr. Prestwich said, watching her. He
was frowning, though, as if he recognized the envelope.

She slid her thumb under the flap, but before she'd even
scanned the first of two pages, Mr. Prestwich spoke.

"It's the inheritance tax bill, isn't it?"

She looked up, her heart pounding. If the numbers on the
bottom of the page were correct, she was in trouble.

"How did you know?"

"I received one myself just like it. May I?"

She handed it to him, and he nodded.

"How soon do I have to pay it?"

He glanced at the second page. "It says upon receipt, but I
would imagine a lawyer could get an extension."

"A lawyer . . . demanding yet another fee."

Handing the letter back to her, Mr. Prestwich smiled—so
serenely she dismissed the first thought that came to mind, that he
might be happy over her predicament. He'd proclaimed he'd been
wrong to welcome his inheritance, but that didn't mean he'd given
up his animosity for the part he believed her father played in his
parents' troubled marriage.

"I have a solution, if you'd care to hear it."

———

If Jonas still believed God cared about the personal lives of human beings, he would have thanked Him for the timely arrival of the tax bill. Although he knew Arianne could barely afford the sum owed, he guessed she would have to narrow any purchases while continuing to meet the orders she already had—a questionable feat. He also knew this was one more worry in an already uncertain time in her life. She may be fully capable of producing the quality paper this mill was known for, but not the quantity. And without filling all of the roles her father had—worker, salesman, bookkeeper—she was doomed at least to fall behind.

In short, she needed a partner as much as he wanted one.

"As long as it doesn't include the sale of the mill in order to buy you out, Mr. Prestwich, I'm willing to listen to any suggestion."

"Let me pay the bill."

She lifted both brows, looking at him with equal measure of what looked like surprise and skepticism. "Let you? By all means, Mr. Prestwich, pay the bill. Only first tell me what you'd like in return. Equal ownership, I suppose."

He shook his head. It was all making so much sense now. Funny how having just a slice of hope that she might accept him as a partner had changed his attitude about this mill. He wasn't ready to believe their parents innocent, but he was ready to concede there might be some doubt. In any case, he'd meant what he said earlier. The past was past. What mattered now was that she needed him, and he needed a future. Maybe revenge was no longer necessary.

"I'd like you to consider something," he said. "If I were to invest in this mill—to start with, by paying this inheritance tax—then you might consider making some improvements."

She raised a single brow this time. "You don't even know the business and you're ready to offer improvements? This mill runs very well as it is."

"Yes, for what it is. A single-vat, small operation. But I've met with one of the biggest paper producers in Philadelphia, and I've learned firsthand how profitable this business can be. You're well placed, and you come with a ready-made reputation for quality. The foundation is here, all you have to do is build on it."

"What are you saying?" That her voice was more horrified than interested gave him pause, but wasn't entirely unexpected. She didn't know the possibilities as he did—yet. "That we convert to *factory* paper?"

He nodded, following her from the table when she pushed herself away from the meal, the table, the bench. Him.

"Why not? The paper industry grows bigger every year. There are more literate people in this country than ever. People who want the information only paper can bring them. And here you are, right in the middle of the biggest resource in the country." His palm swept the forest around them. "If you never want to worry about the future again, Arianne, all you have to do is accept my help."

"Help! Said the spider to the fly."

She turned away, but he caught and held one of her hands.

"No, no! You have a small market now, but with a bit of modernization you could make a fortune."

Pulling her hand away from his, she said, "I'm not looking for a fortune."

He laughed, both unsurprised and impressed. He'd never met anyone like this woman before him, and he had to admit he found her refreshingly different from the women he'd known in the city. Arianne was the exact opposite of Julia Kitteridge, who knew how to enjoy her father's money. "What about security, then? The knowledge that your father's shop will never be threatened?"

He hadn't quite meant to say that, but knew the accidental words were those she wanted to hear. She might have turned away again, he was nearly certain she'd been about to, but those words stopped her. Now he knew the best tactic to take—though he was suddenly unsure the only reason he wanted to proceed was either strictly business, or even personal in a way that had anything to do with her father. Rather, it had everything to do with Arianne herself.

The truth was he still wanted to see her smile.

At him.

CHAPTER SIXTEEN

Mr. Prestwich's proposal was the last thing Arianne wanted to consider. She was a papermaker, not a factory worker. She'd obviously failed to make him see the beauty in the paper her family had made for generations.

"Have you even looked at the paper we've made here? The paper you've wrapped for shipping? Did you not see the quality, the unique and strong texture? The fineness?"

"I concede such paper has a place, but it's a small place. There is a much bigger market for more practical paper, and here you are in the middle of a forest where wood pulp—not rags—is most suitable for newspapers, books, magazines, everything."

She turned her back to him, but didn't retreat inside the factory the way she wanted to. "Natural products don't allow the strength and durability of our paper, no matter how strong the tree."

"How do you know? You told me the other day you have samples of paper made in your family generations ago. But they weren't making paper from wood, were they?" Even though he was right, she refused to admit it. "Perhaps if your family had made paper from wood pulp a hundred years ago, you would be showing that paper to me, too."

She shook her head. "It doesn't matter, Mr. Prestwich. The people who buy our paper expect it to be made the way we've always made it in the past. With excellence."

"I'm talking about new customers, Arianne. New markets. With the reputation you already have, such an expansion would be simple."

"And we would cease being papermakers. We would be machine workers."

"There is no difference! You work with machines now, only this would be new machines. Better, faster ones. You could produce quantities in a single day your father never dreamed possible."

"I know the difference between factory and handmade paper, just as my father knew the difference." She glared at him. "Something you obviously don't appreciate. Don't bring up this subject again, Mr. Prestwich. I have no intention of changing my mind. Ever."

Then she turned back to the mill, leaving him and her uneaten lunch behind.

But even as she picked up a mould at the vat, making sure the deckles were properly placed, she glanced back toward the open door. She watched him cover the lunch again then walk out of her line of vision.

The tax bill envelope peeked from beneath the corner of the tray, taunting her.

During the next two days Mr. Prestwich worked in the factory as if he hoped to be offered a permanent position. But now that Arianne knew what he really wanted—to forever change the nature of her father's business—she was more determined than ever not to share every single secret of the papermaking process. He had neither the devotion to nor the respect for Casterton paper.

Mr. Prestwich said a paper factory would protect the future of her father's business. But how was that possible if he destroyed the way Papa had carried on, with generations of tradition behind him? Did Mr. Prestwich want to change the method of paper production just to keep the factory going, and to make money, or to destroy her father's legacy? Whatever the reason, Arianne refused to consider such sweeping change.

Between worry over Mr. Prestwich's intentions and her new concern about the tax bill, other unpleasant thoughts continued to distract her. There must be some way to disprove Mr. Prestwich's suspicions about Charlotte and her father. Arianne had no doubt there was some terrible misunderstanding, and by Wednesday she was determined to prove it without waiting for Charlotte's maid to return from Europe. She nearly slapped her own forehead when an obvious possibility occurred to her. She would look for evidence herself. Why hadn't Arianne thought of it before?

Since the accident, she hadn't stepped foot in the bedroom her father and Charlotte shared, knowing it would only remind her they weren't returning. If they had any sort of illicit relationship before they were married, there might be some memento giving it away, some sentimental note or gift dated before Charlotte's first marriage ended.

Although Arianne was confident she would find no such proof, she couldn't ignore the idea even though she hated the thought of rifling through their things on such a repugnant task.

Instead of going to the mill, Arianne returned upstairs after breakfast. She would do this alone, not trusting Mr. Prestwich. Nor would she tell Binny what she was doing—there was no sense sharing Mr. Prestwich's outrageous suspicions with anyone.

Binny had kept the room dusted since the accident and if she heard Arianne in there she might mistakenly assume she'd sufficiently adjusted to her grief, at least enough to sort the belongings and give whatever she chose to charity. That was something Arianne expected to do . . . someday. Just not yet.

Closing the door quietly behind her, Arianne looked around. Her heartbeat sped, as if she were invading someone else's privacy.

Wasn't that what she was doing? If her father and Charlotte did have a secret, was it any of her business? It was between themselves and God.

The thought nearly made her turn around and leave. It was neither her place nor Jonas Prestwich's to pry. Yet knowing he judged them so harshly prodded her forward. Surely they were innocent?

Arianne opened the wardrobe, the very same one she'd emptied when her mother died so many years ago. Arianne had kept some of her mother's clothes, expecting one day to grow into them. But Arianne had grown right past them, being considerably taller than her mother. All she'd been able to wear was a shawl and a hat or two, and Leta had gently scolded her sentimentality because they were so out of fashion.

Opening the wardrobe that had so briefly belonged to Charlotte ignited a piercing pain to see her familiar clothing. Charlotte had looked prettiest in light blue, and among the gowns and dresses were several in such a shade. They hung on specially made hangers that protected puffed sleeves or skirt pleats. Arianne touched a golden gown, the one Charlotte had worn on the day she'd married Papa. She pulled the sleeve closer, nearly hugging it. Charlotte had been so dear.

Such a reminder nearly sent Arianne from the room. How dare Mr. Prestwich believe something so ill of either her father or Charlotte? It couldn't be true, and Arianne was following a rabbit trail. A rude, insensitive and preposterous tale that couldn't possibly be true.

She retreated, leaving the wardrobe ajar, yet stopped at the bedroom door. She must get this over with. Mr. Prestwich was likely already at the mill, and she intended to have news to share with him—one way or another.

With renewed determination she went through drawers and shelves, searching everything from shoes to unmentionables. She found nothing out of the ordinary—apart from one item that soothed her. Next to her father's Bible was Charlotte's, nearly as tattered and well used as that of Arianne's father.

Arianne's determination nearly failed her at the thought of going through her father's things next, but when she saw his unexpectedly rumpled neckties she was reminded of the inventory taken by the men counting her father's worth. That gave her strength to check and be sure nothing was missing or ill-used.

Her search ended with nothing. If neither of them could support what Jonas Prestwich believed, even he must accept no evidence was evidence in and of itself.

When her gaze fell once again on the pair of Bibles left at the bedside, Arianne grabbed them both on her way out the door. There was evidence, after all.

———

Jonas tested the paper hanging in the drying loft for the kind of rustle Arianne had taught him signified the paper was sufficiently dried. He separated the spurs as carefully as she demanded, readying the stack of paper for the copper tanks filled with dissolved sizing cakes to be put through the rolls. After that the paper would be pressed and dried for the last time before being readied for delivery.

All the while he wondered why Arianne was so late this morning. The silence of the last two days had been more melancholy than tense—a melancholy Jonas couldn't escape. Had he believed he'd find some satisfaction in the accusations he'd spewed against her father? He'd guessed nearly from the moment he met her that she was too innocent to suspect the truth about their parents. At the very least it was obvious she'd been spared any gossip here in Cranbury and hadn't suffered the way he had in the city.

Not that he was surprised his mother and her father had been especially careful to keep their reputations clean in such a small town they would call home. Jonas had once wondered if his own father had started the rumors in Philadelphia, after he suspected the reason for her extended stay in Williamsport. Hadn't Jonas overheard his father in a rare drunken stupor one evening? He'd been talking to himself, a self-pitying rant if ever Jonas heard one, but a rant anyone might have heard. A neighbor. A gossiping servant. He might not have done it intentionally, and if so he might not have expected Jonas to be the only one who would suffer such rumors. If his father had survived his heart trouble he might have come to Cranbury himself to confront them, and then everyone here would have known what Jonas knew.

But somehow the thought brought him no satisfaction.

He heard the door open from down below and separated the last spur of sheets, adding to those being readied for sizing. He turned to the ladder-like wooden stairway but descended only three stairs before Arianne appeared on the steps below. She didn't look up until she was already halfway to him. Taking the last couple of stairs he met her in the middle, despite the close confines of the dim, narrow passageway. The only light came from above and below, but even in shadows he could see her eyes offered a mix of daring and eager defiance—the closest thing to a welcome he'd ever seen on her face.

"I decided not to wait for your mother's maid to return," she said, one hand on the railing and the other on the wall, as if barring him from passing her. "I've gone through every bit of your mother's and my father's belongings. If what you think is true, there would have been some evidence, some clue about the history of their relationship. A note, a letter—something. But there is nothing, absolutely nothing, to hint at anything improper." Now she crossed her arms, an overconfident look on her face. "I'm convinced of it."

Although he rejected her finding with as much assurance as she offered it, he smiled as if he were an indulgent and wiser friend. "It might surprise you to know I thought of doing the same thing, looking for some kind of proof. I thought I could convince my father of the truth if there was nothing to condemn my mother. She left belongings behind in both Philadelphia and Williamsport

that she must not have had room for here: books she had
purchased, correspondence she exchanged with friends through
the years, old photographs." He wouldn't mention those
photographs she'd left behind had represented the former life
she'd obviously wanted to forget, those of his father—and himself.
"I found nothing, either, after she vacated the house in
Williamsport."

"There! That only confirms what I've already said. You have no
evidence and therefore it can't possibly be true."

"It proves only that if there was any evidence, they were careful
to dispose of it." He spoke in little more than a whisper. He no
longer wanted to hurt her in lieu of her father, but neither did he
want her to absolve the man of his part in wrongdoing.

She lifted a brow, still defiant, as if she had some kind of
arsenal tucked in her pocket. "Come with me, won't you?"

She turned to descend the stairs, and he followed as an unexpected thought struck him. He would rather be searching out clues
as her partner than as the adversary she must believe him to be.

The wrapping table downstairs held two books that Jonas
easily and quickly identified. They were Bibles, and one had
belonged to his mother. The familiar leather binding gave it away
immediately.

Arianne picked up the two books with a hint of the first smile
she'd ever aimed his way, albeit in triumph against him rather than
the kind he kept hoping to see.

"This is all the evidence I need, Mr. Prestwich. Your mother's
and my father's faith is reflected right here—something that
wouldn't have allowed them to do what you suggest."

Then, grabbing one closer to her heart, she thrust the other
one toward him. "Perhaps you ought to read this. You might see
how your mother read these pages over and again, underlining
favorite verses. This book proves how devoted she was to God.
She wouldn't have done what you think. She couldn't."

He eyed her a long moment, choosing not to voice the first

words that came to mind. For someone so convinced of being right, Arianne was certainly defensive.

She grabbed an apron and left him for the vat room, where she would no doubt ready the moulds and deckles for another day of work.

CHAPTER SEVENTEEN

The following day, Jonas opened the door to the post office and took a place in the short line. Although he sensed there had been laughter-laced conversation going on a moment ago, the room fell silent once his presence was noticed.

He chose not to acknowledge the chill, instead casually studying his surroundings. The entire back wall was separated by a countertop not unlike the one in the stationery shop. The shelves behind this one were typically small compartments meant for sorting mail. Just now the postmaster finished whatever transaction had been going on before Jonas's arrival had stalled everything.

Finished, the customer turned toward the door, and Jonas recognized her as the one who had shown up at the stationer's shop so quick to defend Arianne whether she needed it or not. He tipped his hat her way, but she walked by as if she hadn't noticed.

The line moved quickly in the new silence, and Jonas soon handed the postmaster his two envelopes. He would have shipped them from Williamsport but hadn't any envelopes at home so he'd purchased the two he'd needed at Arianne's shop. The older woman, Miss Turner, hadn't hesitated a moment to take his money, despite sure knowledge that he already owned a third of every envelope in the shop.

The postmaster held up one envelope then the other as if searching for something dubious about their preparation. Evidently he found something sinister with the second, because he looked over the top of his glasses with eager distrust.

"Does Miss Arianne know you're sending this letter off to another paper factory?"

Jonas offered a narrow smile. "I'm sure you'll be happy to let her know." If only the man would mention the first envelope instead of the second, the one containing full payment for her tax bill. That might even soften the postmaster's opinion of him, though that might be too much to expect. As it was, he hoped it would do something for Arianne's attitude once she found out, although he'd cautioned himself against much confidence in that department.

The postmaster shrugged, fixing stamps to the envelopes. "It's your choice whether I tell her or you do, Mr. Prestwich. Up to you, so long as she knows."

Jonas handed over the coins for the stamps then left the post office without another word.

Outside, the woman he'd spotted at the counter was still nearby, chatting with another pair of women. As he neared they all seemed to hold their breath, making it clear he'd either been the topic of their discussion or they didn't want him to hear whatever it was they talked about.

"Good day, ladies," he said with another tip of his hat. He paused, eying the friend of Arianne's. "I'm sure you already know who I am, but since I'll be spending quite a bit of my time here in Cranbury, I wonder if I might learn the names of some of your residents. Would you do me the honor of letting me know your names?"

Each one seemed either confused or taken aback at the request. One, short and plump, started to speak but a jab to her side from another quickly stopped her.

"Perhaps it would help if I were to tell you I haven't come to either hurt or to steal the Cranbury Paper Mill. I'm an investor, that's true, but I have an obvious interest in seeing the mill succeed." He took a moment for the words to be received, looking past them at the town's street beyond. "Cranbury is such a picturesque town that I can see why so many people from Williamsport frequent the shops here. Plus there is a certain standard of excellence here, isn't there?"

The women exchanged glances, as if none had believed him capable of anything but breathing fire. He smiled as charmingly as he'd done for the elite of Philadelphia while fighting rumors. Then he tipped his hat again and wished them a very fine day before walking away.

———

"You could tell him to stop coming," Leo said to Arianne as he took up another felt. He was acting as Arianne's coucher today, saving her considerable time. With his help she would likely produce twice as much paper as she had in the last few days alone. Mr. Prestwich helped some, but was quite limited compared to what Leo could do.

Leo was an excellent coucher, which required a different sort of delicacy from vat work. Like her father, Arianne could extract just the right amount of liquid pulp from the vat to produce fairly consistent sheets, even using the largest of their moulds. While Leo had learned to do well with some of the smaller moulds, his long reach and gentle touch were better suited to pitching the felts on top of the newly created sheets. Grasping the short end of a felt and holding it well clear of the paper Arianne had just posted, he dropped the felt squarely upon the wet sheet without letting it drag, wrinkle or in any way damage Arianne's work.

"How can I send him away?" Arianne asked while she worked. "He has a legal right to a third of everything, and until we work out some kind of agreement, I can't do anything but let him stay."

"I don't see why he keeps coming here. Is he trying to decide whether or not to make you sell and pay him his share? If he hasn't already done that, he probably won't. He ought to just go back to wherever he lives and wait for whatever you can give him once you've got something to give."

Arianne refused to tell Leo that Mr. Prestwich had more power over her than just one-third ownership. With the suspicions he carried about their parents, even if those suspicions were wrong, a whisper would sully her father's memory—and that would be almost as painful as losing Papa's mill.

Besides trying to figure out why Mr. Prestwich had kept his suspicions to himself, she found herself unexpectedly grateful to him for that silence.

"Ari," Leo said after she'd turned a new sheet on to the asp. He carefully took the mould from her and set it aside, grasping her hands. Looking at him, whatever he had on his mind seemed to produce in him a mix of fear and eagerness, gravity and excitement.

She calmed her breathing, increased not from a thrill but from queasy cowardice. There wasn't a thing she could do to stop or even delay this conversation, one she'd known was on its way for some time.

"My father is anxious for me to decide where I'll devote myself. Here, or in the shop with him and my brothers."

Arianne pulled her hands from his and folded her arms, looking away because she was afraid he might already guess what she must say. She didn't want to see his disappointment. "You know I've always been grateful for your help, Leo. So was my father. You have the right touch with the felts. Remember how Papa always said that? He was right. But Leo." She looked him square in the face now, forcing herself to be brave. "I want you to work where *you* want to work. Which do you enjoy more? Working with wood, or paper?"

He put a hand on each of her shoulders, but she still clung to her folded arms.

"Ari, you know I just like to work. I'm happy doing both, or either. I've always wanted to work here because I admired your Papa, and he was a good teacher and a fair boss. But mostly I came here to be with you. To work with you."

"Leo . . ." She took a step back, and his hands fell away. "I care for you. I always have. But I've tried to be honest, that my fondness for you is as a brother. We've known each other so long, it's always been that way for me."

"Not for me. In time . . . if we were to get married, work here together just as we are today, then you could grow to love me in the other way."

"I already do love you, Leo. Just not that way."

"Tell me what you love about me, then."

She laughed. "Are you looking for compliments?"

"No. If you love me because I'm a hard worker, then that's something a wife needs to think about her husband. If you love me because I go to church, or because I don't spend my money or my time drinking beer the way some men do, then isn't that what a wife needs to know about her husband? Maybe you already love me in the best ways a wife should love her husband."

"Yes, Leo. All of that is true. I admire you. I respect you, too. I love you for all the reasons you mentioned, and more." Then she took one of his hands. "But, Leo, there's one way I've never thought of you. And I'm not sure that can change."

He held her gaze, as if searching for something to prove her wrong. But she knew what he would see: sympathy.

"Is there something wrong with me?"

"No, Leo, no. Of course not. You're a brother to me, that's all it is."

He cast his gaze downward and his shoulders slumped. "But what will you do about the mill if I'm not here?"

"It isn't fair to expect you to work here with hopes of a future I can't share. I'll have to hire someone, and train them the way Papa trained both of us."

He put his hands on her shoulders again. "Ari . . . I can't give up on a future with you. I just can't."

She unfolded her arms and placed her hands on top of his, still on her shoulders. "But I can't give you any reason to hope, Leo."

"Maybe. . ."

Before he could speak another word, she shook her head, and his hands and his shoulders slumped once again.

He looked around the vat room, as if he expected to miss it. "I'll help you as long as I can. I'll help you train someone. But don't send me away for good, Ari. Let me help you as long as I can."

"Only if you give the best of your day to your father. If you don't love papermaking more than woodworking, then you should work with your father."

He sighed. "My Papa thinks I've been indecisive, so now . . . I guess I can tell him I should work with wood from here on. Unless . . . Don't you want to think about it a little longer?"

Arianne took one of his hands and squeezed it, but looked quickly away when his eyes went momentarily shiny. Surely he wouldn't cry, not in front of her! "I'm sorry, Leo."

"So am I."

Then he let go of her hand and stepped away, turning back once more. "If you don't mind, I think I'll leave off for today."

She nodded, saying nothing more. She'd expected his disappointment, hadn't she? And yet somehow she hadn't. She'd thought Leo would be able to shrug it off and continue working. He was always happiest when he was busy.

Before Leo reached the doorway, Mr. Prestwich's shadow spilled inside.

For Leo's sake—and perhaps her own—she hoped he hadn't been eavesdropping. But once Leo was gone, Mr. Prestwich sent her a too-brief, awkward gaze that hinted he'd heard enough to know he ought to spare her some embarrassment.

CHAPTER EIGHTEEN

Jonas tried walking briskly toward the saul, but his feet stopped obeying his head and listened to his heart instead. His steps slowed and he turned, staring at Arianne from beneath the vat room's archway.

Everything he'd just heard acted as an anvil, crushing the last of whatever resentment he'd tried feeling for this woman. At least she was honest with poor Leo, instead of keeping him on just to enjoy the puppy-dog worship the man displayed around her. Or to take advantage of the work he performed.

The truth was, Jonas believed Leo didn't know how lucky he was to have escaped the bonds of marriage. That was one direction Jonas would never go. Marriage might be a social necessity, but his observation was that it bound two people together who, sooner or later, would grow tired of one another. Leo should be relieved to be spared that fate, at least for the foreseeable future.

"You might as well know I heard enough of that conversation to guess I shouldn't barge in. I wasn't purposely eavesdropping."

"Not purposely and yet not moving away?"

He conceded her point by raising his palm. "I just thought you should know. I also want to remind you I'm willing to take Leo's spot. Working," he added hastily, in case she might see him as the next man willing to risk his heart to her.

"Why would you want to work here permanently, in this measly little one-vat mill when you want nothing better than to destroy it with machinery?"

"I don't want to destroy anything. I want to expand. Why can't we do both?"

His own mouth was full of surprises today! Up until this pronouncement, he'd never given serious consideration to producing *both* handmade and manufactured paper.

Handmade paper would clearly not produce the kind of income Jonas wanted—and, at its current level of production, the income Arianne needed. But had he ever suggested aloud that he wanted to destroy one in favor of the other? If she allowed him to build a new, separate factory, taking advantage of a reputation already in place with the Casterton name, then they could both have what they wanted.

And their partnership would be permanent.

———

Arianne stared at him. Until this moment she'd viewed him only as the enemy. First, to her business and then, more importantly, to her father's memory.

Mr. Prestwich stood before her now with an invitation to something new, something she should contemplate even if the paper artist inside of her resisted. Was there something intrinsically wrong with factory-made paper, as long as she was still able to produce the kind of paper her father had taught her to make? Didn't manufactured paper have a place in society today?

She'd never thought about it. Only in the interest of self-preservation had she rejected the idea of factory paper taking the place of handmade. He'd just issued an invitation to be involved in an expansion, not a replacement of what her family had been crafting for generations.

"I don't know anything about producing factory paper," she said.

"But you know paper. I can learn the process, if you're the eye for quality."

"Such an investment would cost a lot of money."

"I have money. You have the Casterton reputation. We'd need both."

We.

She'd never thought of herself as an equal half of a "we" before. She'd been part of a "we" with her parents, then with her father, then with her father and Charlotte. But always a lesser part, a child's portion.

This "we" felt markedly different—but not unpleasantly so.

And more intriguing than it should.

"No," she said quickly, squelching her own thoughts. How could she contemplate such a thing? This man thought the worst of the two people she loved most in this world. Surely there was something wrong in the idea of partnering with someone who thought so little of her father and his own mother.

"No?" He echoed the word as if it had been the last one he'd expected to hear. "You're not even considering it. Why not?"

She turned her back on him, grabbing one of the moulds. "No."

"And that's all you have to say on the subject? Just no?"

She wanted to forget this exchange had ever taken place. Erase it from her memory and his, too. But he wasn't leaving the room and she knew she would have to say something, if only she knew what.

"Is there anything wrong with producing factory paper?" he asked slowly.

"Of course not. But I'm a papermaker in the way my family has been making paper for generations."

"Yes, but haven't the papermakers in your family used innovation when it came along?"

Arianne dipped the mould but one of the deckles came loose. She nearly lost it in the vat. Annoyed, she pulled the mould out and attached the frame properly. "I cannot work with you distracting me. Please get to your business in the saul, Mr. Prestwich."

"Jonas," he called over his shoulder as he walked toward the other room. "And as we both contemplate our future, I'll call you Arianne."

As if he hadn't been doing that already!

CHAPTER NINETEEN

After a full day at the paper mill, Jonas should have been surprised to find himself so easily passing the livery where his horse waited to take him back to Williamsport. But he kept walking, as if he'd known—not just today, but every day—that sooner or later he would follow this path. As if there hadn't been a single doubt.

He passed the crowded cemetery yard and the church. But once the new cemetery on the hill came into view, those very footsteps that had been so sure to deliver him now stopped altogether.

He wasn't sure which of the two new graves was hers; he saw them both in the distance. It didn't matter which was which, he knew only that she was forever snugly beside Samuel Casterton—at least until the trumpet sounded, as they preached in church. Even from this distance he saw that a single stone, centered between the two still-recent mounds, had been added since the last time he'd looked this way.

A rush of grief took him aback. They were—the two of them—responsible for . . . What? The snickers he'd had to withstand back in Philadelphia. The tainted feeling that went with it, making him abandon certain circles he'd always frequented, making him abandon the last shred of hope that marriage could ever work for human beings too flawed.

He couldn't stand here, but neither could he move. He told himself to approach the grave or leave altogether, yet his feet wouldn't obey.

He began to turn when something caught his eye. Movement from the forest edge, the same forest that had sacrificed some of itself to make room for this town and for the cemetery itself.

It was Arianne, carrying a bunch of flowers. She couldn't have seen him; she'd had her back to him even as she emerged from the darkness of trees. Yet he still jumped within the shadow of the church behind him in case she looked this way. He watched her approach, kneel at the gravesites, remove what was likely a wilted bouquet from the ground and replace it with the fresh one from her hands.

Then, the job done, she stayed where she was, still kneeling. He watched, knowing she must be praying. With some annoyance, he realized she looked comfortable on her knees, a position he hadn't taken for quite some time now. It was still easy for her, she who hadn't suffered the consequences of their parents' behavior. She was so naive she didn't even believe it to be true.

Seeing her action reminded him that he'd nearly been tempted to pray last night. He'd carelessly left his mother's Bible on the table beside his bed, and not feeling as tired as he'd expected he'd started thumbing through it, reading until his fatigue grew at last.

It occurred to him now that his father wasn't the only one buried alone. Arianne's mother, too, must be buried away from Arianne's father. There was no other gravesite near them, not even an old one, so she must be somewhere else, apart from the husband who'd given her Arianne.

He turned to face the old cemetery behind him. Surely she must be here somewhere; he hadn't searched every grave the last time he'd been here. Leaving the shade of the church, he approached the nearest aisle, but after searching one row of headstones after another, he came away confused. There wasn't a single Casterton among them.

"She isn't here."

The voice came softly from behind, closer than he expected to find someone. When had she approached?

He turned to Arianne, eying her with a narrowed gaze. "I wasn't looking for my mother, if that's what you're thinking. I was looking for yours."

"Mine? Why?"

"Because she's buried alone, isn't she? Like my father?"

Though she'd stood only a short distance away, Arianne took another few steps until within an arm's length. She looked at him with such interest he wished he hadn't been so honest about why he was here.

"My mother's family is from England. She wanted to be buried there, and so my father took her back after she died—ten years ago now."

"But didn't she want him buried next to her?"

"That was their first intention, but my father regretted she was so far away. He made arrangements several years ago to be buried here, where I . . ." She looked back toward the other cemetery, her eyes suddenly glistening. "Well, not so far from where I could visit from time to time."

"It must be nice to hold such fond memories," he whispered, "even if he doesn't deserve them."

"Mr. Prestwich—"

"Jonas."

"This morning you proposed the idea of a partnership between us. You know I can't afford to buy your share of the inheritance, which means I have little choice except to agree to your terms. But —" She was shaking her head, perhaps because he'd been unable to prevent the eager smile from forming on his face at the idea of her agreement, albeit reluctantly, to their partnership. "If there is any hope of us working together, you'll have to agree to my terms, too."

He guessed what she was about to say but didn't interrupt, especially when she took yet another step closer and her face took on an edge of warning. He was nearly tempted to take a step back ward—not from cowardice but because her close stance ignited a surge of welcome he would rather not feel, particularly since she was obviously hoping to be more threatening than friendly. But he held his ground, and her gaze remained steady.

"If you ever—ever—again speak ill of my father or your mother, I'll do everything I can to break whatever partnership you propose between us. Do you understand?"

He nodded, continuing to enjoy her close proximity. She really was lovely. No wonder Leo was in love with her. For a moment he felt sorry for the man, realizing to lose her affection would be a great loss indeed.

———

The man was infuriating! He hardly looked serious at all. Was nothing sacred to him? Neither his mother nor papermaking. He didn't even go to church! How in the world was she to partner with such a man?

She walked away without another word, not caring if he followed. She couldn't change what he thought, but at least she could stop him from expressing those thoughts.

"Wait," he said as he fell in step beside her. "So do I understand correctly that we're now partners? Officially? Willingly?"

"Yes, Mr. Prestwich."

"It's time to call me Jonas, Arianne. We're equal partners now."

She stopped short, a new surge of anger coursing through her. "Equal? Do I have to remind you that I own two-thirds, and you own only a third?"

"That might be true right now, but as soon as tomorrow I plan to invest a considerable amount of my own money in expansion. That will equal things pretty quickly."

While his words did abate her anger, a new thought struck her. "If you want to build a factory paper mill so badly, *Jonas*, why don't you build it in Philadelphia?"

He laughed. "Because this will be an expansion—a Casterton

product—not a new business. It's important to use the reputation you've already built, and proceed with the foundation already established. Besides, there are plenty of paper mills in the city and we have everything we need right here: the forest and water power. I may not know everything I need to know yet, but I'm not too modest to say I'll soon learn. Practically speaking, we're already on our way to greater success than your fath—than you—ever imagined."

She raised a brow, wondering if she ought to give him credit for catching his ready reference to her father. Maybe he could learn, after all.

CHAPTER TWENTY

After Jonas left for Philadelphia to make plans for the expansion of the paper mill, Arianne started each day wondering what changes he would bring. She kept pushing those thoughts away, clinging instead to the routine of working in the only way she knew. She was busier than ever since Leo rarely came by to help.

She missed her friend, and certainly missed his assistance, but knew it was better for Leo to stay away. Realizing he didn't share her passion for papermaking reminded her that he wasn't settling for a lesser choice of vocation.

Mostly she didn't want to see him until he could stop staring at her with the dreadful sadness she'd seen in his eyes every time she'd happened to pass him in town. If a future with Arianne had been the only thing tipping the scale toward papermaking, the final decision for him to take a place in his own family's business was not only inevitable, it was permanent.

By the fourth day on her own Arianne found herself resenting Jonas's absence. He might not have been the most efficient help in the mill, but he was better than nothing. The least he could have done was stay here in Cranbury long enough to ensure funds for her to hire someone to help. What in the world was keeping him away so long, anyway?

She refused to admit to anyone, not to Phoebe or even to Leta, how often Jonas came to mind. She barely knew him, but sensed if she could get him to cast aside his suspicion and resentment of his mother and her father, she could easily come to care for him. She had the feeling he wasn't as hard-hearted about his mother as he tried to portray. In fact, she wondered if his problem was more that Charlotte had removed herself from Jonas's life than with whatever misconception he had about her behavior.

By the sixth day of his absence, Arianne determined she would find a way to break through Jonas's resentment and make him face his true feelings about Charlotte. Because if they were to be partners, she already knew she couldn't forget what he believed. So she must rid them both of such suspicions and the only way to do that was to convince Jonas he was wrong.

When Arianne arrived for dinner that evening, she saw that Binny had left an envelope on her plate. A letter from Jonas.

It was brief, surprising her in its businesslike tone. All it said was that he would return the next day. She set the note aside, guessing he likely thought himself a veritable expert on paper-making after a measly week of investigating where and how best to expand.

Silent and sullen despite Binny's attempt to converse, she realized the true source of her sour mood. If they were partners, why wasn't he consulting her? Why had he run off to Philadelphia without her, to learn what he needed to know? He should have taken her with him! He was proving himself just like every other man. With no more than one-third authority in this business and his own resources, he likely believed he was entirely in control.

Humph.

Arianne went upstairs after dinner, but not to her own room. Instead she went to the room her father had shared with Charlotte. Having been in here once, she was no longer hesitant about entering again. She'd decided days ago that, although Jonas was legally entitled to one-third of even her father's belongings, she knew he was not going to demand fulfillment of that part of the will.

He was, however, entitled to some of the things his mother had left behind. Arianne had already given him her Bible, but that might not be the only thing he might one day use.

She went to Charlotte's jewelry box. Her father had been generous but sensible in his gifts, and other than a wedding band he hadn't given Charlotte any of the jewelry she'd left behind. Although Jonas himself wouldn't be interested in such things, wouldn't he someday want to give gifts of jewelry to his bride, particularly jewelry with such sentimental value?

Jonas might resent Charlotte's memory now, but Arianne hoped between prayer and her own stubborn goal of pointing to the truth, Jonas would eventually welcome such a link to his mother's memory. Perhaps this could be a start.

She removed only one item, the ring the undertaker had taken from Charlotte's hand, the one her father had put there. The other items in the box she left intact, closing the lid.

On her way toward the door, her father's Bible caught her eye. Having her own Bible, she'd returned his to this spot, next to the softly cushioned chair he'd kept lamp-side. She didn't like the sour mood she found herself in so often these days, and knew what she needed was a word from God. It was so easy to look to the Bible for guidance on how best to act: reflecting God's love couldn't be done well in the kind of funk she'd been in lately.

So, setting aside the jewelry box for now, she sat where she'd so often seen her father, and took in the Word of God.

———

"That's right, Mr. Phipps," said Jonas to Cranbury's only newspaperman. "We'll supply all the factory paper you'll need for your newspaper just as soon as our facilities can accommodate the orders. But that's not the reason for my visit. I understand you're the best photographer in town."

The man hadn't stopped eying him suspiciously since he'd arrived a few minutes ago on this bright and early morning. Jonas's promise to supply him soon with ready, nearby, reasonably priced paper products evidently made little difference.

"I should hope I'm the best photographer in town," said the man, "but being the only one I guess it's not such an honor."

Jonas laughed amicably. "I'd like to hire you for a pictorial history of the paper mill's expansion. This is going to be important to town history, and you'll want to have a record of it, won't you? I've heard the original paper mill helped to expand Cranbury from a few homes, a grocer, a couple of businesses and a church to what it is today. Well, you can look to the mill for the next expansion, too."

"That so? And our Arianne agrees to all these highfalutin changes you've got in mind?"

Jonas nodded. "As I've been saying since I first came to town, I have no intention of harming Arianne's business. My intention is to make it grow." Did it really matter that she hadn't agreed to the details yet? This was all part of the expansion she *had* agreed to. And having spent a considerable amount of time investigating the process of factory paper, not to mention several long lunches with Mr. Fitzwater, Jonas was more hopeful than ever. Mr. Fitzwater seemed as interested in pursuing this expansion as Jonas himself.

So far, he'd assured the liveryman with whom he'd left his horse that he would soon have enough business to purchase a second Canary and another driver beside Mr. Tummers. He'd then gone to the hotel to let them know they should expect to rent rooms to men who would be working on the expansion of the mill, and then to the cafe to see if they could be depended upon to serve lunch to the crew he planned to bring in before the month was out.

His last stop before going to the mill would be to the post office, where he intended to warn them about the amount of deliveries expected in the near future.

Such local visits would likely have met a warmer reception had Arianne made them, or at least had she been at his side. But he hadn't been afraid to test the waters of the town on his own. They might not be warming, but at least they weren't any icier than they had been before.

He had yet another reason to hope this town might accept him, after all. Although none had shown any enthusiasm about prospective changes to the mill, not a single merchant had thrown him out, not even the hotel proprietress.

He couldn't help but feel well-pleased on his way toward the mill. Maybe it wouldn't be long before Arianne accepted him, too. Professionally and personally. He'd always thought friendship between partners made decisions easier—even if this was an unprecedented kind of partnership.

Not for the first time, Jonas cooled his thoughts that were so easily warmed regarding Arianne. His decision not to marry had unfortunately done nothing to lessen his attraction to women in general, and in particular to Arianne. In Philadelphia, Julia Kitteridge had heard of his return and invited him to their typical old haunts. But he'd found those places, and surprisingly Julia herself, easy to avoid. He'd never fancied himself in love with Julia, but he had been fond of her, not to mention drawn to her beauty. Having his attention absorbed by this new project—and Arianne— only proved how fickle was the human heart. Even his.

He found Arianne in the vat room, just where he expected her to be at this time of the day. But she wasn't bent over the vat, she was at the table with her back to him, a tin of Vaseline opened in front of her.

Though he set the leather satchel filled with plans and forecasts quietly on the table beside her, she jumped as if she hadn't expected his arrival. Hadn't she gotten his note last night?

Without a word, he took the seat opposite her at the table, only then seeing the handkerchief she held in one of her hands, one dotted with blood. Before thinking, he reached across the table to take her hand in his, seeing where the skin had broken open.

"What's this? What happened?"

"Nothing." She slowly pulled her hand away, continuing to rub the oily substance into her damaged knuckles. "Just a byproduct of working in the vat. Water doesn't hydrate after all."

"You're working too hard," he said, dipping his fingertips into the rectangular tin and proceeding to reclaim and minister to the hand she'd refused him. She'd so hesitantly withdrawn he couldn't help but believe she hadn't been all that keen on taking her hand back. "It's time to hire someone to help you here, so you can go back to the work you did when your father ran the vat." Looking up at her face, he saw a hint of a first smile beneath the shock in her eyes over his uninvited assistance. "You can go back to water-marking. Wouldn't you like that?"

"What are you doing?" she asked, but in a soft rather than challenging tone.

"Helping to protect the tools of the mill." He lifted her hand, indicating that was all he was doing; nothing personal. "It's what partners do, isn't it? You should wear rubber gloves."

Her gaze went to the cubbyholes on the wall in the corner. He'd noticed the gloves stored there before, which was why he thought of them now, but they were still there. "I haven't any that fit me. My father's keep falling into the vat."

"We'll have to find some that do fit, then." He kept talking as if his action deserved no more explanation, even as he set aside the one hand and reached for the other. To his surprise, she gave it to him and he set about applying cream to this one as well. "I've been almost as busy as you. I met with a Philadelphia papermaker who is a friend of mine and who was generous enough to help develop plans. As a matter of fact, he and his family are eager to meet you. Mainly because they're familiar with your watermarking skills. Evidently Mr. Fitzwater collects paper from all the mills in the state, and he came across one of yours with the image of a man. Stationery from a Mr. Eliot Wardman, who must be a customer here. Do you recall the one I mean?"

She nodded.

How could he admit it had been the first time he saw what she meant, that paper could be art?

"I think it's important to have you return to watermarking as soon as possible. As much as I'd like to take your place here at the vat, we both know it would be wiser to hire someone who can take the job longer term. Did you have anyone from Cranbury in mind? Other than Leo, that is?"

"I'm the papermaker, Jonas. Watermarking is only part of the job."

He smiled because that was the first time she'd used his name as if it fell naturally from her lips. "Tell me, Arianne, what would your father have done had you gotten married? Would he still have expected you to work here in the mill, and tend your husband and children as well?"

"I . . . suppose he would have depended more upon Leo."

Jonas wanted to snort but contained himself. "And if you'd married someone other than Leo?"

She reclaimed her hand, which even he had to admit had been well-salved moments ago. Perhaps she'd enjoyed receiving the massage as much as he'd enjoyed giving it. "I see your point." Rubbing the excess of petroleum jelly onto the handkerchief, she then set it aside to replace the lid to the tin. Finally she eyed him with nothing less than suspicion. "This friend of yours in the papermaking business. What does he expect in return for the advice he gave you?"

Taking up the handkerchief to wipe off his own hands, he grinned at her. "Your sharp business sense is precisely why our partnership will be successful. They want to invest in our expansion—in us."

"But you said you had all the money we needed!"

He nodded, standing because she had. "And so I do. But can it hurt to have someone already in the business offering a helping hand?"

"A competitor?"

"Isn't it better to have them on our side, than competing?"

"Not if they want to swallow us whole."

He stepped around the edge of the table so they were only inches apart. "I won't let that happen." Taking one of her hands again, it nearly slipped from his hold in spite of taking it firmly. "I promise you, Arianne. Nothing is going to hurt your mill."

CHAPTER TWENTY-ONE

Instead of getting to work, Arianne sat back down and listened with increasing trepidation as Jonas pulled from his satchel the plans he'd brought back for the expansion of the paper mill. He wanted to add an entirely new wing to the factory, and bring in huge, heavy equipment that would remove every bit of artistry from the entire process.

Innovation? Yes. But it all seemed so new, so different. So impersonal.

Just when she was about to speak up, to protest, to demand a stop to his agenda, Jonas set aside the pile of paperwork and rested one of his hands on her forearm.

"Arianne," he said quietly, "all of this is the latest modernization in papermaking. I can assure you the product will be worthy of the Casterton name. But it'll remain separate from what you do here. You understand that, don't you?"

"Yes, you keep saying that. But this is a full-fledged factory. It looks like a behemoth, ready to devour every bit of the resources we have around here."

"Not true! I've already spoken to one of the lumber mills in Williamsport. They're ready to send us their pulp at a reasonable price. Wood pulp is the future, and where better to be than right here in a Pennsylvania forest?"

She rubbed her temples, wishing for the thousandth time that her father were here to make this decision instead of her. She and Jonas had just spent the better part of an hour going over the plans he'd prepared in Philadelphia, and she was no closer to being confident about the changes than she was before he'd returned.

Wasn't there a reason her father had never made such an expansion on the mill himself? Was it only because he could never have afforded such a thing, or was it because he feared the same thing she did, that somehow the new way of doing things would stamp out the old?

"I can see you've worked hard on these plans, Jonas, but it's overwhelming. I'm not even sure I should have agreed to this partnership, and now I see why. Nothing will ever be the same if we go forward with these plans."

He frowned. "Life is that way, Arianne. Nothing ever stays the same."

"I know that." Her father's loss reminded her of that every day.

"Do you? Why do you still have doubts about partnering with me? Haven't I convinced you that I'm a good businessman?"

"It's not that." She looked away from him, uncertain this was the time to bring up everything that had been on her mind. Yet it was entirely possible she would never want to speak of the burdens on her heart, so now was as good a time as any. "It's more than just a transformation from what I've always known in papermaking. I'm afraid of a partnership with you because of two other things, Jonas. Your lack of faith in your mother, and also in God."

A breath escaped him that teetered on impatience. Was he so annoyed with this topic, the only thing that consumed her ever since he'd first revealed his suspicions? How could she work side-by-side with a man who didn't believe in God but did believe something so erroneous of his mother and her father?

The problem was, at least as far as Charlotte and her father went, she'd been unable to uncover anything assuring her that Jonas was in error. In fact, just the opposite. It might be true that Jonas only reminded her of these new doubts, but she couldn't deny this shadow over the idea of partnering with him. How would she ever forget the suspicions with his presence as a constant reminder?

"I never said I didn't believe in God," he said at last. He pivoted on the bench he occupied on the other side of the table, so that he could lean forward and away from her, elbows on his knees. When he ran his fingers through his dark hair it sprang back into place just the way Arianne thought it might if she had done such a thing with her own fingers. Then he raised his gaze, and she was surprised to see a sense of vulnerability there, not the confidence he normally wore. "You can't be angry with someone if you don't think He's there."

"You're angry with God?"

"Why shouldn't I be? He let my father die of a heart attack when we all thought he'd live till he was ninety. Then a few months later He took my mother, just as suddenly. If only God holds the power over life and death, who else should I blame?"

"I'm not sure we should blame God for illnesses and accidents. Starting with Adam and Eve, we all chose our own way instead of His."

"Look," he said, "I know I'm not the picture of sainthood, but I'm not a heathen, either. You don't have to worry I'll make business choices that are opposed to the things you believe."

"You mean the way you think your mother and my father made their choices?"

The question, softly issued, was met with silence. All she could hear was the churning of the fibrous pulp being macerated in the next room, by wheels spinning on the power of the river below.

Arianne watched him closely, not because she'd meant her question to challenge him but because he might reveal something to suggest her own growing doubts could be as wrong as his.

At last he met her gaze and in his, she found not a trace of anger or accusation or self-defense. She saw only sadness. "I can't change what I believe, even if I want to."

Before she could prevent them, tears stung Arianne's eyes. She wanted to insist he was wrong, scold him again for holding so tightly to an ugly suspicion.

But she couldn't, not with her own growing doubts—doubts that incited the tears welling in her eyes so ready to overflow down her cheeks. Ignoring all embarrassment, she folded her arms on the table to hide her sudden and unstoppable tears.

In a moment, she felt herself pulled from the nest of her arms and to her feet, into Jonas's embrace. He held her close, gently not tightly, as if unsure at first if she would allow such contact. But she had no strength to resist. It had been so long since she'd been comforted in such a personal way, and never by a man other than her father or Leo.

"I—I was reading my fa-father's Bible," she confessed, only to interrupt herself with a gulp of air and more tears. He let her pull away, but still held on to her arms. Even though she feared she must look a sight, she couldn't wipe away her tears any more than she could retract them. "The verses he marked with a 'C' were all about guilt! And forgiveness! And . . . And I don't know what to believe any more."

Pulling her close again, he stroked her hair. She'd tied some of it with a ribbon that morning, away from her face so as not to be a bother when she leaned over the vat, but most of it was free and flowing down her back. Had anyone ever touched her so, other than her father when she'd been a child?

"I'm sorry," she heard him whisper, not once but twice.

"Why—why are you sorry?"

He repositioned her to arm's length again. "Because if I hadn't brought up my accusations, you never would have had these doubts in the first place."

She reached for the only handkerchief nearby, already soiled by the petroleum. Finding a dry corner, she wiped at her face. "That doesn't make it untrue."

"I still don't think it makes a difference anymore, whatever my mother and your father did. It's in the past now."

She waved the handkerchief at his words as if to erase them, even though she could tell it still made as much a difference to him as it did to her. "Oh! How can it not make a difference? That they could have ignored everything they supposedly held dear? Their faith, to start with! And us. If . . . If their faith meant so little to them, what does that mean to—" She cut herself off, unwilling to bare any more of her soul to him.

He offered her a lopsided smile. "Better be careful, Arianne, or you'll doubt your faith the same way I did. Let me assure you, it doesn't do any good to feel that way."

She collapsed back onto the bench. Every ounce of energy seemed to have been flushed out with her tears. "And here I'd hoped when you returned from Philadelphia that I would help to restore your memory of your mother, instead of making the chasm even wider." She welcomed it when he sat beside her instead of on the opposite bench. "I have her jewelry, and thought you might want it someday."

Leaning back on the table behind them, he shook his head with a grin. "Probably nothing I'm likely to wear."

Laughter welled up inside almost as uncontrollably as her tears had a moment ago. "Not for you, but someday . . . You may want to make a gift of her things to your wife."

"Marriage isn't for me."

He said it so quickly, so surely, she was taken aback. "Why is that?"

"The marriages I've observed, especially my parents', haven't made it look like a very good idea."

She leaned back on the table too. "My father once told me marriage was the greatest gift God has ever given us."

"Were your parents happy, then? Can you remember?"

She nodded. "Yes, they were. And so were my father and Charlotte. They made me hope for a marriage of my own someday, because it all seemed very romantic. Maybe because of that I've been a little too picky."

"So picky that even stalwart Leo can't live up to your hopes."

Perhaps she should take the observation as an insult either to her or to Leo, but because it was likely true she just nodded.

"I'm sure marriage is romantic," he said, but his tone was anything except tender. "At least in the beginning."

"But not later?"

"If marriage is necessary for a stable society, then families should go back to arranging them for their children. Business arrangements offer more realistic expectations. Marrying for love is romantic, all right. Unfortunately it blinds people only long enough to get them a little past the marriage ceremony. Then it goes away, and all those silly expectations no longer have any hope of being met."

"What a sad thing to believe," she whispered. But then a fresh jab of pain and uncertainty over what Charlotte might have done inside her marriage made Arianne wonder if Jonas's view might be right, at least in some cases.

He held her gaze, suddenly serious again. "You should keep my mother's jewelry, Arianne. I'm sure that would be what she wanted."

She let their gazes stay locked, realizing after too many moments passed how intimate it felt. She stood again, rubbing her palms on her apron despite all remnants of the Vaseline having long since disappeared. "I should get to work."

Going to another apron still hanging on the hook beside the door, he looked ready to do so as well. But he made it no farther than the entry to the glazing room before turning back.

"If I come to church with you this Sunday, Arianne, will you come to Philadelphia with me? Next week? Meet the paper manufacturing family I mentioned?"

A simple visit to a local church might not seem much in trade for a train ride all the way to Philadelphia, but Arianne couldn't think of a better swap.

She nodded, heart thumping.

Partners.

CHAPTER TWENTY-TWO

The week went quickly for Jonas as he learned more about the handmade papermaking process, albeit indirectly. Arianne had hired a local boy by the name of Gideon to work in the mill. He was a sturdy youth, already taller than Arianne despite his young age, and possessed the long arms she said were just right for something she called couching, a method of tossing felts between sheets of newly formed paper.

To his consternation, she trusted the boy at the vat after only two days of work, something she had yet to trust Jonas himself to do. He might not see his future as that of a handmade papermaker, but he possessed just enough stubbornness to want to try learning the craft anyway. He didn't care whether this new fascination was because he didn't like the idea of his partner knowing more than he did or because the interest was genuine. He listened attentively to all of the training Arianne offered Gideon, determined to try each and every step just as soon as Arianne could be convinced the idea was worthwhile.

He'd hoped he might bring it up today, but when she arrived at the mill with a frown already in place, he decided against any new plans just yet.

"Something wrong?"

"I'll have to work in the shop today. Phoebe is unwell."

"Nothing serious, I hope?"

"A headache, something she's suffered off and on for years. She cannot get out of bed without emptying her stomach."

Having arrived a few minutes earlier, Jonas had already donned the leather apron he always wore in the mill. But he untied it and hung it back where he'd found it.

"I'll work in the shop today."

"What? You?"

He refused to contemplate why she continued to think him incompetent in every area of business until he proved himself. "I can't very well take up training Gideon since he already has more experience than I do, but I can add sales figures and make change. If I have any questions, I'll send Binny for you."

He walked from the mill, half expecting her to chase after him with some sort of alternate plan. But Gideon arrived just then, and all she did was ask if he was ready for another day of work.

Jonas had never pictured himself working in a shop of any kind, but after the very first customer of the day he had reason to think he would be more effective here than in the mill. He not only had the confidence that everything in the shop was the best quality, the job offered him the opportunity to present himself to villagers as helpful and polite—the opposite of what people still seemed to think of him.

To his delight, anything that wasn't already priced was listed in a ledger with a price neatly recorded next to it. And since numbers had never daunted him, Jonas knew the day's work would be easy.

Only when the woman from the dress shop came by did he fail to produce a smile. Not that he didn't try, since he guessed she was a frequent visitor and a friend of Arianne's. Still, he was able to erase her frown when he complimented her hat.

There was a remarkably steady stream of customers thereafter, right through to the afternoon.

"Now, young man," said an older woman who introduced herself as Mrs. Jenkins, "I'm here to buy a greeting postcard, but only one." She placed two postcards on the counter between them. "It'll be sent to my niece whose birthday is coming up next month, but I can't decide which of these two is better for someone just turning sixteen. You're closer to that age than I am, so I want you to decide for me. Make the choice, young man, but make it right or you'll hear from me again."

Imagining what went on inside the head of a sixteen-year-old girl was like trying to figure out Samson's riddle without benefit of the story behind it. However, confidence being worth more than half the value of anything, he did little more than look at the text on each card before holding up one of the two.

"This one, Mrs. Jenkins, is exactly right for any girl of that age."

She glanced at the card and, to his relief, she lifted her brows with approval. "Why, that's the one I was thinking, too, only I wanted a second opinion. Thank you!"

"Greeting cards are just what this country needs," he said as he received payment and counted out the woman's exact change. "They deliver not just a paper product, but a smile from one person to another, from your doorstep to theirs. Not to mention the postage stamps that support our country. It's too bad more people don't have your gentility and patriotism, Mrs. Jenkins. Just think if everyone in the country sent one greeting a week, we could probably support the entire government without a single tax."

Not only did she laugh, she reached across the counter to pat one of his hands as if she were his kindly old aunt. "Now how did you know my very own brother is the Cranbury postmaster? And my father before him! Of course, back then my father didn't have a real post office. He just used a little corner of the grocer's shop. My, oh my, it's nice to hear someone appreciate the postal service instead of complaining about it."

Waving to her once she reached the door, Jonas wondered if God's providence had anything to do with his working in the shop today. Ever since he'd promised to go to church with Arianne this Sunday, things had been looking up.

Not that he thought God bargained with people. He'd learned that didn't work a long time ago, or else his parents would be buried side-by-side today.

"Excuse me."

Jonas looked at the newest customer, a stern-faced but well-dressed woman, standing with such erect posture he guessed her to be a school teacher type, determined to set an example for her students. He rounded the counter and joined her at the table filled with stacks of various paper: bound tablets and loose writing sheets both flat and folded, a variety of envelopes and two decorative boxes labeled *papeteries*, a kind of box he'd learned held stationery and matching envelopes inside.

She held up a small stack of loose paper, all that was left of its kind on the table.

"I'm interested in this paper, but this isn't enough. Do you have another stack stored somewhere else?"

There were shelves in the little room separating the shop from private quarters, and he had indeed noticed paper being stored there. He nodded and went in search of what the woman wanted.

Wide shelves covered three of the four walls in the little closet. Several boxes on a generous countertop were already wrapped and addressed, ready to be taken to the post office. Other inventory included packaging material, everything from brown paper and twine to tissue paper and something resembling clean, fine straw.

It took him several minutes to search each shelf before finding a box high up, of loose paper in a canvas-covered box, wrapped inside with tissue paper as if it was to be shipped somewhere. But without a note, address or order sheet it was likely more stock. Counting out fifty sheets for the woman, he trimmed it to stationery size on the guillotine then grabbed an extra handful to place on the table in the empty spot.

Pleased with himself for keeping the shop running so smoothly, Jonas saluted to the woman on her way out the door.

On Sunday morning, Arianne chose her clothing more carefully than she had in the past. She still wore black in mourning for Charlotte and her father, but rather than the plain black blouse and skirt she normally wore, this time she reached past the old-fashioned shirtwaist with ballooned sleeves to a blouse Leta had recently dyed for her. The puffs on these sleeves were higher, and the bodice itself pleated, which was not only fancier but the reason she'd hesitated to wear it yet. Leta had chosen which of her shirtwaists would take best to dye, and she'd insisted there was nothing improper about adding a little style to mourning garb.

For each moment she spent fussing over her appearance, Arianne called herself a fool. *Marriage isn't for me.* His unflinching words rang through her mind more often than she wanted to hear them.

Marriage! She was a fool just to think of the word, let alone in connection to Jonas.

Still, there it was. On her mind. She might as well admit it: Jonas was on her mind far too often for just being a business partner. And she was far too eager to sit beside him at church.

As usual, she met Leta just outside her dress shop, where Leta lived upstairs the way Arianne did, above the shop itself.

Arianne saw immediately that Leta hadn't missed the change in Arianne's wardrobe. She offered a wink as Arianne approached. "If anyone can look stylish in mourning wear, Ari, it's you." Leta leaned forward to land a kiss on Arianne's cheek. "You look a hint of your old self for the first time since the accident. I'm proud of you, getting through all of this so well."

Rather than fortifying her, Leta's words nearly made her cry.

"Oh, now look what I've done," Leta said, pulling out a lacy handkerchief hidden beneath her cuff. Dabbing at Arianne's eyes, she said, "I know you'll live with an ache from here on out, my dear friend, but you're accomplishing it with grace. Now let's walk, and I promise not to say anything more to bring that ache to the fore."

"It isn't that, Leta." How she wanted to talk to her friend, to tell her all of the doubts Jonas had brought with him from Philadelphia. But she knew she couldn't betray her father's memory. Still, she could admit to Leta she was failing to squelch feelings for a man who could only hurt her if he truly intended to avoid marriage. Not to mention one who thought so little of her beloved father! Better to confess and rid herself of these budding emotions before they took too deep a hold on her. "I fear I'm the most foolish woman in the world."

Leta took Arianne's hand as they walked. "What nonsense is this?"

Arianne looked ahead, with a clear view of the church at the end of town. Though he was still far off, she recognized Jonas waiting outside the church, just as she expected. She'd had no doubt he would fulfill his part of the bargain, which included sitting next to her. "I—I spent a half hour on my hair today, and in case you haven't already noticed I'm wearing the face powder you gave me for Christmas last year. And the rouge! Worse than that, I actually kissed rose colored crepe paper this morning to pick up the dye."

Leta squeezed her hand. "I did notice, you silly goose, and you look lovely. It's not the first time you've worn makeup. I don't care what Mrs. Jenkins says, makeup is perfectly respectable when worn properly and not overdone."

"But don't you find it odd that I've decided to do all this when I'm in *mourning?*"

Leta winked at her again, then to Arianne's confusion cocked her head in the general direction of Jonas. "I'm pretty sure it has to do with your new partner, but I wasn't going to say anything until you did."

"Oh, Leta!" Arianne heaved a sigh of relief. "That's the most ridiculous part of all."

"I'd think you were ridiculous only if you'd been working with that handsome man all this time and didn't start to feel something for him. He served me in the shop yesterday and I swear the man could charm a snake right out of its skin."

"But . . ." How could she tell Leta it wasn't so simple? That she wasn't at all sure she should feel an attraction to a man who would be her step-brother had their parents lived any longer than they had? It wasn't only Leo who should seem a brother to her!

More importantly, he wanted to change so drastically the business she loved that she wasn't even sure she'd recognize it by the time he was through. And he might claim to believe in God, but going to church was hardly evidence of a life well lived. Worst of all, Jonas believed something dastardly not only of her father but of his very own mother.

Oh, there were so many reasons not to encourage these feelings for Jonas, not the least of which was his attitude toward marriage. If she were smart, she would turn around right now. Yet she couldn't change the direction of her feet any more than she could the direction of her heart.

"But he says marriage isn't for him."

Leta laughed outright. "My mother used to say men are born with that attitude. It's up to us to change their way of thinking."

If Arianne could admit why Jonas held such an opinion, she was fairly certain her friend wouldn't be laughing away such a worry.

"Be happy, Ari. He's Charlotte's son, so there's bound to be good in him. And he wants your business to succeed. He's not trying to take it away from you. No one believes that anymore."

"It's true," she whispered, watching him just as he watched her approach. "I received a receipt in the mail yesterday. He paid my tax bill."

"There! Now go and greet him. I'm not ready to make him feel so comfortable as to think he's been enveloped into our town just yet. It'll keep him eager to please you if he knows he still has to work for it. You sit with him, and I'll see you later."

Then she was gone, and Arianne was left to greet Jonas for the first time outside of the realm of business.

———

Jonas had to admit that sitting next to Arianne distracted him right through the opening hymns, but somehow the words of the sermon penetrated through the fog of undeniable attraction he felt for this woman.

The sermon was about forgiveness. A simple word, something even a child could understand. That's what the pastor said. How had he known this was one topic Jonas most wanted to avoid . . . But perhaps most needed to face?

Forgiveness was only given to those who'd done wrong. Forgiveness extended toward those who needed it was often the hardest to give. Forgiveness wouldn't be forgiveness unless it was undeserved. One jab to Jonas's heart after another. The pastor might as well have said right out loud that Jonas needed to forgive his mother and Arianne's father.

He nearly wanted to bolt out of the place, but knew he wouldn't be able to explain that to Arianne. She wanted a partner who shared her values, her faith. He didn't blame her for that.

But oh how he wished he could ignore all that went along with this portion of their partnership.

CHAPTER TWENTY-THREE

After the service ended, Jonas politely tipped his hat toward others but expected to shake hands only with the pastor. However it was Mrs. Jenkins who seemed to let loose the floodwaters of friendliness from other Cranbury residents. She introduced him to everyone, even those he already knew, as if she'd personally invited him to town.

Not even an open glare from Leo Levick prevented others from letting Jonas know they were glad to see him at church.

But now that the last of the parishioners were dispersing to their homes for Sunday dinner, Jonas was glad to have Arianne to himself. "I rented a buggy from Williamsport and hope you'll share the picnic lunch I had my housekeeper pack. Enough for two. You don't mind, do you?"

She shook her head, though he would have preferred a smile rather than the pensive face she'd sported almost all that morning. He knew she was a thoughtful, responsible person who took her faith seriously. Church wasn't just a social outing for her. He knew, too, that she had a great deal on her mind these days. Added to all that, she was still in mourning—a period he refused to acknowledge himself. But he still very much wanted to make her smile.

He'd fought all through the night with the idea of today's

picnic. There was something irresistible about the idea of spending the day with Arianne, even though for every thought in favor of such a thing he cautioned himself this was a relationship to be carefully nurtured. She was, after all, his business partner. While he had no idea how a professional relationship with a woman might look, he had every reason to believe theirs would be successful. But what if a personal relationship one wasn't?

Just outside of town, Jonas came to the main road. "Right or left?" he asked. "You've lived here all your life, Arianne. My guess is you have a favorite spot. Will you share it with me?"

"Right."

He guessed the spot almost before she instructed him to pull the rig to a stop. He'd passed this way many times between Cranbury and Williamsport, and more than once had noticed the view. A series of open, farmed hills on one side and forest hills on the other, the wide, flat river below was the only respite from various shades of green. From this height the sky wasn't hindered, and he could see farther than any vista in the city.

He had no idea what Olice's wife had packed for lunch, but felt confident it would meet Arianne's approval. Having never eaten anything Binny had made, he had no idea how proficient she was in the kitchen. But Mrs. Brown could compete with the best, of that he was sure.

The basket came complete with a blanket as well as a sheath of brown paper, evidently in case a table could be found and he needed a disposable tablecloth. This paper from a Williamsport shop was marred with knots and splotches—not nearly as fine as that from Arianne's inventory, even among packing paper. While he considered it suitable for such temporary use he was also aware of his own heightened instinct for quality when it came to paper these days. He was picking up more than he'd guessed.

After laying out the blanket and unfolding the paper to accommodate the food between them, he knelt beside Arianne as she took a seat nearby. He'd done nothing more than withdraw a plate covered with paraffin paper when he heard Arianne gasp.

"Oh! I hadn't thought . . ." She raised an unsteady hand to wipe away a quick tear. "I'm sorry. I just realized your housekeeper must be the very same woman who worked for your mother."

"That's right," he said, offering her a plate. "She's been with my mother's family since she was a child."

"I can tell from the bed of flowers beneath the sandwiches," Arianne said softly. "She used to pack butter that way. My father and I met Charlotte for picnics sometimes, and she knew he liked fresh bread and butter. She always made it look so pretty."

Jonas waited to speak, afraid whatever words he chose would be wrong, at least based upon the first thoughts that came to mind. Had his mother picnicked with them while still married to his father?

Maybe Arianne was right about the reminders of the past getting in the way of any sort of partnership between them, even a professional one. He looked away, remembering for the first time since getting to know her why he'd resented her in the first place.

He settled back on the blanket, leaving the rest of the basket contents untouched.

Silence between them drew out, but Jonas was too caught up in this unexpected resurrection of ill feelings to feel any awkwardness. He scoffed at himself. All he'd wanted to do was produce a smile in her, and now he found it impossible to produce one in himself.

"Did you listen to the sermon this morning, Jonas?"

He raised his gaze to her, surprised by her gentle tone of voice. He'd expected her to feel what he felt at the reminder of their parents' sin. Yet on her face was nothing but peace.

He nodded.

"Then you know what we both must do. I'm not even sure it's our place, but we both seem to be harboring anger. Is it our place, really? Whatever our parents did, is it we who need to forgive them? I thought it was, but now I'm not so sure. We weren't wronged. Only God—and your father—might have been. But us? We haven't any right to be angry."

Jonas sucked in a deep breath and offered a shallow laugh. "What's this? You, comforting me about the past?"

Instead of letting him lighten the topic, she placed a cautioning hand on his arm. "Jonas, there is something I should have told you right away, the minute I met you. It's about your mother, about those last moments before she died."

He couldn't have spoken even if he'd thought of something to say. So he waited, wanting to look away as if whatever she intended to share couldn't make a difference, or didn't mean much to him. But he stared at her so intently he knew she must guess he needed to hear anything she had to offer.

"I didn't understand at the time, I thought she was confused, talking about making a will. But at the very end, just before she died, she said your name. You were on her mind, Jonas."

He frowned, unable to welcome the news as she obviously hoped: as some kind of evidence of his mother's love for him.

"She spoke of a will?"

"That's nothing. What's important is that she spoke your name. I'm sure she wished she could have seen you again."

Jonas withdrew his arm from her touch, looking away. "My mother was savvy about wills. She learned from experience that inheritances could be unfair. She must have thought for me to inherit anything would be unfair to you."

"Even if she did, that doesn't take away from the fact that you were in her heart, on her mind. The very last word she spoke was your name! If you could have heard the *way*—"

He stood, appetite gone. He wanted to leave altogether, but knew to stalk off now would make him appear as immature as he felt at the moment. Insulted yet again by the memory of his mother. Why did he still need evidence of her love? He was a grown man now, no longer in need of a mother.

"Arianne," he said without looking at her. He knew what he must say, and even though it was the last thing he wanted to do, he forged ahead. "I knew the inheritance was wrong. You should have received everything from your father. I knew it and now, from what you said, it's obvious my mother thought so as well." He turned to Arianne, ready to look at her. "If you want me to leave, to stop all of the plans for the expansion, to refuse the inheritance, I will. Only say the word."

———

Arianne stared up at him, any reaction frozen in confusion. She'd meant to comfort him! But what had she done except make him somehow resent his mother even more than he had a moment ago?

What had he just said? That he would free her from his portion of the inheritance? Wasn't that what she wanted? For things to go on as they always had.

But they couldn't. Since her father had died, she'd worked harder than she ever had in her life. Still she was far from up to date in her orders. She was sure the shelves in the stockroom were emptying. There was no possible way she could continue her father's business on her own.

She may not have a clear picture of the changes ahead; she may not even welcome all of them. But she knew one thing. She couldn't avoid it. The fact was Jonas's plans were likely for the best.

"I can't run the mill on my own," she admitted. "If I were perfectly honest, I'd admit that I need you. Frightening plans and all, I realize if you hadn't stepped in, paid that tax bill, I'd be in danger of losing everything by now."

He knelt once again at her side. "You're sure, then? Ahead we go, as partners?"

She nodded, taking his hand in hers, unable to let pass what she'd said earlier. "I don't know what Charlotte was thinking about the will, Jonas. But I do know the way she said your name was maybe with regret but not because of a will. She said your name with love."

He started to pull away, as if wishing she would let the topic— and his hand—go. But she held fast, willing him to stare at her.

After a moment she received her reward. He offered a lopsided grin.

"Between you and the sermon this morning, I have a feeling God isn't finished with me yet. I guess He doesn't want me to keep denying that I loved my mother. Because in spite of everything, I did."

"Oh, Jonas," Arianne whispered, "this is the first time you've ever acknowledged you're mourning your mother. In spite of everything."

"Of course I am." The words seemed choked out of him. "I miss her every day. I can't help it."

Arianne leaned closer, arms outstretched. She wanted her tears to encourage his, but feared he would never allow himself to be so vulnerable.

———

Tears stung Jonas's eyes, and he knew if he let them go she wouldn't think less of him. In fact, she might think better of him after evidence of love for his mother. He did love her; he did miss her. He wished things had ended differently between them.

Only one thing held him back from showing the great, dark grief that his mother's death had left inside him. If he let it show, if he shared the depth of it with this woman, it would be like admitting he needed her to find his way through his grief.

Jonas had not only sworn off needing his mother, he'd convinced himself never to need any other woman, either.

So he let Arianne cry in his arms but refused to do the same in hers.

CHAPTER TWENTY-FOUR

Arianne and Jonas left for Philadelphia early Monday morning. Mrs. Taylor, the proprietress of the Cranbury Inn, had at last agreed to rent Jonas a room, and so he stayed the night in order to accompany Arianne to Williamsport in the morning where they would take the train to Philadelphia. None of the shops, including her own, had yet opened after being closed as usual on Sunday but Phoebe had sent a note last night that her headache had passed and for Arianne not to wait to open the shop in the morning; she would take care of it. So the road was quiet as Jonas directed the rig outside of town not long after the sun had risen.

Arianne wasn't sure which she felt more: excitement or nervousness. The prospect of traveling with Jonas was undeniably exciting. But a business trip—her first ever—created as much tension as it did anticipation.

"The Fitzwaters are eager to meet you," Jonas said, "and to have you as their guest."

She wanted to smile; she wanted to say the interest was mutual. She knew she couldn't stay at Jonas's home—that was out of the question—but the fact was she'd expected to stay in a hotel.

"Are you sure I won't be an inconvenience? I'm not even a

family friend, just a . . ." She had trouble saying it aloud, "a business associate."

"Their home is large enough to offer you every comfort," he said. "I thought you'd welcome that instead of a city hotel, so far from home."

It was true she wouldn't have especially looked forward to that, either, since she was without an escort or chaperone. But if she was to be a businesswoman did she really need such a thing? Never before had Arianne realized just how sheltered she'd been all her life. Secure in her father's love, knowing she was another tightly fitted thread in her close-knit hometown village, confident in the talents she contributed through her work, she hadn't spent much time wondering what it would be like outside the safe surroundings of Cranbury. She might not be a friend to everyone in her little town, but she was at least the friend of a friend to everyone.

Philadelphia was a city of strangers who likely didn't know or care about each other, let alone one more visitor.

Soon they were as quiet as the forest around them. She wondered if this trip was a test. Not only for the obvious—herself as a businesswoman—but for whatever personal portion of this partnership they seemed to be creating, in spite of themselves. Once he oversaw his investment in the paper mill in Cranbury, managed the expansion until it was running, Jonas was likely to return to Philadelphia. Why shouldn't he? The city was his home. But if they continued to develop a friendship as well as a business partnership, he might expect her to visit him from time to time, for business if not personal reasons. He would likely visit Cranbury to make sure everything kept running smoothly, but if the manufacturing process ran as easily as he seemed to think, anyone could oversee it day by day.

Still, she wondered what would happen if marriage entered the picture someday. The thought took shape as it always did, suddenly, without warning, and uninvited. Might he invite her to live in Philadelphia as well?

As she chided herself for such premature and dreamy notions, the words Jonas spoke that day not long ago once again dispelled her thoughts: *marriage isn't for me.* It behooved her to protect her heart from hoping for something Jonas obviously wasn't prepared to offer. Ever.

———

Jonas disliked the silence between them. He had every reason to believe this trip wasn't just necessary, it would be the first of many. Perhaps he needed to make his optimism more clear.

"I've known the Fitzwater family for years through Clarence. We went to school together. My father knew the family through business, too, which must be at least partly why Mr. Fitzwater is happy to help us. He was so impressed with your watermark I've been wondering ever since if he might try convincing you to work for him in Philadelphia." He sent her a wink. "He could make you the most famous watermark artist in the city."

She laughed, and he found himself watching her rather than smiling along. At last! Not just a smile, but a full-fledged laugh. And he had created it! "Do you know I've been working for that nearly since the day I arrived in Cranbury?"

She eyed him with confusion. "Working for what?"

"Your smile."

He was glad when she offered not just another, but the light touch of her fingertips to his hand, the one folded in his lap while the other still gripped the rein. He grasped her gently and for a long moment kept his gaze locked on her.

"I know the way we met was anything but ideal, Arianne, but I'm glad we know each other now. Working together on a shared goal is more fun than I imagined."

"All of this has taught me something, Jonas," she said. "I think it's fair to say neither one of us expected to feel anything but resentment for each other because of—well, because of the nature of our parents' relationship. And yet we've grown fond of one another in spite of that. Doesn't that make it possible to understand, even a little bit, how emotion might have clouded what happened between our parents? How unexpected emotions can be?"

He frowned, coldness washing over him. "Of course emotion clouded their decisions! But emotions shouldn't direct a person's actions. Not emotion alone, anyway." He might have gone on, been graphic in his explanation that if he allowed himself to act on emotion alone he would likely have tried kissing her long ago. He restrained himself even now. "If I can hold myself up to a certain standard, why couldn't they have done the same? I'm young, of an age that a certain amount of foolishness is expected. But they were older. Old enough to have known better."

To his annoyance she laughed yet again, only this time he didn't welcome the sound. Was she laughing at him?

She squeezed his hand. "I thought the same thing, at first. When I saw that I'd become only a secondary reason your mother liked to visit, I was shocked. Embarrassed, even, because I'd never thought of my father or frankly your mother as anything except parental material. But, honestly, does love ever limit itself to a certain age?"

"So you're excusing them? That easily?"

His words effectively erased any hint of the peace he'd seen on her face a moment ago, so thoroughly he almost regretted pressing the issue. Finally she pulled back her hand and shook her head, looking away at the passing countryside. The silence returned.

She might be right to want to forgive them if they could, but he was glad to see it might not be any easier for her than it was for him. If someday she changed, forgave their memory, it was only because she'd never had to suffer the consequences of what they'd done. She'd never felt any censure in the idyllic little town in which she lived, and a taste of that would undoubtedly make extending forgiveness as impossible for her as it was for him.

———

Arianne's spirits were considerably lower than they'd been when they'd first set out. Why did she feel as though she were betraying her father's memory each time this topic rose between her and Jonas? Somehow they must settle the past, but for now she knew that would only happen once they spoke to Charlotte's maid—after she returned from Europe.

She was sorry she'd spoken about it, and wondered at her own motives for doing so. Perhaps it was the only way to follow what she'd warned herself to do earlier: protect her heart. So far, she didn't know any other way to do that except to remind herself of all this unpleasantness every time she felt closest to Jonas.

CHAPTER TWENTY-FIVE

A coach and driver from Jonas's home met Arianne and Jonas at the Philadelphia train station, taking them the short ride to the Fitzwaters. She looked up at the house in front of them, immediately aware that *house* was far too humble a term. This was a mansion. Three stories of rose-colored brick, with long, bevel-edged windows, a wide front porch complete with Roman columns. The doors themselves were giant-sized, reaching as high as the entire first floor. Doors that just now were opened by a man in a formal black suit, who stood at attention awaiting them as if he'd been anticipating their arrival at this precise time.

"Good afternoon, Mr. Prestwich," he said as Jonas led her forward. The man then ushered them inside, through a wide foyer with marble floors and wood-paneled walls. He went to another set of doors that were almost but not quite as tall as those through which they'd just entered.

This room was a parlor of some sort, although with a piano resting in the light shining through an impressive row of windows, she wondered if it might have a more specific name like a music chamber. Certainly there were enough rooms in this place to each have its own name and purpose.

Arianne clutched her purse, knowing this moment wasn't likely to be the only time she wished she'd never left home. This place was twice the size of the Wardmans', where she knew only the staff. She might be intimately acquainted with Mr. Wardman's face, but had never met the man himself and was only marginally acquainted with Mrs. Wardman who'd commissioned Arianne to create the watermark from a small portrait.

She swallowed nervously. What was she doing here? How was she to fit in, even as only a business guest, to such a place?

She turned to Jonas, nearly taking him by the hand to lead him back out the door and insist he take her to a hotel instead. But while he did accept the hand she'd extended, he merely smiled amicably as if trying to reassure her.

"I'll stay with you until you're comfortable."

She tried erasing whatever alarm must be showing on her face for him to offer such instantaneous reassurance, but feared she failed when the sound of quick footsteps echoed through the foyer.

"Don't tell Father yet that she's here, Didier!"

"Oh, no, certainly not," said another female voice, this one more mature. "He'll be sure to monopolize her and we'd like to get to know her first. And don't tell Mother, either, or she'll tell Father."

The girls whose voices heralded their arrival entered in a rush of activity, followed closely by the tap of a dog's paws behind them. They were both young, one short and the other tall, and both wore clothing fancy enough to be photographed for a magazine. The shorter one must be considerably younger, judging by the girlish hem of her gown, but amid their smiles they swooped so close to Arianne she took an automatic step closer to Jonas.

"You must be Arianne Casterton," said the taller of the two, ignoring Jonas as if he weren't even there. She held out her hand and Arianne had to drop her hold on Jonas because first the tall sister took one hand and then the short one claimed the other.

"We're Lydia and Hannah," said the taller. "I'm Lydia, and this is my little sister Hannah."

They fairly pulled her to the couch behind them and each took a seat beside her. "Didier," called Lydia, "have Wilson bring in some tea, won't you?" She looked at Arianne. "Are you very hungry after your travels? Will sandwiches and sweet cakes be enough? Or perhaps you'd prefer coffee!"

"I—I like tea," she said.

"Jonas told us all about you being a papermaker," Hannah said, sparing him a quick glance. "Although now that we're all grown up, Mother says I should call him *Mr.* Prestwich. But that just sounds so silly! Jonas said you can make paper all by yourself, and Lydia and I couldn't imagine a woman working in a factory. That's why we couldn't wait to meet you."

"Yes, and they said you've carried on your father's business by yourself, too!" Lydia said.

"What an astonishing thing to do, Miss Casterton!"

"However have you been managing all on your own?"

Arianne opened her mouth to answer, to say that she hadn't been entirely on her own, but the sisters kept taking turns speaking, not allowing her to respond beyond a nod or a word or two at a time.

She glanced at Jonas, who appeared content to be ignored.

———

Jonas had expected the Fitzwater family to welcome Arianne, but hadn't realized Clarence's younger sisters would demand all of her attention. He was likely to blame for that, having mentioned to Clarence that Arianne would need to be greeted by a friendly face if she were to enjoy a visit to a place so much bigger than Cranbury. If friendly included the talent to out-talk any living being, then Clarence's sisters were very friendly indeed.

He waited for an opportunity to say something, but even Arianne couldn't speak, which soon annoyed him. They kept talking right through the delivery of the tea, which sat unattended after Hannah sent the maid on her way. He'd forgotten how exhausting the Fitzwater sisters could be, just listening to all of the words they used in any given conversation. As eager as he was to leave their company, he was reluctant to leave Arianne's.

He was never so glad to see Mrs. Fitzwater as today, when she entered the room and clapped her hands like a schoolmarm to gain her daughters attention.

"Girls! Girls!" She smiled at Jonas then at Arianne. "I must apologize for my daughters' enthusiasm over our company. But girls, one would think we never have guests for your lack of manners. I could hear your voices all the way from the stairs, and never once did you allow Miss Casterton to speak."

"Yes, Mama," said both girls, instantly and unexpectedly quiet.

"Now," said Mrs. Fitzwater to Arianne, "is the tea not to your liking? Or have my girls let it sit without serving?"

The censure in her voice was unmistakable, and even if her assumption was correct, disapproval seemed to come easy to her. The silence that followed was more uncomfortable than the chatter had been moments before.

But Mrs. Fitzwater gracefully served the tea, and Jonas accepted a cup hoping Arianne didn't think it had been a mistake to come here instead of a hotel.

―――――

"Now tell me if it's true, Miss Casterton," said Mrs. Fitzwater, "that you are a watermark artist as well as a papermaker yourself."

Arianne nodded carefully. "My father taught me to make paper, just as his father taught him."

"But surely he didn't expect you to work in the factory yourself? A woman? When God Himself created you for something far greater—to be a vessel of life?"

It took a moment for Arianne to decipher what Mrs. Fitzwater meant, and when she did she felt her cheeks warm. She couldn't help stealing a glance in Jonas's direction; he only smiled reassuringly.

"Papermaking is a calling in our family, Mrs. Fitzwater. A life's work, you might say. I'm sure my father meant to allow certain seasons in my life, but he also equipped me with something that will be mine whenever I can devote myself to it."

The older woman offered a smile that was as polite, it seemed, as it was both insincere and disapproving. But then she looked at Jonas and her smile became more welcoming.

"Now here is a man of ambition." She sipped her tea. "My husband is quite impressed that you've grown into a businessman, Jonas. Not that I would know anything of such matters, of course, but I can tell when someone has caught my husband's attention. And you have certainly done that."

"It's an honor to be working with someone so successful in the industry," Jonas said.

"There is no one who knows the paper industry better than my husband."

"Yes, I learned that not only through his factory, but when he produced a copy of Arianne's—that is, Miss Casterton's—watermarked stationery. Evidently your husband keeps a close eye on everything in the industry."

"Father has been collecting competitors' paper ever since we can remember, hasn't he, Mother?" said Lydia.

Mrs. Fitzwater aimed a narrowed gaze at her daughter, though whether she disapproved of Lydia's statement or the way she'd entered uninvited into the conversation was hard to tell.

"My husband is eager to meet you, Miss Casterton," said Mrs. Fitzwater, responding no further to her daughter. "Which is why he should be here at any moment. He isn't content to wait until tomorrow night's reception to talk to you. There will be a number of business men competing to meet so rare a woman as one in business, so he welcomes having the advantage of offering you our home for as long as you're in the city."

"I'm grateful for your generosity." Arianne's voice wasn't much more than a whisper, but she still feared saying or doing the wrong thing under the force of this woman's presence. As Mrs. Fitzwater continued to steer the conversation, Arianne wondered if she would have missed her own mother so much during the years of her awkward journey from childhood to young womanhood if she'd been anything like Mrs. Fitzwater.

CHAPTER TWENTY-SIX

"Well, so this is the artist!"

Mr. Fitzwater's voice fairly boomed an announcement of his entrance into the parlor. Jonas stood upon the older man's arrival, glad to see Clarence at his side. The two had already shed their top hats and gloves, and both approached with eyes only for Arianne.

"Allow me to welcome you to Philadelphia," said Mr. Fitzwater, taking one of Arianne's hands and kissing it. She looked a bit surprised by the old-fashioned gesture, and even Jonas was glad when Clarence didn't follow suit.

His old school mate did bow in front of Arianne when his father introduced him, and afterward his gaze never seemed to leave her face. Even when Jonas nudged his friend in the rib, Clarence only spared him the briefest glance. His attention was clearly glued in place, directly upon Arianne.

"You're quite a talented young lady, Miss Casterton," said Mr. Fitzwater. "And you ought to know right away that I have an eye for such things because whenever possible my hope is to capitalize on the talent around me. Consider yourself invited to my staff any time you choose."

Arianne looked no less embarrassed by the invitation than she had by all of the attention leading up to it, murmuring a thank you but nothing more. Jonas hadn't expected the offer to come so soon after their meeting. He may not know everything he wanted to know about Arianne, but he did know one thing: she wouldn't be happy living anywhere but Cranbury.

Jonas only half-listened as the Fitzwaters continued to ply Arianne with questions about her ability to make paper. Instead, he watched Clarence—who was still watching Arianne. He had such a schoolboy look about him that Jonas knew his old friend had become instantly besotted. So he elbowed him again, if only to make Clarence aware of himself and his rude staring.

"You didn't tell me she was so pretty," Clarence whispered, as if that was excuse enough for his behavior.

Jonas wanted to pull the young man aside, hint that there was already one lion in this den and he had every intention of pursuing his own plans with Arianne.

Yet the very notion of announcing himself as Arianne's partner both professionally and personally made him stop short. He'd genuinely renounced any intention to ever marry and hadn't expected those plans to change. Were they now? Was he actually willing to risk his heart—his life, his future—on a contract of marriage that could easily be compromised?

And if he wasn't, was it fair to Arianne to continue enjoying her company—outside of the business relationship they needed to continue? He was as eager to monopolize her company as any one of the Fitzwater clan, and yet his intentions were murky, even to himself.

As he sat watching the Fitzwaters preen in front of Arianne, he told himself he should be grateful for this eye-opening opportunity. What was he up to, really, when it came to Arianne? He knew he wanted only good things for her. But he knew, too, that he couldn't very well encourage a deepening friendship unless she understood exactly what he intended.

Problem was, he had no idea what that might be.

———

"You'll stay for dinner, won't you, Jonas?" asked Mrs. Fitzwater.

Arianne looked at Jonas eagerly, hoping he agreed. He'd said he would stay as long as it took to see her comfortably settled, and that had yet to happen. As friendly as the entire Fitzwater family seemed to be, even Mrs. Fitzwater in her reserved yet demanding sort of way, Arianne was among a family who knew each other's ways, but their way was utterly unfamiliar.

To her relief Jonas agreed to stay, and she hoped they might be seated next to each other. She was disappointed when his friend Clarence claimed one side and Hannah her other. Jonas sat opposite, however, nearer Mrs. Fitzwater.

"I cannot tell you how dedicated my father and I are to your success, Miss Casterton," said Clarence. He was a pleasant-looking young man, with his brown hair and eyes and ready smile. Just now he kept his tone low, as if he wished to keep the conversation only between the two of them.

"I'm very grateful," she said. "But Jonas, that is Mr. Prestwich, will be overseeing the factory while I continue focusing on the work I know best. Handmade paper."

He patted one of her hands, which she'd let hover near her napkin while waiting until someone else unfolded theirs. She didn't intend to do anything without seeing someone else do it first. Now, feeling his warm hand linger over hers, she glanced up at him, startled. He wasn't as talkative as his sisters, but given his bold touch just now he wasn't likely as fearful of their mother, either.

She withdrew her hand, deciding to keep both safely in her lap until the last possible moment.

"Father was entirely serious about having you join us here in Philadelphia," Clarence went on, as if he hadn't noticed how fleetingly she'd allowed his hand to cover hers. "What do you think of this city?"

"I've visited before, but have never been here long enough to form much of an opinion."

He leaned closer, and she stiffened.

"There is only one remedy for that lack of opinion, of course," he said with a wink. "You must stay with us longer than just two days. My friend Jonas asked us only to open our home until the day after tomorrow, after his reception introducing you to everyone in our business world. But of course you must stay longer."

"An excellent idea, Clary," said Hannah on Arianne's other side. "A month, or two! At least."

"Oh, I couldn't possibly stay away from my own responsibilities back home," Arianne said. How could she tell them she could barely afford to stay away these few days?

Mr. Fitzwater, at the head of the table, evidently had been listening, too, despite Clarence's attempt at relative privacy. "Now that you're expanding your business, Miss Casterton, you'll find yourself using your time differently than before. Your role will necessarily grow to that of an investor. Investors take a bird's eye view, which is impossible while working within the walls of any given business. Just ask our partner here. How long did you work with your father in textiles, Jonas? Long enough to know how things are done."

"I agree there is a difference between overseeing and working on the floor of any factory," Jonas said, eyeing Arianne rather than Mr. Fitzwater. "But this is an unusual case to say the least. Miss Casterton doesn't intend to step away from handmade paper, which will continue to be produced in the Cranbury mill. She's particularly reluctant to leave watermarking, which I'm sure everyone agrees will benefit the company."

"Yes, of course," said Mr. Fitzwater. "It's one of the things I have no intention of forgetting." He spared a glance toward his frowning wife but went on. "I suppose we shouldn't be discussing all of this at the dinner table, but considering we must handle details in mixed company anyway, I'm afraid I don't know where else to discuss it."

Arianne exchanged glances with Jonas as Mr. Fitzwater continued.

"I have great hopes for the future of your mill, as you both know. I wouldn't invest in it if I didn't. But I must also confess that

I hope to depend upon Miss Casterton's watermarking skills now and then for my own company. Partners, eh? An exchange of services?"

Arianne felt the ripple of something up her spine, like the tip of an icicle drawn from bottom to top. She was to accept another partner before she'd gotten used to the idea of the one she had? And yet here she sat, swept away in a business momentum she had no way of slowing, let along stopping altogether.

"In time," Jonas said, his gaze still on Arianne. Did he see her reluctance to agree? "Once the Casterton name is recognized, we'll be better able to explore other opportunities for greater expansion."

"Yes, of course," Mr. Fitzwater said softly. "Just remember, the recommended equipment, the sales avenues, the advice I offer lends itself to partnership. It will go both ways."

Perhaps Jonas was used to dealing with such men who could make a statement sound simultaneously friendly and threatening, but Arianne was not. Was there no way of expanding the mill to suit Jonas, but without help from Mr. Fitzwater?

That was a question she would him ask just as soon as she could.

As it turned out, Arianne had no chance to speak to Jonas alone. He stayed well past dinner, but the entire family stayed together first in the dining room and then back in the parlor, where coffee, chocolate and hot milk were served as the evening grew late. When at last Mrs. Fitzwater claimed their guest must be ready to retire for the evening, she had Hannah take Arianne to her room without allowing her a private moment with Jonas, even for farewell.

She would see him tomorrow. The idea of a business reception in his home had intrigued her from the start, but now she knew whatever eagerness she had was solely because she hoped to see

Jonas in his Philadelphia home, not because she hoped for a greater taste of the business world.

As she lay awake in bed that night, she wished she hadn't come. She reminded herself she'd felt foolishly left out the first time Jonas had come to Philadelphia without her. She was still the greater partner then, but now her share felt even more diminished.

Yet what else could she do? She knew she couldn't have run her father's factory all by herself, even if it remained a one-vat operation. Still, there might have been a way to keep it closer to what it had once been under her father's loving hand than she feared it was becoming under Jonas's.

————

Jonas stared at the globe he'd kept in his room at home long after his studies at school had ended. It had been a gift from his mother when he turned ten, along with a note that had said she believed the world was his because of his talent. She'd loved him then, and he hadn't doubted it until the day she'd refused his care in favor of an obscure papermaker from a little town called Cranbury.

Looking at it now brought a mix of comfort and sadness. Comfort because he thought somehow his mother would understand why he'd enlisted Fitzwater's help to secure his own first step in a business different from the one his father had started. And sadness because even if she had, none of this would have come about had she not known Samuel Casterton the way she had.

This entire day at the Fitzwater residence disturbed Jonas. He saw Arianne's growing unease, and couldn't deny the same feeling in himself. Yet wasn't this the wisest course, the one that offered a solid path to success? Not only the most solid, but the quickest path to success. Why not follow the track Fitzwater so willingly put before them? Nothing he'd suggested today had been outrageous, not even his implication that he would like to use Arianne's watermarking skills for his own business purposes. One service in exchange of another.

Until today, Jonas had imagined the Fitzwater involvement would be minimal. He fully intended to keep true to that impression.

Jonas's gaze left the globe for his mother's Bible, something he'd started reading each night before going to bed. He lifted it again now, but before opening it realized business matters weren't the only thoughts delaying his interest in sleep tonight.

A familiar feeling had crept between his thoughts all evening as he'd watched Clarence Fitzwater practically consume Arianne, at least with his eyes. These feelings in Jonas were selfish, as if Arianne were his and no one else's, for now and forevermore. But what right had he to such feelings? They were for someone who believed in marriage, the kind that lasted forever.

He shook his head as a breath escaped that resembled a sigh. Whatever distance Jonas hoped to keep between himself and the idea of marriage was unexpectedly—and all too quickly—narrowing.

Marriage.

He'd silently insisted that observing Clarence's behavior was no different from watching Leo Levick mope over Arianne. Had she looked any more welcoming toward Clarence than she had Leo? Not in the least. Amazingly enough, Jonas himself had created a smile more freely bestowed than either of the men whom he was sure would welcome such a thing.

The fact was, her reception of their interest—or her lack thereof—didn't matter. What did matter was that sooner or later someone was sure to come along who would stir in her a more favorable response. And unless Jonas was willing to risk his heart by giving it to her, he had no right to stand in the way once that man arrived.

CHAPTER TWENTY-SEVEN

The following day began later than usual for Arianne. Though she woke at seven as was her routine, and used the private bath attached to her room to freshen and dress, she then waited more than two hours until hearing anything to indicate the rest of the household was astir.

Hannah came at last, tapping on her door to escort Arianne to breakfast.

"Good morning!" Hannah greeted, but a dent appeared in her smile when her gaze passed Arianne to the clothing she had hung on the wardrobe door behind her. The simple black damask skirt and pleated gray shirtwaist had seemed appropriate when Arianne had packed it in her suitcase. This was, after all, a business trip. Now she realized how plain it must seem in comparison to the Fitzwaters' love of fashion. The frothy green day dress the youngest Fitzwater wore just now was prettier than anything Arianne had ever owned. Not that Leta hadn't often begged Arianne to let her sew something just as fancy, but it was a plea Arianne had never entertained. Seeing Hannah's disappointed gaze now, she suddenly regretted never listening to Leta's fashion advice.

Still, she was in mourning and that was reason enough not to wear any other kind of attire than what she'd brought. She stepped outside her room, shutting the door to hide the source of Hannah's disappointment.

"Tonight is something of a challenge to me, Hannah," Arianne confessed as the girl led the way down the wide, carpeted hallway. "My visit here is neither all business nor all social. And I'm still in mourning for my father and his wife, so I brought clothing I thought was appropriate."

"Oh, I didn't mean to—" Hannah stopped, turning to Arianne. "You'll look lovely, no matter what you're wearing. That wasn't on my mind in the least. It's rather . . ."

She stopped again, even though a moment ago whatever she'd wanted to say had transformed her face from placid to eager. Now she looked downright worried.

"What is it?"

"I shouldn't say. It's something I wasn't supposed to hear, and besides it's none of my business and something I don't even understand myself."

She started walking again, but Arianne caught one of her hands. For someone who couldn't find a limit to her words yesterday, at least when her mother wasn't nearby, Hannah seemed suddenly reticent to speak. "But it must have something to do with me, or you wouldn't be thinking of it right now. Is it something about the reception tonight? That I'm a woman in a man's business?"

"Oh, no, that's not it. Even if it were, no one would dare say a word against you being in the paper business after all the bragging my father has been doing about your skill."

"Then what is it?"

She diverted her gaze. "I was being silly, that's all." She stole a glance as if to test how much she could hide of whatever she struggled to say. "It was just about the clothing." Then she looped her arm through Arianne's. "We have the entire day ahead of us. Why don't we ask my mother if she wouldn't mind a trip to our favorite dress shop? Our dressmaker is a wonder! She keeps dozens of gowns already made, as samples for women to see her handiwork. If you wanted to, I'm sure we could find an evening dress for you. Oh, I know it'll still have to be proper attire to reflect your loss, and I am sorry about that loss too—since I haven't said so before —but my guess is tonight will be more social than business and maybe you'll feel better if you wear something a little fancier . . . Or less business oriented, anyway."

Evidently Hannah had found her energy for words again, because she prattled on about the talents of the woman who had sewn every dress she, Lydia and their mother had worn for the last five years. Now and then she mixed in how hard it must have been for Arianne to lose her father just a few short months ago. The barrage of words might be common behavior from Hannah, but Arianne had the distinct impression the girl wasn't sharing what was really on her mind. Arianne was tempted to press her, but between having just met her and being a guest in her family's home, she was reluctant to risk being rude.

So they joined the others in the vast dining room, where a buffet of ham and eggs, fruits and cheese, muffins and jam, tea and coffee awaited.

Hannah had to do little more than mention their dressmaker's name before Lydia joined in with an enthusiastic vote to visit the shop. And Mrs. Fitzwater was all too eager to comply, so before the morning was out Arianne found herself on the way to a favorite place of business, at least for Mrs. Fitzwater and her daughters.

Despite her worries about how she would avoid purchasing something she hadn't brought money for—she had little to spare these days, particularly for something as frivolous as a dress she didn't need—the girl's enthusiasm was almost contagious. Especially when the dressmaker brought out a gown that seemed to have been made for her.

It was black damask, with just a hint of silver thread sparkling along an embroidered bodice. The collar was high and lacy, the sleeves neither too full nor sagging, and completely of lace. The cinched waist proved a perfect fit, while the rest of the gown flared attractively and in the height of fashion.

"Now, Miss Casterton," said Mrs. Fitzwater just as Arianne turned back to the dressing room to remove the gown, "Mrs. Gallbraith will deliver the gown to our home, after it's inspected one last time for any loose stitches or other little flaws."

"Oh, no, Mrs. Fitzwater! I do love the gown," she hastened to say to the seamstress nearby, turning back to Mrs. Fitzwater, "but I didn't come to the city prepared for shopping. And as lovely as this is, I'd have little reason to wear such a gown in Cranbury. We live so simply there."

Mrs. Fitzwater raised a brow that Arianne already recognized as disapproving. She stepped closer, taking Arianne's shoulder as she directed her back toward the dressing room. "Think of it as an investment, then, my dear. This isn't likely to be your only visit to Philadelphia now that you've taken on the expansion of your mill. Now go on. There is no charge, you know. We'll simply add it to our account."

"I couldn't let you do that," Arianne insisted. She might have allowed the purchase had the Fitzwaters been a relative, or even a close friend to whom she would one day have the opportunity to offer some kind of recompense. She knew only that she didn't want to be indebted to the Fitzwaters. "You barely know me, and you've already been more than generous by letting me stay with you."

"Think nothing of it, my dear." Then, with her gloved hand Mrs. Fitzwater took Arianne's chin and held her steady. "You are in partnership with the Fitzwaters now. And as such we can't have you looking like a poor relation, now can we?"

Arianne couldn't have looked away if she'd tried, with the woman's skeletal fingers holding her tight. "Only on one condition, then," she whispered. "That you allow me to send you reimbursement."

Just as soon as she had more in her purse than the price of a ticket home . . . But she didn't admit that aloud.

———

As Jonas readied himself for the reception that evening, he was confident about the condition of his home, the excellent punch, the extensive buffet and the quartet that would perform in the background. He knew everything was well prepared, because his staff had been trained by his parents.

He'd never forgotten the awkwardness Jonas felt hosting his first business dinner. He'd taken on the event to prove himself worthy of assuming his father's position and had asked Julia Kitteridge to play hostess. All the while he'd resented his mother's absence. She would have been the natural choice to carry on in the social realm of his father's business. But she'd never come home from Williamsport.

That evening had been the first time the rumors reached him from a source different from his father's drunken lips.

The shadow of those unpleasant memories played only a small part in Jonas's anxiety. He easily reminded himself no one from that other dinner party would be in attendance tonight, not even Julia who didn't know he was back in town. The business associates expected tonight had no connection to Julia or her family, and he had no intention of mixing the two groups.

The one aspect of the evening ahead outweighing his unease was that Arianne would soon be here.

He'd spent the darkest hours of last night trying to talk himself out of it, dozing but not sleeping. By morning he guessed it was too late to ignore the truth: he was well on his way to loving Arianne, and doubted he could stop the inevitable.

Last night's realization had left him weaker than a child, as vulnerable as a baby. Love had kept Jonas awake. The irrefutable knowledge that he'd succumbed to the one thing he'd sworn off.

He must face her tonight for the first time knowing he loved her, and wasn't at all sure what to do about it.

CHAPTER TWENTY-EIGHT

Arianne was never so glad to don gloves as she was that evening, knowing her work-worn hands had already been noted by Mrs. Fitzwater. A tin of hand cream had been sent to her room once everyone disappeared to dress for the dinner ahead.

Eyeing herself in the glass now, seeing her hair swept up into a fashionable chignon under the expert touch of a borrowed maid, Arianne was surprised by her own reflection. It was herself she saw looking back, yet she appeared far more sophisticated than the Arianne Casterton of Cranbury, Pennsylvania.

She tried to see herself as Jonas might. Would he be surprised this little town girl could look so thoroughly citified? Or would he think, as she privately did, that she was playing a part for a costume ball and this image was nothing more than pretend?

Perhaps it would prove a wiser decision than she knew to have let Mrs. Fitzwater insist on this new dress. At least its loveliness might help to take her mind off Arianne's other worries. And she had many beside the condition of her hands or even what Jonas might think.

There was an aura surrounding the Fitzwaters that continued to disturb her. She seemed to be less a business associate than their newest acquisition, ready to be shaped, molded, and prodded forth into the evening for her first taste of their world. Mrs. Fitzwater knew which guests would be in attendance as thoroughly as if she'd planned the invitations herself. Perhaps she had. Arianne had no idea how far Jonas welcomed the Fitzwaters' involvement in this expansion, so he may have asked her opinion about such a thing.

She raised a worried hand to rub across her face but stopped just in time, remembering her face powder would rub off on her white gloves. What was her place this evening, really? She'd all but handed over control of the mill to Jonas. Surprisingly enough, she even trusted he wanted what was best, at least according to his vision. His plans were certainly more progressive—not to mention expensive—than either she or her father might ever have hoped for, but as long as he allowed the vat of handmade paper to continue its production, why didn't she just hand over the rest and be done with it?

Only one thing prevented her from doing just that. If this new addition would take on the Casterton name, as Jonas promised, then she would have to be involved. She couldn't lose sight of what happened in her father's memory. The paper factory was, after all, the only legacy that would carry his name, even if she did marry.

Thoughts of marriage brought an uninvited rush of warmth and anticipation as she wondered yet again what Jonas would think when he saw her. Calling herself childish over such a worry, she left her room to wait for the Fitzwaters in the foyer, where she'd been told to meet them.

The Fitzwater carriage was a five-glass landau, which barely accommodated Mr. and Mrs. Fitzwater, Lydia and Arianne. Hannah, being just fifteen, was not to accompany them. Clarence sat atop with the driver, so they were able to take just one vehicle.

Arianne couldn't help but gaze out the window beside her, eager to see Jonas's home. She knew he didn't live far from the Fitzwaters, that he was considered a neighbor. And so she expected his home to be similar to the Fitzwater mansion.

When the carriage stopped only a few minutes later, Arianne leaned forward to take in the sight. She saw first that the porch was graced with huge potted plants, a reminder to a bricked and paved city that greenery was far more lovely.

The door itself was not as large as the Fitzwaters', nor she guessed was the house itself. But it still earned its spot within a respectable radius because of its three stories and generous allotment of mullioned windows—each of which was lighted just now, with lacy curtains pulled aside.

She swallowed with a painful reminder that this had once been Charlotte's home, too. A home she likely helped to decorate and certainly oversee. An unhappy home, yet like Charlotte herself, Arianne could already tell it would be lovely.

And now it was Jonas's. A place he probably found far more comfortable than had his mother.

———

Jonas expected the Fitzwater family to arrive first, as partners in business to greet the rest of the guests. The Fitzwater name alone added an immediate layer of respect, given their position in the paper industry. They had offered to host the dinner party themselves, but Jonas insisted having the evening here.

It wasn't any of the Fitzwaters Jonas was eager to greet after his butler answered the door. Though he dutifully welcomed them all, his gaze returned again and again to Arianne, like a bee to a flower.

That he should want to stare didn't surprise him, but his new, unfamiliar shyness did. The moment he saw her he felt the transformation. Had he ever called himself confident? Charming? Self-assured? He was none of that now, facing this woman who had easily captured the love he was so unwilling to give. The vulnerability that came with this newfound love perturbed him, but he knew he was helpless to change it. And that perturbed him more.

He spared a brief glance toward Clarence, who was hovering behind Arianne as if he alone had escorted her there.

"Miss Casterton," Jonas whispered with a bow her way. How foolish he was, so awestruck he couldn't even call her by name. He was callow and inexperienced; hesitant and unsure. He wanted both to be in her company and flee from it, especially when he saw a hint of surprise on her face at his formal greeting.

Was it only his newly recognized love that made her the most beautiful woman he'd ever seen? She *was* markedly different tonight, with her hair wound up in a way he saw on women from the city. Her gown might represent mourning but was somehow different from her usual manner of dress, even her Sunday best. The material was soft yet crisp, and offered a glimmer of light reflected from some nearly invisible thread. In it she represented an aura of refinement meant for the largest possible audience, not a small town.

Thankfully more guests arrived, and he was able to escape just far enough to try recapturing his composure yet still enjoy her presence. He introduced her to others, all the while astounded at how lovely she was in comparison to everyone in the room.

To his annoyance, Clarence stayed nearby, ready, it seemed, to take Jonas's spot. Only when Mr. Fitzwater took Arianne's elbow did Clarence let her go. Mr. Fitzwater's brother was in attendance, another business holder whom Fitzwater had already introduced to Jonas on his last visit to the city.

So many guests arrived in succession he was about to take a silent count—there should be sixteen, the number of guests his dining room could comfortably seat—when he felt rather than saw someone approach him from behind.

"Jonas, how nice to see you tonight."

The voice, too close for politeness, catapulted any hope of recapturing his composure. He hadn't invited her, yet the owner of that voice was unmistakable.

Julia Kitteridge.

Knowing the speed of his pulse couldn't be measured by anyone but himself allowed Jonas hope of hiding further damage to his self-command. Turning to her, he had an immediate urge to show her out the door.

"Why, Jonas," Julia whispered as she leaned in to kiss his cheek, "you look a bit pale. Aren't you feeling well?"

Withdrawing the hand she'd claimed while kissing him, he saw Terrance Macpherson at her side. Terrance—whom they all called Titan because he could outrun or out-wrestle any one of their friends. Terrance the Titan, the one friend to bridge both business and pleasure circles, had been too weak to refuse once Julia obviously heard about the invitation.

Terrance lifted a shoulder and looked away, evidently agreeing with Jonas's silent assessment as to how Julia had wheedled her way into the party.

"Now," Julia said, the diamond pin in her hair catching the light and momentarily matching a gleam in her blue eyes, "you're without a hostess tonight, aren't you, dear? Titan is more than willing to loan me to you for the entire evening, aren't you, darling Titan?"

Another shrug.

"This is a business dinner, Julia." Jonas kept his tone polite. "If you haven't already been informed—" he spared another glance Terrance's way, who likely had told her details of the evening—"I have a business partner who is filling the role of hostess."

He took a step back to excuse himself, but Julia rested a hand on his forearm. "I'm eager to meet her—this business partner of yours." She let her gaze roam the area, narrowing once she reached the spot where Arianne stood next to Fitzwater. "Why, Jonas, she's lovely. I wonder which of her parents she favors . . . Her mother?" Now she looked at Jonas. "Or her father?"

Jonas took the words for the warning they were. He squared off in front of her. "I thought we were friends, Julia? What are you doing here?"

Her face froze when Jonas identified their relationship as friendship, but she was quick to recover herself. She offered a small, breathy laugh. "Of course we're friends. I came here to support your new investment. To let you know I'm looking forward to doing business with you."

"I wasn't aware you had any business transactions outside the racecourse. Or are you using your father's money for more productive pursuits these days?"

She leaned closer. "Tsk, tsk, Jonas. Your business partner hasn't been a very positive influence if this new rudeness is any indication. I always thought we both enjoyed the fruits of our parents' labor."

"It's time I've earned some of my own."

———

Arianne struggled to keep up with the conversation around her. She might have found the topics fascinating had her attention not been arrested by what was obviously an intimate conversation going on across the room. Jonas stood with a strikingly lovely woman whose pure white skin and golden hair squashed whatever confidence Arianne brought with her from her moment before the mirror—a sense that was first chipped away when Jonas had greeted her as formally as if they were strangers.

Perhaps this woman was the reason. He must have been anticipating her arrival and didn't want to give the impression that their partnership was anything other than standard business.

Marriage isn't for me . . . His words replayed in her mind. Perhaps he'd given her fair warning because he enjoyed the company of many women and couldn't settle for just one. Maybe he was just trying to protect her, or any other woman, from hoping he might be talked into marriage the way Leta's mother said most men had to be.

"It's exactly the same method any vat man uses when he dips a mould into the vat of pulp," said the man Mr. Fitzwater had just introduced to her. Reed? Leed? She couldn't remember. "Only of course we're free to create any size, we're not limited by what one man can hold."

"Yes, yes, man," said Mr. Fitzwater with some impatience, "but what about the cylinder-mould? The one that makes paper that compares with handmade. That's what I wanted you to tell Miss Casterton all about. It may be something she'd like to try herself." She felt his gaze turn to her and she had no choice but to stop looking Jonas's way. "Deckle edges and strength in two directions, if the machine is run carefully. Isn't that right, Leeds?"

"Yes, indeed. The diluted pulp passes over a flat strainer while the cylinder mould rotates. Felt on both sides, you see, fed through a bronze top roll and rubber-covered bottom—all run by precision-cut gears that start and stop at the same time. It's taken right through to the drying cylinders, all connected on the same machine . . ."

The man went on, describing the entire process that sounded like what Arianne did yet mechanized and unfamiliar. How could a machine make paper that compared with handmade?

"We don't presently have such a machine on this side of the Atlantic," Mr. Fitzwater said, "but I'm considering making an investment in one right here in Philadelphia. I've seen the water-marks on this kind of machine, and I'm impressed with the clarity. Far better than any dandy-roll, let me assure you of that!"

Movement across the room once again grabbed Arianne's attention. Jonas walked away from the woman, a look of dissatis-faction on his face she hadn't seen since the early days of knowing him. And he was headed this way. Was he annoyed that he must act her partner here among his friends, annoyed to be leaving the other woman's side?

Pretending she'd heard each and every word of the present conversation, she looked directly at Mr. Leeds. "I have yet to see a sample of this cylinder-mould machine paper, but even if the difference to handmade is minimal, there is something else to remember." She acknowledged Jonas's addition to the group with a quick nod, but nothing more. "There is a measure of satisfaction in creating something by hand that can't be replaced with machinery. I know machines can make everything from fine stitchery to woven rugs. I know there is a place for machines to make life easier. But what if the old ways are forever forgotten? Hand sewn dresses and scarves—like handmade paper—have something in them that machine-made materials never will: the soul of the creator."

Mr. Leeds cleared his throat. "All of that is fine if you're a hobbyist. But we're businessmen, Miss Casterton. Surely you wouldn't suggest housewives—women of your own sex—return to spinning cotton and sewing the clothing for their entire families, beside all the other tasks they do?"

Arianne shook her head. "No, nor am I suggesting factory-made paper doesn't hold a place in society. I'm only saying that a strawberry grown and nurtured in one's own neighborhood is somehow tastier than one grown by some unknown farmer and purchased at a grocer." What had made her say such a thing? That she recognized Jonas might prefer a woman from his own back-yard? She couldn't look him in the eye, only adding another less personal thought: "I don't wish to see society become so imper-sonal that everything is run by machines. Some traditions are worth keeping alive, whether or not they're sold for hefty profits."

CHAPTER TWENTY-NINE

Jonas had no time to contemplate who frustrated him more: Terrance for bringing Julia, Julia for finagling her way into an invitation, or himself for letting Julia's presence wobble the already unsteady bridge he navigated ever since realizing the depth of his feelings for Arianne.

Afraid too much attention directed her way would make Arianne the target of Julia's unfriendly nature, Jonas found himself unable to stand in the way as Clarence Fitzwater rarely left Arianne's company. Much as he resented that, it did give him the chance to seek out Terrance. But the man caught sight of Jonas coming and turned away, evidently to leave the room altogether in an attempt to avoid him.

Jonas followed him, pleased to catch up in the relative privacy of the hallway leading to his library on the opposite side of the house.

"Why'd you do it, Titan?"

"Do me a favor and don't call me that."

"Why did you let her manipulate you? Don't tell me you still hope to marry her someday."

Terrance scrubbed his face as if the thought tortured him. "I can't help it." Then he eyed Jonas and a new light entered his eyes.

"I'm not a complete traitor, though. Remember Fred Boyle? He worked with your father."

Jonas nodded; Boyle had been one of the managers who went to work elsewhere in the city after the partners had moved the textile business to Atlanta.

"When I told him about tonight he said to give you a warning about Fitzwater. Sounds like if you weren't going to partner with him he'd have found a way to buy you out."

"What are you talking about? The Cranbury mill is too small to be anything he'd want. I was the one who came to him for help."

"Boyle said Fitzwater has put two other mills out of business in the last few years. He undercuts their prices and when their business flounders because they can't match the price, Fitzwater swoops in and buys them for less than what they're worth."

Jonas frowned. "He's ambitious, I'll give you that."

"Ruthless might be a better word for it. Just ask the owners who had their businesses practically stolen."

Jonas looked back in the direction of the parlor. Was it safer to have Fitzwater on his side, as he'd once told Arianne? Better a partner than a competitor? Somehow it didn't feel better, not at all.

With the confrontation over, Terrance rejoined the guests along with Jonas. To Jonas's disappointment, Clarence's attention to Arianne continued right through dinner. Mrs. Fitzwater had arranged the seating, and Jonas found Terrance on his left and Julia to his right. Arianne sat where he'd expected as his partner-host, but he hadn't recalled just how long was his table until seeing her seated so far away at the opposite end. With Clarence right by her side.

Mrs. Fitzwater had suggested most of the evening's social time to be before dinner, claiming the after-dinner tradition of having the men and women separate was compromised by the fact that Arianne wasn't the traditional hostess but a business partner instead. And so she'd elected to serve coffee and tea in the parlor shortly after dinner, eliminating any separation of the sexes.

At last the guests made a slow progression back into the parlor, where the staff had set up a table filled with sugary selections and a variety of beverages.

Despite Fitzwater's praise of Arianne's talent, which offered immediate respect and interest in their upcoming business, Jonas was more anxious than ever to leave Philadelphia tomorrow, with Arianne at his side. Maybe their absence from Philadelphia would slow down a partnership that seemed to be proceeding at break-neck speed.

———

Arianne welcomed Lydia's company, more so when she delivered a message to her brother that their father wanted to speak to him before the evening was out. As attentive as Clarence had been, Arianne grew tired of his near constant attempts at flirting.

"Is it terribly awkward for you?" Lydia whispered once they were relatively alone. "Having her here tonight?"

"Her?" Even as she pretended not to know, Arianne's gaze followed Lydia's straight to Julia Kitteridge at Jonas's side.

"Everyone knows Julia's been waiting for Jonas Prestwich to propose. But now that Jonas has you for a partner . . . A woman . . . Perhaps that proposal won't be coming, after all."

Arianne stiffened. Marriage! To Miss Kitteridge? Who had started that rumor? If Jonas could be believed about his opinion of holy wedlock, it certainly wasn't him. "The evening isn't awkward for me at all. If Mr. Prestwich would like to propose to Miss Kitteridge, that means nothing to me."

The words came out with such assurance she almost believed them herself, at least for a moment. No sooner had the words faded away than she knew not a single word was true. Not only had the evening been awkward, seeing Julia Kitteridge fawning over Jonas had revealed just how jealous Arianne could feel. Telling herself she had no right to such a thing made not one little bit of difference. It was eye-opening, however, to realize she had such an

unwelcome streak inside of her. Something she would have to peti-
tion God to help eliminate.

"I suppose I should have warned you," Lydia went on. "But it
was none of my business, and of course Mother has never
approved of gossiping. Still, if there *is* any sort of friendship
between you and Mr. Prestwich—and how could there not be,
working together and planning such a big expansion, and both of
you unmarried—then I thought you ought to know there was
another woman invested in him."

Arianne told herself to speak again, hide behind an empty
proclamation that whatever Jonas Prestwich did with his personal
life was none of her business, either. But she didn't have the
strength to make such a lie sound believable.

" . . . Not that I think you're any less deserving of his interest,
of course. I'm just glad he's never looked my way. I doubt I could
resist him, if you want to know the truth. And wouldn't that make
my father just too happy. A merger! Business and family. Not that
Father isn't hoping for that sort of thing between you and my
brother Clarence. Clarence is always too happy to do anything for
Father. Oh! Not that I don't think Clarence would just love having
you as a wife, I can tell that by the way he looks at you. All I know
is that my father will do just about anything to have you as his
watermark artist! I've heard him say so to my mother."

Arianne had tried not to listen to Lydia's prattling ways, but
everything she'd just said astounded her. That Julie Kitteridge had
some kind of personal expectation regarding Jonas was obvious;
that Clarence Fitzwater was spending far too much of his attention
on her was just as clear. But that Mr. Fitzwater might have insti-
gated Clarence's behavior revitalized the icicle along her spine.

There was nothing, absolutely nothing, that appealed to her
about the Fitzwater investment in the paper mill's expansion. If it
were up to her, she would break any ties between them.

She only wished Jonas would agree.

———

"Step outside, won't you, my boy?"

Jonas agreed, not because he wanted to leave his own party, or be away from keeping his eye on Arianne, but because Julia couldn't follow him out. Not when Fitzwater was already pulling a cigar from his vest pocket. Cigars remained one of the few walls between the genders. And he'd so sufficiently ignored Arianne all evening that he'd convinced himself Julia wouldn't spend a moment's notice on her.

"Now look here, Prestwich," Mr. Fitzwater said after lighting the tip of his cigar. "I've made arrangements this very evening for a crew of my best men to be dispatched up to Cranbury and start work immediately. You needn't worry about the expense. Leave that to me. They'll do first rate work, I guarantee that."

Jonas had no sooner taken his eyes off the door behind them when the man's words took effect. An immediate twist to his gut made him want to object, but the business sense his father taught him forced him to remain calm.

"I planned to hire a crew myself, some who worked for my father."

Fitzwater waved away the smoke between them. "My men are familiar with exactly what we need. Why use anyone else? Besides, I thought you were eager to go forward with this expansion?"

"I am. Only as you might have guessed from talking to Miss Casterton, she might think tomorrow a bit hasty."

"The sooner she gets used to factory paper, the better. That's just a simple matter of investment opportunity. Now her watermarks are altogether another story. Do you know how widespread her watermarks will be one day, with my help? Even she won't object when her talent is seen from here to Paris."

That Fitzwater could have so completely misread Arianne flummoxed Jonas. "I'm sure Miss Casterton will welcome the opportunity to return to watermarking, but I'm not sure either fame or fortune are of special interest to her."

Fitzwater sucked in a deep puff from his cigar. "Oh, I heard that nonsense about satisfaction and the like. Just wait until she has a taste of what her talents can bring. She doesn't know how to appreciate her own gift yet, but she soon will, I guarantee you that."

Fitzwater and all that came with him, including business associates currently in Jonas's own parlor, didn't seem so much a collective group of partners as one giant boulder, ready to forge a path of its own design. Was this what Arianne had first seen in him?

More importantly, was Jonas himself part of the Fitzwater boulder, or merely in its way? Either option left him with another twist to his gut.

———

"Miss Casterton, at last a moment to speak to you!"

Julia Kitteridge approached with a smile aimed only at Arianne, as if Lydia beside her did not even exist. She obviously had no expectation of Lydia making a proper introduction as she unnecessarily told Arianne her name, all the while facing Arianne as if her cold shoulder alone could withhold Lydia from the conversation.

Thankfully, Lydia did not leave.

"I'd heard Jonas inherited a share of a paper mill, and that it came with a partner. My, my, how could he resist a woman such as yourself in need of help with her business?"

"I had no idea he had inherited until we met."

Julia smiled, but her eyes were glacial. "Really? Is Jonas another part of Charlotte's life she kept a secret? Besides still being married to Jonas's father, that is, while she knew your father?"

Arianne tried to swallow, but her mouth was too dry and her throat nearly closed. She glanced at Lydia, wishing after all that she had taken Julia's impolite cue to leave them alone. The girl looked on with slightly widened eyes. Was she surprised by the innuendo, or merely shocked that Julia had mentioned it?

"It's lucky for you Mr. Fitzwater has taken Jonas under his

wing. He can't be blamed for the scandal, of course, but people do remember these things. Seeing that you and Jonas have partnered will certainly resurrect the talk, though. Not that you have anything to worry about. I'm sure Mr. Fitzwater's influence will have all that sort of gossip quickly squashed. But you would have been stepbrother and sister, you know, had your parents lived, and that's hard to forget. You wouldn't even have met had his mother not left his father for yours, but now something good will come of all that. A new, improved business. One that Mr. Fitzwater will remake into a grand success. "

Arianne had no reply, and no wish to continue the awful, one-sided conversation. Nor had she any wish to stay a moment longer. She looked beyond Julia, catching a glance from Mrs. Fitzwater who seemed to be gazing across the room at her with disapproval. Did she know? Arianne looked around the rest of the room, seeing Lydia's surprise had already been replaced by a simpler look of discomfort. Did they all know? Others certainly hadn't heard Julia's words just now, but had every person in the room already jumped to the same conclusion Jonas had about their parents, if such rumors were commonplace?

"If you'll excuse me," she said, refusing to allow herself the freedom to release tears too ready to fall. Without thought for repercussions, Arianne grabbed Lydia's hand and led her from the parlor.

"Oh, Miss Casterton," breathed Lydia. "Arianne . . . I'm so sorry for Miss Kitteridge's rude behavior. She ought never to have brought up such a thing!"

In the hallway, well beyond the arch leading to the parlor, stood a footman near the door. Arianne asked him for their belongings, half expecting him to demand she wait for the rest of the Fitzwater family. But when he went off to do her bidding, Arianne grabbed Lydia's other hand.

"Then you've heard those horrid rumors, too? They're not true! Not about Charlotte, and certainly not about my father."

Lydia squeezed Arianne's fingers. "I did hear Mother say something to her maid, but honestly I've never heard of anyone being so awful as Miss Kitteridge was just now. I only barely knew Jonas's parents, and I'm ever so sorry he lost them both in so short a time."

"I'll not stay here another minute," Arianne said, glancing back toward the parlor. Through the archway she saw Julia, laughing with the man she'd arrived with. She imagined them tittering at her father's expense and it only confirmed her resolve to leave. "I know your house isn't far from here, but I'm afraid I might not find it on my own. Will you take me there?"

"What's this?" Clarence's voice reached her from the direction of the parlor, nearing as he added, "You're not leaving!"

Arianne closed her eyes, any urge to cry now replaced with frustration. She turned to face him. "Yes, Mr. Fitzwater. I—I've developed a pounding headache."

Just then the footman returned with two shawls, and Clarence sent him back for his hat and gloves. "I'll accompany you myself, and send the carriage back round for my mother and father later. Lydia, why don't you tell Mother what we're up to?"

"You—you wouldn't leave without me, though? What will Mother say if you take Arianne home alone? She'll never forgive you!"

"Go on," Clarence said. "It'll take a moment to have the carriage brought up anyway."

As soon as Lydia walked off, Clarence put a solicitous hand on her arm. "This is awfully sudden, isn't it, Miss Casterton? Is there anything I can do?"

Arianne shook her head. The last thing she needed was someone to act in her defense, giving Julia the chance to repeat what she'd said.

No sooner had the footman handed Clarence his hat and gloves than he directed her outside, where another servant said their carriage had already been summoned. Arianne welcomed the cool evening air; her cheeks had been aflame ever since Julia approached. She breathed deeply, grateful to be away even though such an abrupt departure was likely rude even here, in a city so big all kinds of behavior must be seen every day.

Would Jonas even notice her absence? He'd acted so carefully all evening, so proper and businesslike. Perhaps he feared Julia would assume he was more than Arianne's partner if he acted any other way.

So be it.

CHAPTER THIRTY

When the carriage arrived before Lydia returned, Clarence moved as if to leave without his sister. For one desperate moment Arianne was almost willing to go.

Yet she was reluctant to throw away not only all sense of caution, but decorum. She couldn't leave alone in Clarence's company. "We'll wait for your sister, if you please."

He grinned at her. "You've read my interest correctly, Miss Casterton, if you don't trust me alone with you. I'm not even sure I trust myself."

He laughed as if to make light of his own words, but she couldn't welcome his attention. She'd just told herself she didn't care what the others thought, but clearly adding her own scandal to that of Charlotte and her father would confirm the worst they already believed.

Thankfully Lydia returned a moment later, hurrying down the stairs and nearly dropping her shawl in the process.

"Mother is fit to be tied!" Her voice was breathless, but her face was clearly excited and perhaps a bit pleased, if Arianne correctly read the sparkle in the other girl's eyes. "First she said we should wait until she can talk Father into leaving, but I told her you'd already called for the carriage and that we'd send it right back for them. So now we'd better hurry! She wants others to think we came separately and we'd all planned to leave now anyway."

Arianne had no trouble leaving quickly, glad when Clarence told the driver to lose no time in taking them home and making the return trip. She might have minded that Clarence claimed the seat beside her after directing his sister to sit opposite them, but relief to be away was stronger.

"When did your headache come on, Miss Casterton? You seemed perfectly fine for most of the evening."

She glanced at him, having forgotten her excuse even though her head did pound. Lydia opened her mouth and Arianne prepared herself for the girl to tell all, but then she unexpectedly clamped her lips together and Arianne slipped her a grateful smile.

"I'm not used to so much attention, I suppose," Arianne whispered.

Although Clarence had likely heard the same awful rumors, Arianne had no desire to hear the two talking about it anymore than she'd welcomed hearing it from Julia Kitteridge.

Jonas returned to the parlor with Mr. Fitzwater and quickly sensed Arianne's absence. She might have gone to the water closet, but when Mrs. Fitzwater approached with obvious tension, Jonas guessed something was wrong.

"We'll need to leave right away, Robert," she said to her husband. She sent a narrow gaze Jonas's way as if whatever she was about to say was somehow his fault. "Evidently you failed to prepare Miss Casterton for the social requirements in business. She's left already without a word to any of us, and now we must make excuses."

Jonas let his gaze roam the room again in useless hope of finding Arianne anyway. When he spotted Julia looking at him with a look of unmistakable satisfaction, he didn't have to ask what had happened. Whatever it was, Julia had a hand in it.

He had the equally irrational desire to leave his own home just as suddenly as Arianne had. He might have carried out that desire had Mrs. Fitzwater not been standing in his way, even placing a cautioning hand on his forearm.

"She obviously possesses an artist's temperament," Mr. Fitzwater said, "which you can imply when you explain she's already gone. Many of these guests are some of my most influential associates, and potentially your best customers, Jonas. You'd better handle this tactfully."

Jonas knew exactly what the older man meant, particularly issued in such a grim tone: don't follow the instinct to run after her. Whether Fitzwater truly did have the best interests of business in mind or wanted something else—the knowledge that Clarence, too, was missing didn't sit well with him—Jonas knew he couldn't do as he wanted.

So he started with Terrance, telling him he ought to start the trend of calling for his carriage. The evening was clearly over, albeit a little more suddenly than most might have expected.

———

Arianne packed her bag. It was too late to go to the train station tonight, but she was determined to find a way there before the Fitzwaters breakfasted in the morning. She had no intention of waiting until the rest of the household roused, or taking another leisurely meal with them.

Although she'd had a maid's help dressing, she managed to remove her new gown without too much trouble. She hesitated to add it to the belongings in her satchel, but knew to leave it behind would only add to the insult she'd already extended.

Yet how could anyone, even the Fitzwaters, think she would want to return to Philadelphia? If she'd known they'd all whispered about her father and Jonas's mother, she never would have come here to begin with. Jonas had said there were rumors, but she'd never imagined how widespread those rumors had been.

A tap at the door startled her and she'd barely left the bedside with her bag on top than the door opened uninvited. Unfolding the robe she'd just been about to pack, Arianne put it over the chemise she wore.

Mrs. Fitzwater stood there, tall and regal. She left the door ajar behind her, folding one hand over the other at her slim waist as she assessed Arianne in a long moment before speaking.

"Your behavior tonight was unwise, my dear."

"I suppose I shouldn't have acted so hastily, but my head—"

"You may indeed have a headache, but that isn't why you fled. You let whatever that nasty little Kitteridge girl said upset you."

Arianne couldn't have denied it if she wanted to. She wasn't used to hiding the truth.

"You're a very curious child. You're determined to continue your father's business, but not for any reason I can understand. Don't you want it to be successful?"

"I want to work the way he did, the way his father did before him."

"And did they so lack ambition that they were content to live no better than each generation before them? Do you?"

"Their ambition—my ambition—is to produce the loveliest paper that we can. I see nothing wrong in that, and I won't apologize for it."

Mrs. Fitzwater stepped closer, her face hard and far older than she'd appeared earlier that evening when her powder was fresh. "You cannot mean to look around at what I have, what my children have, and not want it, too." She let out a sigh laced with impatience. "Don't you know why I insisted you wear that gown tonight? So they would have one less thing to snicker about. Listen to me, Arianne. My husband is giving you and Jonas the opportunity to make a fortune in the paper industry. Don't let anything stop you. Not an irrelevant scandal from the past or some silly girl intent on embarrassing you."

If only the rumors were irrelevant . . . But something else was suddenly clear to Arianne. Mrs. Fitzwater was entirely mistaken in believing they could ever agree about the best path for Arianne to follow. However, it was also clear the woman wanted what she thought best for Arianne.

"Thank you," she managed to whisper.

Satisfied that Arianne must have capitulated to her way of thinking, Mrs. Fitzwater turned back to the door with the hint of a smug smile.

"I hope you won't mind if I borrow your carriage and driver as early in the morning as possible. I'll be returning to Cranbury and will need transportation to the train station."

Mrs. Fitzwater stopped at the door, looking over her shoulder with a hint of surprise. Arianne wasn't sure if she saw disappointment or respect grow in the lift of her brow. But she only nodded then closed the door behind her.

CHAPTER THIRTY-ONE

Jonas arrived at the Fitzwater home unsociably early, practically barging in on their breakfast. He was both surprised and disappointed to realize Arianne must still be in her room, making it even more difficult to keep his voice to a civilized tone. She should have been long finished with breakfast if they were going to make the train.

Instead of a greeting, Jonas asked, "So were you able to stop your assessment crew from leaving for Cranbury, Mr. Fitzwater?"

Fitzwater must have just taken his seat, because he was still in the process of unfolding his napkin. He did so carefully, laying it across his lap and taking up his knife and fork.

"Have some breakfast, Jonas," he said amiably. "You'll feel better on a full stomach."

"I feel just fine. Did you stop the crew?"

A footman poured coffee into the cup Fitzwater held up. "Of course not, my boy. As I told you last night, crews aren't always available, at least not the best of them. This crew is available now, so it's in our interest to employ them before other jobs claim their time."

Jonas gripped the back of the chair in front of him, although when Clarence approached from behind to take that very seat, he was forced to step aside.

"Then I'll wait to speak to Arianne, if you don't mind. I'd like to prepare her for the hurried schedule."

"Hurried!" Mr. Fitzwater laughed. "We're right on schedule. I thought you'd appreciate my efforts to get started immediately."

"In any case," Clarence said, twisting in his chair to look at Jonas, "Arianne—that is, Miss Casterton—isn't here. Hannah went to her room a few minutes ago and found it empty."

"What!"

Hannah, across the table, nodded. "Not to worry, though. I stopped in to tell Mother, and she said she talked to Miss Casterton last night. She planned to take the first train out of the city this morning. Of course Mother disapproved, but I think it's bold and brave of Arianne to travel on her own. We've become good friends, you know, Arianne and I."

Since Mrs. Fitzwater was the only family member not present, Jonas couldn't ask for more information. He was sure whatever had prompted Arianne to leave his home so abruptly last night was also to blame for her early departure this morning. Maybe she hadn't fled only because Julia had been rude. That had been his first guess, but there was definitely another reason Arianne might have been upset. Had Clarence, or his mother, or Fitzwater himself told Arianne of their plans to start construction so soon? Did she think she could stop them? Why hadn't she come to him first, instead of running off without him? Perhaps she thought he was in full support of Fitzwater's plans.

Clarence stood and patted Jonas on the shoulder. "I know, I know, I'm disappointed that she left, too. But we'll see her soon. I imagine you'll see her before I will, but I have every intention of visiting that little village where she lives."

Fitzwater cleared his throat. "My wife says your partner just needs time to get used to the idea of a bigger business opportunity than what her father left behind. She'll come round, don't worry."

Clarence, who'd rested his hand on Jonas as if he needed the consolation, patted his shoulder again. "She'll thank us when she can afford to move right in to this neighborhood."

Jonas had never been more tempted to call someone a fool, but he just stared at Clarence a full moment without a word. Some portion of his thoughts must have shone through his gaze, though, because Clarence frowned as he slowly withdrew his hand, then turned and sat back down.

———

To Arianne's surprise, Tummers and his Canary were outside the Williamsport train station when she disembarked. She was especially glad to see him, since she'd spent her last dime on the train ticket and would have had to walk all the way to Cranbury without enough money to hire someone to take her there. At least Tummers would trust her to pay him on the other end of the fare.

That he seemed just as surprised to see her confused her. "Then why are you here?"

He pulled a note from his pocket. "Miss Phoebe got a telegram early this morning that a crew of men were coming on this train, and she was to let them in the mill. When I heard about it, I jumped in the Canary to pick them up. They're from the city, so I can charge city rates. It's your mill, Ari. We thought you knew all 'bout this. Who else woulda' sent that telegram?"

She nearly dropped her satchel at the news. Men were arriving to start on the factory already? Without her even knowing it? If she hadn't returned unexpectedly early, they might have begun work before she was even there!

Before she could reply she noticed a group of three men getting off another car of the same train. They approached the nearest Canary waiting at the station, but Tummers beckoned them with a whistle and a wave.

"Hi-ho!" he shouted through cupped hands. "Goin' to Cranbury?"

The men didn't hesitate, they just walked toward Tummers.

"You can sit up here with me, Ari," Tummers said. "No sense sittin' in the back with a pack of men."

She had no intention of sitting anywhere just yet, or allowing these men to go to Cranbury. Who had sent them? Had Jonas told them to be here so quickly? She knew nothing, absolutely nothing, about the work these men had been sent to perform.

She faced the trio before they could step around her from the train platform.

"I'm afraid there has been some mistake," she said.

All eyes stopped on her with a mix of curiosity and suspicion. "Are you talking to us?" the most suspicious one asked.

He was the youngest of the three, and wore a relatively new sack coat, unlike the others whose workingman shirts were tucked into baggy trousers and beige shirts barely covered with less stylish coats. None wore ties, not even the man who seemed reluctant to remove his hat and take the time to speak to her. Each of them carried leather satchels that looked heavy.

"If you're here to work on the Cranbury paper mill, yes, I'm talking to you."

"And who might you be, miss?" asked one of the older men.

"I'm Arianne Casterton, the owner of the paper mill. I'm not prepared for you to begin working yet. There is a matter of getting caught up on my present work before I allow the disruption of an expansion to get in the way."

The suspicious one grinned. "If I might say so, miss, you're just a part owner, and we've been guaranteed jobs by Mr. Robert Fitzwater. It would be pretty hard to turn us away when we're already here. At least without talking to Mr. Fitzwater."

"It'd be a shame to turn away a paying fare, Ari," called Tummers from his seat, "so maybe we can work this out in Cranbury. Let them do what they's plannin' to do, and take up the argument later with whoever it was that sent 'em."

Arianne spared him an annoyed glance before eying the younger man she guessed to be the foreman. "I suggest you telephone Mr. Fitzwater from here at the station," she said. "Tell him

I'd rather he'd have checked with me first and that you'll have to come back at a later time."

Now he crossed his arms, his hat dangling from one hand. He didn't look worried, just amused, and saw no apparent need to turn back to the station. "I don't think you've had much experience working for Mr. Fitzwater, miss. He hired us to bring him preliminary plans and we're here to do it. By tomorrow, if the ground is sound, there will be a dozen more men on their way, not to mention a load of material and equipment. You might want to believe me when I say Mr. Fitzwater isn't going to turn all that—and us—around now."

"If you won't telephone him, then I will," she said, turning back toward the station house. When she didn't hear footsteps behind her, she stopped and spun around. They were already boarding the back of the Canary, and Tummers wasn't doing a thing to stop them.

If she didn't want to walk all the way back to Cranbury, she had no choice but to join them.

CHAPTER THIRTY-TWO

Upon arriving in Cranbury, Arianne jumped off the Canary before Tummers could lend a hand. By the time she rounded the back of the carriage, the men had already exited. Just being back in her own town gave her all the confidence she needed to face them anew.

Standing between them and the direction of her shop, she folded her arms.

"Now that you're here, gentlemen," she said, "what do you suppose you're going to do? The factory is on my property, and I have a right to deny access."

The man she'd spoken to back in Williamsport didn't reply, just stepped aside to pay Tummers the fare. Another one faced her, perhaps the age of her father. In fact for a moment he reminded her of him, his skin thickened with age, hair sprinkled with silver. But she refused to let the comparison soften her mood.

"My name's Dobry, miss," he said amiably. "And that man you spoke to back there is the foreman, Ritter. He's got a hard head when it comes to the job he's hired for, so you ought to go ahead and make that call to Fitzwater yourself. Ritter only takes orders from him."

Arianne frowned. "There are no telephones in Cranbury. Mr. Ritter will just have to listen to me."

The man shook his head and the other behind them grinned as if in anticipation of a show. The one named Ritter climbed the carriage rung to retrieve an oblong bag from the top rack of the Canary, reaching for Arianne's satchel at the same time. Then he hopped down and approached her, handing her the bag belonging to her.

"We're ready to see the property, miss. We need to assess the land for the factory foundation, do some measuring, maybe even start some clearing." He glanced around the town, no doubt eager to begin.

"As I said, Mr. Ritter—"

"Just Ritter," he corrected.

"As I said, I have no intention of allowing this expansion to start. I'm sorry you've come all this way, and perhaps you can take that up with Mr. Fitzwater, but if anyone had consulted me first, all of this could have been avoided."

Ritter folded sturdy arms across an impressively wide chest. "I don't think you have all the facts, miss. I was scheduled for another job up in New York when Mr. Fitzwater summoned me. He went to considerable trouble—and expense—to make sure we took this job before starting another. If we leave for that other job instead, it'll be that much longer before we can come back here."

She folded her arms, too, and met his stare. "Then I suggest you go on to New York and do that job."

He laughed. "You think Fitzwater will welcome a change to his plans?"

"To be perfectly honest, I don't care what Mr. Fitzwater will say. The job he hired you to do here is not ready."

Ritter appeared to have more to say, but the fatherly one put a hand on one of his shoulders. However, instead of speaking to him, he aimed his words at Arianne.

"Here's what we'll do, miss. We're here. We might as well take advantage of that. We'll do our preliminary study of the work site

—just to see what kind of job it'll be—to make sure the plans Mr. Fitzwater hired us to do will work out. We won't get in the way."

Ritter was already shaking his head. "But if the ground is workable, we'll start digging today."

The other man raised a weathered, cautioning hand. "You were going to talk to Fitzwater when we'd finished this morning anyway, Ritter. You can still report about the land and whether or not the area will work for the kind of building and equipment he wants. Only you can add this here miss's concerns to the conversation, can't you, before we get to work?" He eyed the town around them. "And you'll start by telling him you had to go all the way back to Williamsport to find a telephone. And I don't see no electric lines, either, so you might want to let him know about that, too."

Ritter ran his broad hand through his sandy colored hair, finally nodding. "All right then." He eyed the area then, too, and shook his head as if confused. "I don't know what the hurry was to get here. He must have thought Cranbury was closer to Williamsport." He sighed and looked again at Arianne. "I don't suppose you'll want to show us the way, but since we'll just pester you until you do, you might as well save us all some time and aggravation."

Arianne knew he'd already offered all the compromise she was likely to get, at least for one day, and so she nodded. She bypassed the shop altogether, even though she saw Phoebe staring out the window with wide-eyed concern. She led them down the path to the factory by the river, a sense of heaviness marring her contentment at being back home.

———

Jonas looked again at the clock on the mantle in Fitzwater's parlor. He'd long missed the train he'd originally planned to board with Arianne. As it was, she must be well on her way back, or perhaps nearly there if she'd found a train leaving as early as she'd hoped.

Mr. Fitzwater had insisted on finishing his breakfast before agreeing to discuss any further business. Jonas knew he couldn't leave without settling this. What had begun as an opportunity to accept the help—just help, that was all—of a more experienced businessman in the same industry had become a nightmare.

Jonas refused the invitation to join them at the table, telling them he would wait in the parlor. And there he paced, the only clear thought in his mind the urge to pray. If ever he needed divine guidance, it was now.

What had he done? Last night, in addition to hearing what Terrance had to say, Jonas had talked to various business acquaintances of Fitzwater's. The man was not just respected as the fiercest competitor in the paper industry, his goal seemed to be to have his name the one and only synonymous with the product.

And Jonas had all but flagged Arianne's company by bringing it to Fitzwater's attention.

Despite wanting to chase Arianne this morning, he knew he couldn't until he broke whatever bonds Fitzwater had been all too eager to establish between himself and Arianne's mill.

Jonas stopped pacing when Clarence entered the room and, though he looked for his friend's father, Mr. Fitzwater was nowhere to be seen.

"Father is finishing up," Clarence said casually, setting aside the coffee cup he'd carried in with him. He eyed Jonas. "You look more worried now than you did before final exams, old man. What's the matter? Don't we all want the same thing?"

"I'm not sure any more."

Clarence laughed. "You came to me and my father for help to enter the paper industry. We're doing that. We'll all be the better for it."

Jonas doubted it—maybe Clarence was right monetarily, but for personal reasons, Jonas couldn't agree. He kept that declaration to himself, looking again at the archway between the parlor and empty foyer. "Look, Clarence, I may need your help to talk your father into withdrawing his involvement with the Casterton mill. I was too hasty in accepting his help. Arianne is willing to expand, but I think we'll be better off making the changes on our own schedule rather than being swept into your father's business."

Clarence shook his head, all trace of friendliness gone. The shift in mood reminded Jonas why they'd never been closer friends: Clarence had often been swift to change his mood, even as a boy, especially if he didn't get his way. "He's not very likely to back down now, Jonas. And don't forget you came to him. Not that he wouldn't have found your factory by himself sooner or later. He was already interested in the watermarks."

"If you'll remember, Clarence, I came to you for advice, not for a partnership or even money. He doesn't have any legal right to take over this expansion."

"No, but I wouldn't try competing with Father's sales circuit if you try establishing a business on your own. You'll have to go pretty far afield if you want to sell to anyone without my father's blessing. You'll never beat his pricing if you try producing factory paper."

Voices from the hallway drew Jonas's attention, though Clarence's warning was immediately troubling. He looked to see not only Mr. Fitzwater enter the room, but Mrs. Fitzwater as well. Her arm was through her husband's, a united force to be sure. Mr. Fitzwater, as usual, looked jovial. Mrs. Fitzwater, on the other hand, carried a familiar look that made the skin under Jonas's collar prickle. Disapproval? He dismissed the thought, even though that was what he used to feel around her when he was still in school. This felt different, somehow. She had the look of a queen, as if she could control him the same way she controlled the rest of her family.

"Now, Jonas," said Mr. Fitzwater, "I'm sensing some reluctance on your part to go forth with plans to make the little Casterton Mill one of the most successful business ventures in the northeast. What's gotten into you? Small town thinking?"

"I'm concerned about Miss Casterton," Jonas admitted. That was certainly true, but he wondered if he would still want to be involved with this man in a business venture even without Arianne.

The way he'd pushed his way into their partnership made Jonas wonder if any opinion counted other than that of Fitzwater's himself—or his wife's.

"I'm sure we all want what's best for Arianne," said Clarence.

Mrs. Fitzwater raised one thin hand, as if dismissing both statements. "All that lovely partner of yours needs, Jonas, is to look in the mirror more often. Once she's finished wearing mourning colors, she'll come to enjoy the splendid wardrobe she'll be able to afford when her business is more prosperous. And living in Philadelphia will give her ample opportunities for that."

Jonas knew money was important to Arianne only as far as it allowed her to do what she wanted to do: make the finest paper she could.

"I don't think she'll be coming back to the city any time soon," Jonas said. "What she really wants is for her business to remain the kind her father left to her. And I'm beginning to think she's right."

Mr. Fitzwater neared him, the cheerful facade fading. "She won't last on her own. Her father ran the vat, and ran it well, too, from all accounts. But she can't keep up the way he did. It would be best if that ancient way of doing business closed down. At least it would let her concentrate on the watermarks, which can be more widely used on factory paper. Don't you agree?"

"I'm sure she'd be happy to concentrate on that," Jonas admitted, noticing Mrs. Fitzwater had squeezed her husband's arm, almost as if cautioning him to say no more. "But she won't give up making paper. I'm equally sure of that."

Mrs. Fitzwater took a step closer. "Then perhaps you need to convince her the one-vat mill will fail. We all know it's inevitable. Why wait for it to happen naturally?"

Jonas knew it was true; without help, eventually Arianne's paper mill was doomed. It was already floundering, despite her best efforts and his limited help. Only problem was, he thought the answer had been to add factory paper and hire workers who didn't need quite the expertise required for handmade projects. That would certainly support her needs even if the one-vat factory shrunk to something she could handle. Now he wondered if he'd been wrong all along.

"Tell me, Jonas," said Mrs. Fitzwater softly, her tone crawling like a spider from under his collar, "what would happen if Arianne had no way to support herself in Cranbury?"

He stared at the older woman, repulsed by the coldhearted words and the impassive look on her face. She could have been an iron statue. "We're not likely to find out. She has a lot of friends to help her. And me."

Mr. Fitzwater stepped away from his wife, directing Jonas to the couch. "Sit down, my boy. It's time you were informed of what's really going on here."

"Robert . . ." Although Mrs. Fitzwater cautioned him, Mr. Fitzwater shook his head without looking at her. Jonas accepted the seat, although no one else sat with him, not even Clarence. He had a feeling whatever he was about to hear was better off heard sitting down.

"We might as well tell you, Jonas, that not only have we no intention of building a factory up there, but you'd be a fool if you tried."

"I thought you just sent a crew this morning? How could you know—?"

"Arianne is the only asset up there," Mr. Fitzwater said. "Do you know how much it would cost to build a modern factory in so remote a place?" He shook his head. "It would make no sense, none at all. They don't even have telephones up there!"

"Arianne would be best taken care of if she were to come here to work in Father's mill," said Clarence eagerly. "She would be renowned in the paper industry if she lets Father sell her watermarks."

Mrs. Fitzwater smiled but even an attempt to look friendly had an edge to it, one that made him every bit as wary as he'd been before. "If Arianne's paper mill cannot keep up with production in spite of her best efforts alone, she'll be that much more apt to accept the security we can bring to her. And she'll be allowed to do what she does best. What could be a more satisfying future for her?"

"Then why pretend you're interested in a factory expansion, if you want to force her to work only in watermarking?"

Clarence sat on the couch, too, putting a brotherly arm about Jonas's shoulders. "She has to come to the same conclusion we've come to, Jonas. The only bright future for her is here, working with us. Eliminating the possibility of expanding to factory-made paper is just one of the steps, and Father's crew will prove it. Besides," he added with a grin, "with her here, we can both woo her properly. May the best man win!"

Jonas couldn't stand to look at his old classmate, but his disgust for their plan was matched by disgust for himself. He'd led them all straight to Arianne.

Mr. Fitzwater smiled so broadly that for a moment Jonas wondered if they thought their plan selfish or altruistic. For a moment even he wasn't sure. "We're ready to offer Arianne a grand future. Have no doubt about that, my boy. She'll have everything she wants."

"Don't you think the best future for her would be one of choice?" asked Mrs. Fitzwater. "If her mill fails—no, *when* her mill fails—she may think marriage is her only option. She may be forced into a decision she'll later regret. Trust us, Jonas. If she has a secure future, she'll be much happier."

"I'm prepared to expand the Casterton mill in spite of what you want to do," he told them, finding himself standing again. "It doesn't have to be the size you envision, but big enough to give her all the security she needs."

Mr. and Mrs. Fitzwater exchanged a glance that contained at least a hint of amusement, if he gauged them correctly.

"She left your home last night without so much as a word to you," Mrs. Fitzwater reminded him gently. "It's obvious there isn't any special tie between you. Even if you have developed a shallow friendship by being partners, last night you both acted like partners and nothing more."

"And I was the one to take her home," Clarence said. "I know she was grateful for my help, and I have every reason to believe she could come to care for me if we got to know one another better."

Jonas felt Mrs. Fitzwater's unbroken attention. It was obvious they guessed he had more interest in Arianne than just as a business partner. Clarence himself had already declared a race to gain her affection.

He could deny it; he could lie. Yet having them know anything about his private feelings suddenly seemed like ammunition in their hands. He didn't want to conceal his feelings, not when he was just beginning to realize the importance of God in his life again—and that inevitably came with truth. But he said nothing, immediately aware his silence was as good as an admission.

Mrs. Fitzwater tsked. "You know, if you rescue her the moment she needs you, you'll wonder if she chose you for love or security. Wouldn't it be better if she came here an independent person?"

Mr. Fitzwater put a heavy hand on Jonas's shoulder, pulling him away from the other two. "What matters is that the paper industry is best served. Miss Casterton would be a great asset, and if you continue working with us, you could have your pick of managing any number of my factories. I know you hardly need a job, what with all that your father left to you. But you'll want to keep busy, won't you? Live a productive, meaningful life? That's only found in work, and I'd be happy to give you one of the best jobs in the state. I'm opening a new factory in Pittsburgh, and the plant is yours if you'll take it."

Squaring his shoulders, Jonas looked Mr. Fitzwater in the eye. "Mr. Fitzwater," he said, "as generous as it's been of you and Mrs. Fitzwater to offer Arianne the opportunities ahead, I think I can speak for her when I refuse all of it right here and now." He looked at Mrs. Fitzwater again before bowing once toward Mr. Fitzwater. "Thank you, sir, but you can consider Arianne and me out of your business. We won't trouble you further. I would consider repaying you for the expenses of the crew you sent to Cranbury, but as it appears they were nothing more than a sham anyway, I expect you don't require any such reimbursement."

He walked from the room and retrieved the hat he'd left on a marble-topped table in the hallway on his way in.

Not only did he have to reach Cranbury, he had a good deal of prayer in store. Perhaps only God could stop the Fitzwaters from wanting to acquire Arianne's talents, because Jonas was pretty sure their ambition could easily outweigh any ethics they might hold.

CHAPTER THIRTY-THREE

Arianne was hesitant to leave the men alone down on the bank of the Susquehanna, even to go up to the shop to let Phoebe know why the men were here. So she went inside the mill and found Gideon at work. He was creating a stack of tablet paper that demanded less meticulous care than society or other writing papers. Although he was happy to see her and likely expected she'd returned to work, she told him to continue what he was doing while she returned outside to sit at the table in the garden and watch the crew of men.

Binny soon joined her, a meal tray in hand. Though she brought something for Gideon as well, who joined them after Binny called his name through the open door, she offered nothing to the other men nearby even as they glanced their way with interest. Arianne fought a stab of conscience reminding her to be a better hostess, but in spite of that, not a single word passed her lips. She didn't even feel sorry that the forest slowed their progress as they counted footsteps over fallen logs and measured distances between wide tree trunks obviously in the way.

"Miss Ari," Binny whispered, "what're them men doing over there? Phoebe got a telegram sayin' they was comin' but not why.

And Tummers told us you tried to send them back to the city. Is everything all right?"

Though she'd failed to answer that same question from Gideon when he'd noticed the men earlier, she knew she couldn't keep the truth from them. They would blame Jonas for this unexpectedly quick development, and maybe that was where blame belonged.

"They're assessing the property for the mill's expansion," she said, hoping that would be answer enough.

"So soon? You sure you want to make such a big change already?"

Arianne couldn't nod; all she could do was lift a shoulder as if she were indifferent to the matter.

"You'd best come on up to the shop when you're finished eating and talk to Phoebe. She's been worrying ever since you got back, but won't leave the shop untended. Seems like whatever's on her mind sure isn't any good news."

Arianne sighed. What now? It was one thing to feel as if God were in control and she was only meant to follow and obey. But the overwhelming feeling that someone else had stepped in between her and God was too great to ignore. Was Jonas distancing her from God?

Deciding not to wait, Arianne finished her sandwich on the way up the path. She found Phoebe in the shop, and the only customer Mrs. Jenkins. Seeing her, Arianne assumed news had traveled about the men from the city. Upon Arianne's appearance, the older woman seemed prepared to linger even longer. She perused the shelf of books, glancing over her shoulder at Arianne as Phoebe greeted her with a hug.

"So you're going ahead with the expansion so quickly, then?" Phoebe asked, after Arianne confirmed the men were there on request. She didn't bother to explain upon whose request.

"I'm not sure I have much of a choice," Arianne admitted. "I can't keep up production without my father, at least not until Gideon can master something more elegant than Bristol board."

"Give the boy a chance, Ari," Phoebe whispered. "He's a hard worker."

Arianne nodded. "It'll take time, but he'll be a fine papermaker. Eventually." She only wished the art could be more quickly acquired, but reminded herself when she was Gideon's age she'd already been working over the vat for a half dozen years. "Binny mentioned you had some bad news for me. What is it?"

Phoebe's face clouded over as if the news wasn't as simple as another order they would be unable to fill or the withdrawal of an impatient client. She looked away, first toward the storeroom then toward one of the display tables, as if searching for the courage to tell Arianne the news.

"It's your paper, Ari. Your special paper from your Papa."

Arianne's heart dipped to the bottom of her stomach. "What about it?"

"I don't know how it happened. The other day, the very morning you left for Philadelphia, I came to open the shop just as you expected. I was doing my regular dusting, and when I saw the paper on the table, I nearly died a thousand deaths. A whole stack of your Papa's paper, just sitting out there as if for a normal purchase!"

Arianne's gaze flew to the display table of writing stationary. Her breathing shortened to quick and shallow, her blood dashed through her veins.

"Oh, I put it right away, Ari," Phoebe assured her, as if she thought Arianne was looking for it even now. "But a good portion of it is gone. Over fifty pages! Sold, I suppose. I don't know how it happened."

Arianne left Phoebe's side without another word, going straight to the shelf where she stored her father's gift. She stepped on the stool to retrieve it, then opened it and peeled away the protective tissue. There was no doubt about it; the stack was noticeably shorter than what it had once been. Perhaps as many as a hundred fewer sheets, she was sure of it. Gone.

Myriad thoughts clamored for attention, but only one made

any sense. Binny never filled in at the shop; she hated working with money. Even if she had, she never would have taken this box from its shelf. Beside Leta knowing about the paper, only Phoebe and Binny ever came into this storage room.

Except Jonas. And he'd had the opportunity.

Tears nipped at the rims of her eyes, hot and bitter. Ever since that man had arrived at her door, he'd brought nothing but trouble.

Part of her wanted to flee to the factory, to take refuge near the single sheet of paper she'd left hanging in the saul, a tribute to the last job her father had asked her to finish before he and Charlotte had taken that awful train ride.

But she couldn't go there, and it wasn't because of Gideon's presence interfering with a moment she would prefer spending alone. Those other men were too close by. Maybe not inside the factory itself, but certainly too near to ignore. Men Jonas had arranged to be there. Even if he hadn't hired them himself, Mr. Fitzwater would never have sent them if it wasn't for Jonas.

Carefully tucking back the tissue, Arianne closed the box and returned it to its spot. All morning she'd been careful to keep Jonas from her mind. She ignored visions of him with Julia Kitteridge, of his lavish Philadelphia home, of a future she couldn't even imagine with a factory that produced paper in ways as foreign to her as her ways were to the Fitzwaters. Of partnering with the Fitzwaters, whose goals seemed to be making money and growing more prominent in the paper business but who did not pursue those goals for the love of paper.

Without another word, Arianne left the storeroom knowing there was only one place she could be alone. Upstairs in her own home, a home far more humble than one in which she could ever now picture Jonas.

But it was hers, and she knew she belonged in it.

———

On a train headed only as far as Kimbletown, Jonas pulled out his pocket watch. He'd had to wait several hours for another train traveling toward Williamsport and would have to hire a carriage to finish the route. It would be near midnight if he could even find someone to take him all the way to Cranbury. The sky was already darkening, but not because of the hour. Clouds hung heavy with rain, and that always slowed transportation. He'd likely have to wait until morning to see Arianne.

He may have broken their partnership with the Fitzwaters, but he wasn't at all sure the Fitzwaters' had broken their partnership with them—or at least, with Arianne. A familiar stab of guilt pierced his stomach. He should have investigated the Fitzwater business tactics before blindly walking into their web.

There must be a way to keep the Fitzwaters from further inserting themselves into Arianne's life. Marriage came immediately to mind—too quickly and definitely too easily. She would be officially off the papermaking market, her future secure once he found another investment as he was bound to do. Surely he could find some business that had nothing to do with a viper like Fitzwater in it. The paper mill could continue in any capacity she chose, but at least she would no longer worry about security.

Despite the reluctant affection he knew she felt for him, her acceptance of marriage was anything but guaranteed. She hadn't much trouble refusing Leo, and she'd known him far longer than she'd known Jonas; he had even enjoyed a familiar place in her life.

A second option was more sensible, one he begrudgingly admitted might be best for Arianne. He could do the opposite of what the Fitzwaters suggested: make sure her one-vat mill succeeded on its own, at least as much as it had under her father's diligent work. Jonas wasn't so blind that he didn't see papermaking as the single most important force pushing blood through Arianne's veins.

He was impatient enough to offer all of his own energy to its success. Who better to insure a hard working helper than the only person he could truly control? Himself.

The idea intrigued him as much as it alarmed him. Failure was bad enough when failing oneself. Failing someone he loved was downright unacceptable.

He was certainly willing to dedicate himself to Arianne. The discovery of his love for her hadn't diminished, though he conceded if he could rid himself of this feeling his life would be easier. He could stay in Philadelphia, search another investment opportunity in one of the many businesses flourishing in the city, and continue his life much as he might have before knowing Arianne. That was certainly safer than either option he contemplated now.

But comfort was for old men, weak men. Besides that, life without Arianne would be dark, dull, and cold.

Mrs. Fitzwater had been right about one thing. There was only one way to offer Arianne a real choice for her future. Knowing her father had been every bit as flawed as any other human being gave Jonas hope that he could, with hard work and Prestwich stubbornness, take the man's job and do it just as well.

With enough determination, perhaps a paper artist could be born at any age.

CHAPTER THIRTY-FOUR

Arianne woke with spirits as dark as the skies exploding up above. A summer storm ravaged the area, whistling through the trees, bending boughs and tearing leaves prematurely from their branches. Between downpours she hastened from her home to the mill, joining Gideon in another day's work.

But her mind was on none of it. Where was Jonas? Was he still in Philadelphia, waiting to meet with the men who had measured the area, tested the ground, even explored the town itself for meeting the needs of a full-fledged mechanized paper factory?

Thankfully, they'd left the evening before, ahead of the storm that might have stranded them. They couldn't have known the weather would hamper any work today, so she hoped they'd found some other reason to leave without beginning the job for which they were hired.

That they'd left without sharing their report didn't surprise her, but it did add to her frustration. It only proved how little her opinion mattered in this "partnership."

A crack of thunder startled her and she nearly dropped the mould in her hands. She conceded that same storm might be keeping Jonas wherever he was, but if he'd left the city shortly after she had, if he'd met the train she was to have traveled on with him, he'd have arrived in Cranbury yesterday, before the men had even left, and well before the raging storm.

Maybe he'd stayed in Philadelphia to await the work crew's report. It was entirely possible that Jonas was, right now, meeting with Mr. Fitzwater and deciding how soon they could start construction.

As unpleasant as that was, another thought kept pestering her. Maybe it wasn't business at all that kept Jonas in Philadelphia. Maybe he had stayed to spend more time with Julia Kitteridge. It must have been clear to everyone that, although Julia had arrived at the dinner party with an escort, it was Jonas she preferred.

Thoughts of Jonas permeated every thought, every feeling of worry, anger, frustration and fear. Confusing it all was the fact that she still longed to see him. How could she still crave his company? What was it about him that made it true?

She knew why, at least in part. She'd watched him working in the mill during those weeks he'd been here. Maybe he guessed she was as demanding as her father had been, but he was meticulous, too, all on his own. Whatever task she'd let him perform he'd done well. She'd guessed if she ever allowed him near the vat he could make a passably fine papermaker. Not that she believed he wanted to.

More importantly, despite the protection he'd built in himself when it came to his mother, Arianne knew he loved Charlotte even more than Arianne herself did. She'd seen the depth of his grief even though he'd tried to hide it.

As the rain continued to pour, Arianne plunged the mould back into the pulp. The warm water welcomed her, and the pulp obeyed as it always did. Steady, reliable work was always available, ready to soothe her spirit, employ her mind if she let it, and lend itself to the creation of something lovely.

She had work to do if she was ever to catch up, and missing these last few days only put her farther behind.

———

Jonas set aside the empty coffee cup, staring out the window at the rain slicing diagonally from the sky to the earth below. The driver he'd hired at Kimbletown last night had agreed to take him as far as Williamsport but no farther. This morning he'd foolishly tried hiring a carriage, but the Williamsport liveryman had refused to try navigating the muddy washboard roads in the continuing downpour. Jonas had considered taking a horse, bypassing the roads if conditions warranted, but the rain fell hard again and he knew he was stuck, at least for the time being. The swelling river and over-forested lands around Williamsport made travel unpredictable at best, downright dangerous at worst.

Olice entered the parlor, ready to remove the empty cup and coffee pot.

"We'll see some flooding with a rain like this," he said. "Always somethin'. If it's not a flood, it's a fire."

Jonas turned from the window, offering only a nod to acknowledge he'd heard Olice's comments. Lumber lords had been harvesting the Pennsylvania forests for decades now, leaving the land vulnerable and empty. It was the one industry Jonas hadn't considered investing in with his inheritance. The naked land was more susceptible than ever to flooding, mudslides and especially to fire. Ever since they'd built those rail lines to transport timber farther from any finger of the rivers, the trees left behind were unprotected from the occasional spark shooting up out of the very trains that carried away what remained of the fruit of the land.

But Jonas hadn't thought of flooding until now. Images of the Susquehanna raging through the Casterton mill took quick and vivid shape in Jonas's mind.

He needed to get there—and soon.

CHAPTER THIRTY-FIVE

For the second day in a row, Arianne rushed past the soggy ground to reach shelter inside the factory. Gideon had beaten her to work again this morning; he was already at the press.

She planned to use him as her coucher today, allowing him time to improve the art of tossing. His movements weren't flawless yet —he sometimes added a wrinkle to the newborn pages—but he had a natural grace that needed only the confidence of experience to perfect.

"Good morning, Gideon," she called to him through the archway between the vat and press. He looked up and grinned at her, but kept working. "When you've emptied the press, come to the vat. You can be my coucher today."

He stood straight, a look of eagerness on his face. "Yes, miss!" Then he hurried to squeeze out the last of the water from the pages more vigorously than she'd seen a moment ago.

She wanted to smile at his enthusiasm, but smiling wasn't any easier for her today than it had been yesterday. So she went to work, wishing it would stop raining. The near constant showers of the last two days did nothing to improve her spirits.

But it wasn't the weather affecting her most; Jonas's continued absence felt like a raw wound to her soul. The same questions haunted her again and again. Was it only the rain keeping him away? Or had he found himself too reluctant to leave Philadelphia?

Too reluctant to leave Julia?

———

Jonas could barely see through the rain pelting him. He'd set out that morning with hopes the storm had moved on, but it returned in full force half way to Cranbury.

Since then he'd grown oblivious to the wet. Rainwater drenched every inch of his skin, from the hair on his head after his hat blew off to the insides of his shoes. Droplets running down his collar no longer brought a chill, they just joined the others already clinging to him.

Olice had tried talking him out of going, claiming the worst wasn't over. His wife, Mrs. Brown, came as close as a servant could to forbidding him to go, invoking the memory of his mother and insisting she would have found a way to talk him out of such foolishness. Even the liveryman who rented him the same mare he always used for this trip charged him the entire price of the horse, convinced neither would return if the Susquehanna flooded.

He might be every bit the fool they all believed him to be. Floods always brought disaster, from the epic one at Johnstown ten years ago to the more recent events that had littered the city streets of Williamsport with everything the river carried: boats, logs, cut wood from the booms.

He just hoped he reached Cranbury soon enough to be of any help. Arianne treasured her father's equipment more than anything, and Jonas would do all in his power to save what they could.

———

By mid-morning Arianne stopped working at the vat. She stood beside Gideon at the door watching the rain continue to pour.

They'd both hoped the rains had let up for good, but the clouds overhead were every bit as dark as they'd been the day before.

"I'll make a run for it," Gideon said.

"Be careful of the slope," she cautioned, remembering count-less times she'd offered to do what Gideon had just volunteered to do. How many times had she made a dash to the rain gauge, kept her eye on the metered jar only to lose her footing for lack of care on her approach?

"Don't worry," he said and though she heard his bravado he was off before she could warn him again.

So this was what Papa must have felt when watching her do the same. *Time to check the gauges again, Arianne. See how fast that rain's coming down since last hour.*

Gideon did what she'd done far too many times: he slipped at the last moment, at the foot of the post that stood clear of rooflines or interfering trees from above. He stood again as quickly as he'd fallen, then took a long look at the standard gauge with its cylindrical center, rewound the older tipping bucket gauge and afterward made a quick path back to the mill's door.

"Not more than twenty millimeters higher than last time," he called, even before he'd crossed the threshold.

"Hmm, is that all?" She eyed the rain again. "Looks worse than that."

He shrugged out of his rain slicker. "That's all it is. Both say so."

She turned away, folding her arms and looking around. What would Papa do? They'd enjoyed an early spring this year, which meant much of the snowmelt had already passed. Still, it was early enough in the year to worry about flooding. Would it be wise to move everything up ground, or was she being too cautious?

"We'll wait another hour," she said, "and if it doesn't let up we'll start moving what we can up to the loft and the house."

The horse automatically stopped at the Cranbury livery, refusing to move another step despite Jonas's urging. Exasperated, Jonas dismounted and let the horse find its own way into the stable then he set off to go the rest of the way on foot. The main street through town was soft with mud so he stayed on the wet boardwalks, wondering if the horse had known better all the time. Jonas would likely make better time on the sidewalk than the horse would have in the mud.

"Hey!"

Jonas turned at the call, since he'd expected to be the only one out on such a day.

Leo trotted toward him right through the mud, splattering both sides with every step. "What kind of fool travels on a day like today?"

"I came to help move equipment in case there's flooding."

Leo stopped in front of Jonas, crossing his arms. "So you're finally here to do some good. Come on. I was just going down there myself."

They didn't bother stopping at the stationery shop, even though surprisingly the sign in the window claimed it was open. The path from the street was wider than the mint-laced one behind Arianne's home, for which Jonas was instantly grateful. This one accommodated both of them, eliminating Jonas's fleeting image of a race to get to the mill first.

Light from the window promised someone must be there. He wasn't too late.

Hopping up the two steps into the mill, the water Jonas collected along his way landed in a puddle at his feet. He spotted Arianne at the vat.

Leo was already nearing her. "I came to help!"

"Yes, *we* did," he corrected.

They must have startled her, because she dropped the mould— one of the pieces of equipment he'd come to save—back into the vat.

"That's fine," she said.

"Aren't you moving up ground?" Jonas took one look around at the mill, seeing only business as usual before stepping forward and taking up three of the other moulds nearby.

She put a hand on his forearm. "I'm keeping an eye on the gauges," she said. "The rain has been tapering off for the last two hours."

"That don't mean the river won't swell," Leo said. "I think we ought to move everything up ground."

"Fine," she said, lips a bit thinner than usual. Worse than that, she didn't make eye contact with either one of them.

For this, he'd risked life and limb all the way from Williamsport?

Between the four of them, they soon had most of the supplies and movable equipment transferred to the loft. Arianne directed them to pile the crates and boxes beneath the single sheet of paper she'd insisted be left hanging even when other orders came and went. He'd guessed her father put it there. *Only God can take that one down*, she'd once told him, without further explanation.

She sent Gideon home after that, and Jonas wished she would do the same for Leo. But he lingered even as they put the felts and moulds into two boxes they would take all the way up to the house. The felts and moulds were the most valuable of transportable equipment—if not in monetary value, at least in sentimental as far as Arianne would measure.

"Thank you for coming to help, Leo," Arianne said once they were finished. "It was generous of you to leave the woodshop."

Jonas stepped forward to lift the heavier box containing the many felts, eliminating the need for Leo to tag along. He planned to pile the box with the moulds on top, but Arianne was already reaching for it and started walking to the door.

Good; she didn't expect Leo to come up to the house any more than he did. It was hard to ignore his jealousy of the man even while other thoughts reminded him there was no reason for such feelings. Unless something had changed in the few days of his absence, Arianne had already rejected Leo once. Nonetheless, the sight of them together now looked somehow . . . right. Two people who'd known each other all their lives, well fitted in this tight-knit little community. What a celebration this town would enjoy if two of their own committed to one another. It would be like affirming their way of life. That this town could provide everything needed to be happy.

Maybe it could.

CHAPTER THIRTY-SIX

Arianne wanted to be angry with Jonas. Besides what she suspected he felt for Julia Kitteridge, wasn't she angry with him for the way he and Robert Fitzwater had joined forces against her? If it wasn't for Mr. Fitzwater *and* Jonas, those men never would have arrived to start plans for the expansion already.

And he'd sold her paper!

In spite of all that, it was awfully good to see him, knowing he'd faced the storm for fear of losing some part of the business to the foul weather.

She led the way out of the mill, glad to see it had stopped raining. Maybe her instincts hadn't been wrong, after all. Maybe her father wouldn't have wasted time moving everything to higher ground, at least not yet. If it didn't start raining again, this caution was only a waste of time.

"I'm sorry I didn't get here sooner," Jonas said. The air was still, but the quickened river flow was still loud enough to warrant a raised voice. "I'm glad I wasn't too late to help in case there is some flooding."

"The mill might still take in some water," Leo said, looking beyond Jonas at the river. "Not much we can do about it, beyond what we've done."

"If you had electricity," Jonas said, "you could have the power to make paper anywhere you want. Well away from the river and whatever trouble it brings."

"So now you want to move the factory, too?" Leo cast a derisive glance Jonas's way in case he'd missed the tone, but she could tell from the frown that he hadn't. They'd stopped at the foot of the path, where she expected Leo to leave them. The tension between the two heightened her own, and even though she still considered Leo an ally it might be best if he left. But he didn't move.

"I suppose you know Mr. Fitzwater sent a crew of men to start the plans for the expansion," Arianne said to Jonas. Her tone didn't match Leo's in loudness or contempt, but still carried an unmistakable ring of reproach.

Jonas shifted the box in his arms. The moulds in her box weren't heavy, but she knew the felts were. "Let's go up to the shop, or your kitchen," he suggested. "We have a lot to talk about."

He sounded so serious Arianne wondered why. He looked downright somber. Wasn't he as eager as Mr. Fitzwater to reap the rewards of factory-made paper? Mr. Fitzwater may be only Jonas's partner, and he the rightful owner of only a third, but she had no idea how to stop either one of them.

One thing was clear; everything they had to discuss was none of Leo's concern anymore. Even if she'd married him and handed over her own two-thirds for him to worry about with her, she doubted he could stop them, either. "Thank you again, Leo, for all your help today."

"I'll always want what's best, you know. For you." He spoke so tenderly she wondered at his boldness in front of Jonas.

"I know, Leo. And I'm grateful. I suppose we can be extra careful and wait until we know in a day or two just how high the water's going to get."

Leo still didn't move, only now he aimed his gaze at Jonas as if he wanted to say something. Whatever it was couldn't be pleasant, since Leo's eyes narrowed in the most unfriendly way. So Arianne juggled her box to one arm and patted Leo's shoulder, offering a more direct farewell. "I'll see you later, then."

Leo never took his eyes from Jonas. "You're doing the wrong thing, you know. Pushing a factory on her. She don't want it."

She was about to interject, to remind Leo it wasn't any more his business than the rest of Cranbury's. As Jonas had once said, change was inevitable, sooner or later. They all knew a factory would bring new workers, new businesses, new services, to a little town that seemed content to spend tomorrow much as it had yesterday.

"I know."

She felt her brows lift at Jonas's two simple words. Well, of course he knew she didn't want the factory. She'd told him that often enough. Only she hadn't thought he was listening.

The two words seemed to embolden Leo. He stepped closer to Jonas, stuck out a finger and jabbed it into Jonas's chest. "You know? Then you ought to know a few other things, too. She's the best handmade papermaker this side of the Atlantic, but it's not just paper to her. It's not something you use and throw away. It's something special. It's not a *factory* product. You can throw away that kind and not think twice. But her paper? That's something you use for words and pictures that count."

He leaned in closer, nostrils flaring like a bull ready to charge. "Even if you don't know much about Ari, you oughta know that much. And you know what else? She sings like an angel because that's what she is. She needs somebody who'll sit next to her in church. Every week, not just when he wants to make a good impression."

What was Leo doing, defending her as if Jonas had stormed the citadel for her, or at least openly claimed an interest in her? "Leo, what in the world—"

"Don't stop me, Ari. I seen the way he looks at you and, so help me, I didn't want to see the way you look back, but I did. I'm not going to fool myself. If I can't take care of you as a husband then

I'll do it the way I always have, like a brother. Without your Papa here to protect you, I'm all you've got." He turned back to Jonas, poking him again with his finger. "And you better listen to me, too, fella', because I'm not done. You're going to have to learn a whole lot more about paper than what you think you already know, let me tell you. Not just the factory kind, neither. You don't even know what you did, do you, you saphead? You didn't know the difference between her Papa's identical paper and just any old stack of stationery, did you? You sold it!"

He might have gone on, but Arianne set down the box and put a cautioning hand on Leo's forearm. It shouldn't have surprised her that Phoebe had told anyone, but somehow it did. As much as the loss pained her, she couldn't entirely blame Jonas and didn't want anyone else to, either.

"That's enough, Leo."

"What paper?"

The two statements were issued at the same time, but Leo chose to respond only to one. "It's special paper her Papa set aside from lots of different orders through the years. Same pure white, same weight. Color, texture, best pulp you'd ever see. Identical, those pages were. Each and every sheet. Stored behind the shop, wrapped in tissue inside a burlap-covered box. And you sold it."

"Only some of it," Arianne added.

Jonas looked from Leo to Arianne. "I do remember getting paper from that storeroom. I didn't know it was a special stock."

"Well, it was," said Leo doggedly. "So as far as I can tell you've got some making up to do. You're starting from a little bit farther behind than you know, all right."

Arianne felt Jonas's gaze as surely as if he'd touched her. "I'm sorry," he whispered.

Perhaps even Leo was impressed by his sincerity, because his chest wasn't quite so puffed and he didn't say a word. A gust of wind blew through then, releasing some of the caught raindrops from the trees bent overhead.

"We'd better go inside," Arianne said, picking up the box again and turning back to the path behind them. To her relief, Leo took the other path, toward the main street of town, leaving her and Jonas to go up to her home alone.

CHAPTER THIRTY-SEVEN

As Jonas followed Arianne up the stone pathway, struggling to hold the box under one arm but not daring to take her hand, he stayed close in case she needed assistance on the slippery rocks. He was a fool for having sold something that was obviously special to Arianne. He should have known from the way the paper was stored on the highest shelf, carefully wrapped. But, hang it all, the way everyone loved paper in that shop it was no surprise to see it stored that way. It should have been labeled.

But he voiced no defense, knowing he'd have a hard time forgetting that mistake. Because it was just that, a mistake. His.

One thing Leo's outburst proved, though, was that he must have seen something the Fitzwaters hadn't. Jonas wasn't surprised that his own feelings had been found out; how could he have hidden his growing admiration of this woman? But had Leo seen some sort of answering affection in Arianne? Something Leo must never have seen aimed his way?

It was hard to believe, but Jonas was eager to find out if it could be true.

The kitchen was filled with activity when they arrived. Binny was laughing along with Phoebe at something Tummers the coachman must have just said, who lingered inside the door. They all looked surprised to see them.

"I was just looking for you, young man," said Tummers. "That horse you ride showed up at the livery without ya' so I stopped by to make sure it weren't just him that made it here through the storm."

Jonas smiled at the older man. "Now here's a day to remember," he said. "A resident of Cranbury concerned over my welfare."

Binny folded her arms and looked at him with a scowl. "Is that the best you think of Cranbury? That we ain't got no concern for another human being?"

"No, Binny," Jonas said, offering her his friendliest smile as he deposited the box near her feet. "I only thought I wasn't worthy of the concern, at least around here. But I'm trying to change that."

The box inspired another scowl from Binny. "Now what's all this and what's it doing in my kitchen?"

"A few things we didn't want to risk leaving on low ground," Arianne said. "It'll be here for a day or so."

"Is there water in the factory, then?" asked Phoebe.

"No, at least not yet," Jonas said. He cleared his throat, hoping what he was about to say didn't inspire laughter or even ridicule. "About the factory, Arianne. I know I haven't been as much help as I'm able. But while you continue with Gideon's training, I'd like to be included as well. At the vat."

All eyes went to him then, and even Tummers stopped, removing his hand from the doorknob he'd grabbed. No one laughed, but he did sense a hefty dose of disbelief. Maybe he should have expected that.

"Listen," he said, deciding not to wait until he was alone with Arianne but going ahead to reveal at least the majority of his plans. "I made a mistake asking Mr. Fitzwater for help. I stayed in Philadelphia long enough to talk to him and learned he already knew his crew would come back with a report that this isn't the best spot for a full-fledged factory."

"It isn't?" Arianne's eyes shone with hope, which gave him what he needed to continue. He'd known she'd never welcomed the expansion, but he wasn't entirely certain how she'd received the Fitzwaters themselves. She'd looked so different after spending only a day with them, as elegant as a member of their family. Despite her hasty departure he'd believed she'd become friendly with at least the Fitzwater girls. And she'd likely been flattered by Clarence and his open adoration.

"You can't continue with such limited help," he said. "Gideon will be a great addition, but it'll take time to work the factory as efficiently and successfully as you did with your father. I figure if there are two of us learning all of the jobs, the three of us might find a spot that suits each best. Maybe Gideon and I can do half of what your father did." Jonas might still resent Samuel Casterton for his involvement with his mother, but he could finally admit aloud that the man knew what he was doing when it came to paper.

"You . . . You want to work in the mill? In the handmade mill? As it is?" Arianne's voice was little more than a whisper, and the questions rang familiar. He had to prove he hadn't come to take over her business.

Nodding, he wished he'd waited to speak to her alone if only to take her hand right now and pledge to replace the paper he'd inadvertently sold. Mrs. Fitzwater was right about one thing. If he were going to win Arianne's love freely given, it would have to be from a place she felt strong. That meant she needed the security of a successful mill, and he was determined to make it so. Until then, he would keep his feelings a secret.

"I think we could use another worker, too," he added. "I have the funds to invest until the mill is working at its greatest capacity, and then it'll pay for itself just the way it did when your father was here."

No one said anything, perhaps out of shock. So he continued. "The Fitzwaters should leave us alone from now on. Their market is different, and even if they wanted to compete with some kind of price battle, it wouldn't work. Not with paper that's an art."

Arianne was staring at him with what could only be gratitude. He wanted much more than that, but it was a beginning.

Arianne studied Jonas as if she'd never seen him before. Certainly she hadn't, at least not the Jonas who stood before her now. Handmade paper was worthy to be called an art? And he was willing to try making it himself? Not the factory kind, but the kind she made?

It was such a drastic change she wondered what must have happened to sever a business relationship with someone as successful as Mr. Fitzwater.

She wished they were alone, fearing others might notice her blush. To divert their attention as well as her own suddenly unruly thoughts, she joined Binny in moving the box to the corner.

"Oh, now, this is the worst thing about bad weather," Binny grumbled as she took the box out of Arianne's hands. "Everybody hovers in the kitchen and I can't get a thing done 'round here. It's bad enough I'll have this crate in my way. Go on, Miss. Go help Phoebe in the shop. There's bound to be something to do in there without any customers in the way."

The unfortunate truth was there was precious little to do. Arianne hadn't ordered any outside stock, such as new books or pens, since shortly after her father had died. She'd been too concerned about funds. Display items had grown sparse, as the shelves demanded nothing but a daily war on dust.

Tummers was the first to take Binny's advice about leaving the kitchen, tipping his hat with a farewell. Phoebe obeyed next, leading the way through the storeroom and into the shop. Arianne followed, and she felt rather than saw Jonas do the same behind her.

Phoebe straightened a display of postcards and patted a stack of envelopes, but soon caught Arianne's eye before stealing a quick glance toward Jonas; he was studying book spines. Arianne could tell the woman felt more than a little uncomfortable, even before issuing a strained smile.

"If you're going to be up here instead of in the mill, Ari," she said softly, "and with so few customers . . ."

Arianne nodded before her friend had even finished. "Go home, Phoebe. I'll see you in the morning?"

"Of course!"

Then she disappeared back into the storeroom but only long enough to retrieve her shawl. A moment later she scurried through the shop and out the door, holding the shawl above her head in protection against lingering raindrops.

The shop was quiet but for the steady trickle of water from the roof at the corner, and an occasional thump of movement from the kitchen. Arianne had gotten her wish: she was alone with Jonas.

Evidently Jonas thought they weren't alone enough. He moved toward the storeroom, to close the door between them and the kitchen. Then without another word he walked past Arianne to the customer door. He flipped the sign her father had made of his best Bristol board and marked with his steady hand from the *Open* side to *Closed*. Finally Jonas pulled the shade even though there was almost no light coming in on this dark day. But it did afford a facsimile of privacy; only a facsimile, because anyone could still see inside through the display case windows.

"We have a lot to discuss," he said as he neared Arianne, standing in front of the polished counter. His voice was cordial, businesslike. He didn't meet her gaze. Instead, he pulled out the only chair in the store, the one with a high seat to match the counter, which she kept handy when working on ledgers.

Arianne didn't move. She stood on the other side of the chair, waiting for him to notice she didn't want to sit while he remained standing. When he still didn't look up at her, she decided to start the discussion.

"Tell me what happened in Philadelphia," she said. "Why are you no longer partners with the Fitzwaters?"

Jonas leaned over the top of the chairs' slatted back, bringing his face a bit closer to hers.

"Perhaps you might go first and tell me what happened while *you* were there. Why you left so suddenly, without even a word to me."

She tried looking away, suddenly embarrassed that she'd acted so childishly. Obviously he had learned to handle the rumors about their parents. The fact that she couldn't do the same proved her far less sophisticated. Besides that, telling him Julia Kitteridge was to blame sounded like she was competing with the other woman for Jonas's attention. Even if she was, she wasn't ready to admit such a thing. "I learned I'm not very talented in business, I'm afraid. I was overcome with the desire to be here instead of there."

"No one would have doubted your knowledge of paper," he said softly.

She looked away. "As Proverbs teaches, even a fool can appear wise if he keeps his mouth shut."

"Does it?"

She nodded, though she couldn't claim to know where to find such advice. She was fairly certain she'd read it, though.

"If anyone was a fool, Arianne, it was I. I shouldn't have invited Fitzwater's attention. He's a hawk, ready to take any paper business into his claws. I should have been more careful, more content to help grow your business on our own. Or at least keep it going the way your father did."

"But you've never been willing to settle for such a small business investment," she reminded him. He'd very nearly convinced her progress was inevitable!

"Was I as bad as the Fitzwaters to you, Arianne? Pushing you into something you didn't want?"

She couldn't speak, he was looking at her so peculiarly. He studied her the way she stared at pictures to recreate a watermark.

"Is that what I was to you, Arianne?" he pressed. "A snowball, ready to wrap you up in all my plans no matter what you had to say about it?"

She could lie to spare his feelings, but it would be useless. They both knew his words were accurate. She nodded.

"I'm sorry." He raised one hand briefly toward the closed store-room door. "I'm sorry for a lot of things, but I think I'm most sorry for selling your special paper."

Though the thought of it still tugged at her spirits, she couldn't hold it against him. "You didn't know. I should have told you. I should have been able to produce enough stationery stock for the store so you didn't have to go looking for more."

"Maybe someday I can replace it. I meant what I said. I want to learn how to work in the mill, not just as a layboy." She smiled to think of him in terms of the simplest job, stacking felts and newly formed paper into the presses. "Will you teach me?"

Something had definitely changed since they'd left Phil-adelphia. She wanted to welcome the change, because somehow he seemed to want what she did. Heaven knew she needed his help to stay in business, not only to invest in the shop but more impor-tantly to support her father's mill. Why had Jonas changed? He was far too appealing the way he was now, and warning signals told her to be careful. This was the same man who'd told her *marriage wasn't for him*, the same man who'd treated her nearly like a stranger in his Philadelphia home. The same man whose friends gossiped about their parents, and whose special friend obviously wanted to share a good deal of his company. Julia Kitteridge's face came easily to Arianne's mind, and she couldn't help wondering if it came just as easily to Jonas's.

"I don't understand." Her voice was a whisper even though she knew there was no need to be so quiet, but it was as if a louder tone would threaten the intimacy of the moment. "Why have you changed your mind about everything?"

His hands reached for her, she was sure of it, but the chair was in the way and he withdrew so quickly she wondered if she'd only imagined him wanting to take her into his arms. He stood before her with only a friendly smile.

"Let's just say I learned an important lesson from the Fitzwa-ters. Aspiration isn't always a virtue."

CHAPTER THIRTY-EIGHT

The weather had soon done its worst. The factory suffered little more than a few puddles here and there, which they mopped up. Jonas worked alongside of Arianne and Gideon, glad to feel part of a team.

Jonas wasn't sure if he was a coward or a fool, but he didn't regret not telling Arianne the one thing foremost on his mind. As tempted as he'd been, he hadn't told her he loved her. And he didn't intend to, at least not yet.

Arianne had spent yesterday afternoon acquainting him with every aspect of the business, with sales histories and suppliers, customers and reasonable expectations along with budgets, expenses, and expected profits.

The most fun of the day had been inviting Arianne to write restocking orders on ancillary items, all financed from his bank account. She'd been like a child with a wish list, pulling out recent catalogs and ordering items she'd obviously had her eye on but couldn't afford. She happily accepted his help but only on loan, insisting she would reimburse him once the shop was back up to its full sales capacity.

Jonas was surer than ever he wanted to be involved in the

success of the mill. He might—or might not—become a competent papermaker, but he could prove he wanted to try. He assured
himself he was at least as motivated as Gideon, who only wanted
to make a living. Jonas wanted to make a life. That should count
for something on the day he asked her to consider loving him in
return.

But after his first lesson, Jonas convinced himself he would
need all the help he could get if he was to become a papermaker
along the Casterton model. There was definitely a knack to
dipping those moulds and retrieving just the right amount of pulp
—a knack he had yet to acquire. On his way to the mill for the
second morning in a row, he detoured to the wood shop.

Jonas stepped inside, greeted by a fresh scent of wood and
varnish. A variety of items were on display, everything from tables,
chairs and cabinets to toys, games and decorative boxes. Little
wonder this small town attracted so many shoppers from
Williamsport.

"Can I help you?"

The woman who approached was well past middle age. White
hair piled atop her head looked like a cloud of chalk dust with
wisps escaping here and there, as if it had never known a clip it
would obey.

"I'm looking for Leo Levick," he said.

Her brows lifted. "My son." Those same brows came together
as she looked him over. "You're Charlotte's boy, aren't you? The
one who came to work with Ari."

He nodded, grateful he was no longer known as the one who
came to steal the mill. But if this woman knew of her son's feelings
for Arianne—and how could she not have at least guessed?—she
might not be all that willing to welcome him into her shop. Even
now, as she eyed him, she folded her arms across her generous
waist as if wondering what words to spew at him. She even put
forth one of her feet, tapping her toe at him.

"Well, I suppose I should thank you," she said after a moment.

Those were the last words he expected. "Excuse me?"

"Leo needed someone to show him Ari wasn't going to marry him. I used to hope her feelings would change, or that she'd . . . settle, I guess. But that wouldn't have been best for either one of them."

Knowing an entire town not only watched but formed opinions about all of their observations reminded Jonas yet again he wasn't living in Philadelphia any more. But even as the thought crossed his mind, some small part of him welcomed it. This wasn't the kind of gossip he'd suffered in the city, from predators circling over the foolish or weakened, people who barely knew one another. This could even be called concern. As if this woman cared almost as much about Arianne's future as she did about her own son's.

"You'll find him in the shop," she said, nodding toward a door at the back of the store. "He's working with his father and brothers every day now instead of splitting his time between here and the paper mill. I'm grateful for that, too."

"Thank you," he said, feeling her curious eyes follow him all the way to the door.

The workroom was surprisingly small compared to the amount of inventory filling the store. It was the second time a pleasant scent greeted him; this area smelled strongly of sawdust and was far more inviting to work around than some of the pulp and finishing chemicals used in the paper factory. Leo might not have won Arianne, but at least he worked in an industry that smelled better. A potbellied stove nearby suggested they might be comfortable year round, although it was lit even on this warm day. The heavy iron melting pot resting on top provided another clean scent: glue. Each of the walls was cluttered with hooks and shelves, but in an orderly fashion, boasting a variety of tools.

The sawing and pounding he'd heard through the door stopped altogether as he stepped in the room. An older man bent over a sawhorse looked up, and another man stopped sanding the edge of a perfectly square board. Leo wasn't in sight, but in a moment he came through a wide set of double doors from outside. He carried one end of a long and heavy beam.

"What're you doin' here?" The words competed with a thud as the plank landed on a set of trestles. Though Leo looked at the wood instead of Jonas, adjusting its placement, the three other men stared at him with varying degrees of interest.

"I came to talk to you, Leo."

"So talk."

Jonas looked around at the watchful eyes. No one made any attempt to resume work.

"Can we go outside?"

"Whatever you've got to say you might as well say right here. Sooner or later they'll know anyway."

While that was likely true, especially if Leo agreed to what Jonas was about to propose, he hoped to keep the idea between themselves if Leo refused. Evidently he had no choice.

"I'd like your help in making up for the mistake I made."

The request didn't ignite the interest Jonas had hoped for, though Leo did look amused by the reminder of his error.

"You mean about selling the paper?"

Jonas nodded, cooling his embarrassment with the realization the entire town probably knew what he'd done. The lack of surprise on anyone else's face proved that.

"I need you to help me learn to make the best paper I can. Arianne is willing to teach me, but if I'm going to replace that paper, I'm going to need all the tutoring I can get." He didn't add how hard he expected it be to concentrate with Arianne as his teacher.

Now Leo smirked outright. "*You're* going to replace it? Replace prime paper taken from the best of Samuel Casterton's stock?"

"I can try."

Leo turned back to the wood he and his brother had just brought in. He pulled a measuring tool from the leather belt around his waist, as if he'd been distracted long enough. "Can't be done," was all he said, without looking at Jonas.

Jonas took a step closer, refusing to be dismissed. "I know it won't be easy. I know Mr. Casterton worked his entire life and Arianne's done the same, to become the papermakers they are. You worked at it for years, too. I'm a latecomer, but that doesn't mean I can't learn."

Leo stood tall again, at roughly the same height as Jonas but with considerably larger girth. He would have been intimidating if Jonas didn't know better. "Why should I help you, even if you could learn anything?"

"For one thing, because you said you were going to act like the brother she's always seen in you." Then he added, with a whisper, "But mostly because you love her."

Leo scowled. "That's no reason for me to help you, especially with *that* paper."

"I know the paper was remarkable—"

"It wasn't just remarkable. It was supposed to be a wedding gift. She won't get married without that stack big enough to print an entire Bible."

Jonas's heart sank to the pit of his stomach. He'd delayed the very thing he most wanted to pursue! Ignoring the irony, he didn't take his eyes from Leo.

"You think she deserves to have that paper replaced, don't you? And besides, if Arianne ever does agree to marry me someday, at least you'll always know you did the right thing to make her happy. Whether it's with you or somebody else. And if she doesn't marry me, then everybody in town, including Arianne, will know you didn't do anything to stand in another man's way. Everybody will know all you want is for her to be happy."

"I never heard so much balderdash in all my life," said the brother on the other end of the wood they'd carried in. He'd briefly pretended to tend the wood but now looked between Leo and Jonas. "You want my brother's help for you to win the heart of the woman he loves, too?"

"Hold on, there, Brom," said another brother who'd stopped

sanding. "If Ari's going to make a choice between the two, wouldn't it be better if they both did the right thing?"

The one he'd called Brom slapped the cloth against the beam in front of him. "Just tell him to be the first witness at the wedding ceremony, why don't you? You saw the way the boy's been moping around here ever since he left working with her."

"Yeah, and if there's any hope of mending that heart," the other said, voice raising to match his brother's, "he's got to know he did everything he could to be the kind of man a woman wants. Any woman."

"And you know what kind of man that is? *You*, a bachelor at near thirty years old?"

They both shouted back and forth, and Jonas could barely hear either one of them until the older man grabbed a hammer and pounded it once on a sturdy block. The room fell instantly silent, as if the sons had long ago been conditioned to a familiar sound that demanded immediate attention.

"What's important here? Arianne?" He tossed aside the hammer and stepped to the center of the crowded workshop. "This boy? Leo? The paper?" He approached Leo. "If you said you were going to be the brother you've been to her all these years, then it's your own words you've got to live up to. That's what's important. Your words." He put a hand on one of Leo's strong shoulders. "You don't always do the right thing for somebody else's sake. Sometimes you do it just for yourself. It's in the Book. He'll guide you in the path of righteousness. Don't gain the world while losin' your soul. You know what's right. Now do it."

It wasn't exactly the way Jonas had hoped for his plea to go, but for the first time since entering the wood shop he had some hope Leo might agree.

Leo eyed Jonas, looking none too pleased. "I don't know why you need my help if Ari's agreed to teach you. She's better at it than me anyway."

"She's going to work with me during the day," Jonas said, refusing to admit the rest about being a near dunderhead around her. He was almost hesitant to reveal the next part. "I'd like you to work with me at night. I don't want her to know about it until I can produce my first sheet of paper good enough to replace what I sold."

There was a grumble from one brother, a laugh from another. But Leo just lifted one brow and finally nodded.

CHAPTER THIRTY-NINE

Never toss the paper onto the felt's long nap. Longer, stiff hairs might tear it, or at least leave an imprint. Protect the texture . . . Protect the texture.

Arianne woke with a start. Why was she reliving each of the lessons she'd shared with Jonas? Yet that's what she'd been doing for the last two weeks since he'd begun working with her at the vat. Each moment she spent with Jonas was lived not once but twice. First during the day, then again in her dreams.

She lay awake though she sensed dawn was still far off. Was she too demanding? Too particular to expect a precise sheen on newly formed paper before landing it onto the waiting felt? Not that he wasn't receptive to her direction. Jonas seemed eager to learn the proper way to make paper, more than anyone she'd worked with or seen her father teach over the years.

Jonas had already proven confident when plunging the mould into the warmed and watery pulp, almost as if the action came naturally to him. He'd quickly learned to shake the mould, just the way her father had shown her. She wanted to marvel over his touch, tell him she'd noticed that he was both smooth and firm yet gentle, but feared her secret would soon be out. That secret had awakened her just now, with him already on her mind. The secret that she was so in love with him made her fear she was the worst of teachers.

Constant distractions blurred her focus. Instead of looking at the readiness of the pulp, she found herself appreciating Jonas's strong hands. Instead of making sure the felts were properly placed she admired the way his shoulders moved during the toss.

All of which made her more desperate than ever to hide that he was more than a favorite pupil. Was he really a most talented papermaker, or were her uncooperative feelings marring her judgment? So she kept her compliments to herself. Until she could tell Jonas that he really did have exceptional talent—it wasn't just her own eagerness to imagine such a thing in him—she would keep her enthusiasm to herself.

Restless, Arianne tossed in her bed. It was no use; she was fully awake and she had little hope she'd ever get back to sleep. She'd often used such pre-dawn hours for prayer, thinking there must be a reason for her wakefulness. But since Jonas filled her thoughts yet again, she reminded herself it was dangerous to lie awake dreaming of a future that might not have a chance. He was working hard to make sure the mill was a success, but not because he planned to stay in Cranbury after her mill proved that success.

Determined to better use the hours, she flung off the covers. She might as well work. She'd often made paper under lamplight; there was no reason not to do so now.

She paused only long enough to dress. On her way through the kitchen she glanced at the clock, seeing it was four in the morning. Making her way down the path, her heart skipped when she saw a light from inside the factory.

Who could be there at this hour?

She was tempted to return to the house, to at least alert Binny that she was going to investigate, but decided to peek inside without giving herself away. Carefully and without a sound, Arianne crept to the side of the building, stopping directly beneath the open, lighted window in the saul. Low voices came easily to her ears. Instantly familiar ones.

"I wondered why the sheets had to be rotated before pressed again," said Jonas. "What would happen if we didn't do this a second time?"

"It's all for the texture." Leo's voice was tired but sure. "Skip any one of these steps and the paper won't turn out right. Hasn't she given you a lecture on beauty yet?"

Arianne wanted to march in there and demand to know what was going on in her mill. Confusion—and curiosity—held her back. She knew Leo had just referred to her.

"You mean the one: 'beauty isn't always an opinion?'."

Leo's laugh cut into her spirit. Were they laughing at her? Her pulse quickened for flight to carry her back home so she wouldn't have to hear any more.

"She's right, though." Jonas's voice held her in place. "I can be trained to feel the difference in the finest textured paper, and that's when opinion counts. But beauty itself is one of the true pleasures in life, and that's worth going after. God made a lot of things beautiful, like music and stars and flowers. I think she means that if God created beauty we shouldn't hope to do less."

Leo moaned. "Just shut up and work, will you? Talk like that and I might stop thinking you're all wrong for her."

Arianne sank to a seated position, unable to wipe the spontaneous smile from her face. Leo was tutoring Jonas in papermaking, but Jonas could already tutor her old friend *about her*.

The realization both impressed and offended her. Impressed that Jonas knew her so well, as if he'd been working as hard to know her thoughts as he had been trying to make the best paper. And impressed not only that Jonas was willing to work so hard, but that Leo was willing to help.

Offense rose that Jonas saw the need for extra practice. Was that why Jonas took so easily to the tasks she assigned? Because he'd gone to Leo for help?

Her own heart accused her. So she mustn't have hidden her lack of concentration when around Jonas. He obviously recognized the need to go elsewhere for better tutelage even though some small, overconfident part of herself had thought she'd gotten away with her lack of concentration around him. After all, she'd always believed she could make paper fast or slow, in good health or not, awake or half asleep. Pulp, not blood, ran through Casterton veins.

Arianne retraced her steps back up to her home, more confused than ever.

———

Jonas stifled a yawn after tightening the press on a full set of newly formed sheets. It was a good thing Arianne still assigned him to fill this press, or she might have noticed the sheets already there which he'd made before anyone had arrived that morning. If Gideon had noticed the extra supplies occasionally drying in the loft during these past two weeks, he hadn't said anything. Paper was filling up the factory as if a little elf from the shoemaker's story had joined them.

Jonas worked alone this afternoon, under the reminder that practice made perfect and he welcomed every chance at the vat. Arianne was up in the shop, having received a large portion of the new inventory she'd ordered. Gideon was in the loft, collecting dried sheets ready to be stacked and shipped or sold.

Working night and day had definitely made Jonas a competent papermaker. Merely competent. More than once he'd eagerly compared his paper to the one sheet still hanging in the loft, the page Arianne kept in remembrance of her father. But not a single sheet of Jonas's best effort came close to the light, elegant weight or consistent texture Samuel Casterton had created.

If there was an artist inside Jonas, he had yet to discover him.

"Well, well, so this is the little mill."

Clarence Fitzwater appeared as out of place as a fish that had jumped too high out of the river and somehow landed in the middle of the vat room. He wore polished shoes, white spats and gloves, a high top hat and dove gray suit. He even carried a fashionable walking stick. He was nearly a mirror image of what Jonas had once looked like living in Philadelphia, making him grateful to be wearing his old plain trousers and white cotton shirt, with sleeves rolled to his elbows and out of the way.

Instead of greeting his old friend, Jonas neared him with the first question that came to mind. "Does Arianne know you're here?"

Clarence looked around. "Someone called Tummers drove me from the train station in Williamsport and said I'd most likely find her here at this time of day. Isn't she here in the mill?"

Jonas wiped his hands on the towel hanging from a loop at his waist. "What do you want, Clarence?"

Clarence shot him a smile that Jonas suddenly realized was all too familiar but not as sincere as he'd once believed. "You should welcome me, old friend! I came to help inspire Arianne to move to the city." He looked around the mill again with a gloved thumb beneath his nose. "Get her away from this little old hamlet stuck in the last century."

"Maybe this is exactly where she wants to be."

Clarence eyed Jonas, his gaze lingering on Jonas's apron and old shoes. "No one should be confined to such a backward place. You wouldn't consider it yourself, would you?"

If Jonas was to divert attention away from Arianne, it wouldn't help to have a target on both of their backs. A surprised enemy was a defeated one.

"No, never. I'm here only as long as it takes to make the mill profitable."

Clarence's smile broadened. "Then we all want the same thing —you, me, my father. We all want Arianne in the city. I admit my father doesn't care if she comes as my wife or yours, or even someone else's for that matter. Or no one's. He only wants to make sure she has nothing to keep her here."

Jonas folded his arms, caution gathering in his chest as easily as pulp gathered on the moulds. "Forget that, Clarence. She wants to stay right here." He turned to walk back to the glazing rolls as if finished with the subject, but he silently conceded that without allowing them some hope they might not leave her alone. "If your father wants to hire her as a watermark artist, have him send her a proposal in the mail. There may come a time when she can lend her talent elsewhere." Not that he really believed she wanted to be involved with the Fitzwaters again, after all Jonas had told her of them.

Clarence came up behind him so quickly Jonas was surprised when the other man grabbed his arm. He should have been prepared for Clarence's sudden change from amiable to unpleasant, but somehow he wasn't.

"That might be fine with my father, but not with me. And it shouldn't be fine with you, either. If you want a fair contest for her, you'll have to get her to the city."

He shrugged free. "If you want to woo her, go ahead. But you'll have to do it here. She's not going anywhere."

"Huh. If this place caves in on itself, she won't have a choice, will she?" He turned around to take another look at the humble factory. "I'd hoped nature would have taken care of this with the rains a couple of weeks ago. Look at those water stains. Looks like it wouldn't have been the first times this place flooded. One more might have been the straw breaking the camel's back."

Jonas ignored him, going back to work, something Clarence seemed to notice for the first time.

"Say, look, what are you doing? You're not actually working in this place, are you?"

"Why not? I own a third of it. I want all of my investments to succeed."

"You're an idiot! The only way to get Arianne to the city is if this place fails."

Jonas shrugged. "I never said I wanted her in the city."

Suspicion took over Clarence's face. "So you don't care if she stays here? Even though you're going back to Philadelphia?"

"That's right."

"I thought—"

Jonas faced him. "You thought wrong."

He'd put lying behind him, yet those words couldn't be farther from the truth—words he couldn't have issued so convincingly except for all the practice he'd had pretending gossip about his mother hadn't touched him. Lying might not be right, not even now, but he had no intention of admitting the truth to Clarence.

Clarence must have believed the foul words, because in a moment he smiled again. "Well, then. That clears the path for me, doesn't it?" He saluted Jonas with his walking stick, a quick tap to his forehead.

"Don't count on it," Jonas whispered, but doubted Clarence heard him. The man was already leaving the room, evidently headed up to the shop in search of Arianne.

CHAPTER FORTY

Arianne pulled out the remaining volumes from the box that had just been delivered, *Red Badge of Courage* and an English translation of a Polish novel called *Quo Vadis*. Both books were hard to keep on the shelves, they were purchased so quickly. Sighing with delight, she filled the last two remaining spots on her book display. It was good to see the shelves so full again.

"I know I could have asked you to handle all of this," Arianne said to Phoebe, who had just restocked their supply of pens, "but I have to admit this feels like Christmas."

"Christmas!" Phoebe shook her head. "Hard to imagine on a hot day like this. And you won't get to keep a single item for yourself."

"But I feel like Santa Claus, seeing others get what they want." She laughed. "Things they don't even know they want until coming into this shop."

Phoebe's sigh echoed Arianne's as she looked around at the gleaming, well-stocked store. "It is nice to see things nearly back to normal. And none too late for summer shopping."

Although the strawberry festival opening the summer season was long since passed, they were still enjoying the town's busiest time of year.

"I can't wait to see our regulars from Williamsport back again, once they know things have improved here. That advertisement in the Williamsport papers was a good idea, Ari."

A jingle at the door sounded and Leta came in, soon followed by Mrs. Crane and Mrs. Jenkins. Everyone was eager to see the store renewed to its full capacity—and get a first glimpse of the goods before a flock of Williamsport shoppers came in to buy it all away.

Arianne stayed to enjoy the company of her neighbors, but knew she ought to go to the mill. Jonas and Gideon were likely hard at work. Each time she imagined working with both of them at her side, her heart warmed. She'd once thought the mill had no hope for a productive future, but that was changing. Together they were producing more paper than she'd ever imagined. Thanks to Jonas working nearly round the clock.

The door had been jingling all morning, but when a deep voice called her name, she turned with surprise.

Clarence Fitzwater tipped his top hat her way.

"Mr. Fitzwater," she said, covering her surprise with a welcome she did not feel. "I didn't expect to see you in Cranbury."

He skirted displays and tables to reach her, and she found herself wishing she'd left a few minutes earlier. But it wasn't likely he came all the way from Philadelphia just to shop, so an escape to the mill would have been nothing more than a delay.

"I came for two reasons, Miss Casterton. One, because I couldn't stand another day without your company. And two—" he looked around at the others who didn't bother hiding their well-aimed stares—"is something not nearly so obvious as my affection for you. Is there somewhere we can talk?"

Those were the precise words to fixate every ear in the shop. "I don't have any secrets, Mr. Fitzwater." Immediately she regretted the words, knowing her father and Charlotte might have. But surely Clarence Fitzwater hadn't come about that! "Besides, I thought Mr. Prestwich ended the business association between us?"

"Oh, he did, much to my regret." Clarence smiled in a way that made her think he had no intention of giving up his personal interest in her. "My father and I will always welcome your watermarking talent. Never forget that. You could be famous! And we could bring that fame directly to the hem of your gown."

"Is that why you came all the way to Cranbury, Mr. Fitzwater? I'm sorry you've wasted so much time. I'll be devoting myself to my own mill for the time being."

"But there is a much more serious reason for my visit—tragic, you might say." He hushed his voice to a whisper. "I came to warn you."

Arianne doubted anyone had heard his last words, despite the craned necks, cocked ears and total silence while everyone watched their exchange. Her pulse picked up, convinced he must, after all, be talking about the one thing she most hoped to forget. Perhaps he'd learned her abrupt departure had nothing whatever to do with a headache.

"Follow me," she said, then directed the way through the storeroom and into the kitchen. Binny had left behind the morning dishes to enjoy the store's new stock and plentiful company, so a filled sink and messy table greeted them. She turned to Clarence. "What sort of warning are you talking about?"

His study of the untidiness only made her impatient to have him say whatever he'd planned to share and then depart. She didn't care that he disapproved of the way she lived. At last he looked at her again, and the distaste in his eyes turned to distress.

"I assume it hasn't arrived yet, then."

"What hasn't arrived?"

"A letter—anonymously sent, to the Cranbury post office. Addressed to the entire town in care of its newspaper."

The pulse battering her veins throbbed painfully at her temples. Still, she clung to one last hope that the nature of the letter wasn't what she'd feared. "I cannot imagine what such a letter might say . . ."

"I'm so sorry, Arianne," he whispered, casting aside any

pretense of decorum not only by calling her by name but by stepping so near the scent of his cinnamon bay rum filled her nostrils.
"My sister told me the Kitteridge woman upset you the night of
the business reception. So I paid Julia a visit to tell her she ought
not have been so rude. That's when she told me what she planned
to do. I tried talking her out of it, of course, and I think I did
delay things. But when I saw her yesterday she told me she went
ahead and sent a letter filled with tales about your father and
Jonas's mother."

Arianne grabbed the edge of the sink behind her, dizzy. "Why
would she do such a thing? She doesn't even know me, or my
father."

Clarence leaned even closer, encircling her by placing a hand on
each side of her. "I'm afraid she's intent on ruining your business.
Without an investment so far away in Cranbury, Jonas will go back
to the city and to Julia, where she thinks he belongs. Evidently she
thinks he's taking too long to come home."

Arianne's grip on the sink tightened. "But why hurt my father's
memory—and his business—just to hurry Jonas's return, if the city
is where he truly belongs?"

"Let's leave up to me where I belong, shall we?"

Arianne peered around Clarence at Jonas, who closed the
kitchen door firmly behind him and stepped farther inside the
room. Pushing aside one of Clarence's arms, she slipped away and
approached Jonas.

"Clarence says there is a letter on its way from Julia Kitteridge,
addressed to the Cranbury newspaper. It's about—"

Jonas held up a hand even as he never took his eyes from
Clarence. "I can imagine what it's about." The grim edge on his
face didn't soften, even when he looked at Arianne. "Right now
I'm not sure who wants to hurt the mill more. Clarence or Julia.
But it's clear they only have one weapon: the rumors about our
parents. We can try stopping them, but—"

Arianne nodded eagerly. "Yes! We can tell Mr. Phipps about the
letter, only not to open it. We can destroy it!"

Jonas was already shaking his head. He looked again at Clarence. "If the letter doesn't work, my guess is they'll just tell everyone some other way."

Clarence lifted both of his palms as if he had nothing to hide. "Don't include me, Jonas. I came to help, not to hurt."

"Sure you did." Jonas's tone mocked Clarence's words. He turned to Arianne. "We're going to have to weather this storm. If rumors are all the ammunition they have with which to try ruining your business, it'll pass."

Arianne stared at him, aghast. "How can you say such a thing? Don't you care that people will talk about your mother and my father in a way that isn't true?"

His brows gathered—but in sympathy, not the indignation she felt. He still believed the worst of their parents! She stepped back and looked from one man to the other.

"I want you both to go. Now."

Both opened their mouth to speak, both took a step closer, but Arianne only turned her back. "Please just go."

Someone reached for her, and with a glance she saw the glove on Clarence's hand. "I'll do as you ask, Arianne. But I truly want to help. You know that, don't you?"

She nodded, only because she thought he might not go away if she didn't. She heard the door open then close, sensing rather than seeing Jonas still in the room.

"I wouldn't be surprised if Julia did send the letter, Arianne," he told her quietly. "But it was likely with Clarence's blessing, if not his idea altogether."

She eyed him over her shoulder. "Accusing someone behind his back shouldn't surprise me, since you never confronted my father for what you think he did before he died."

"Was it my place to do that? It was my father's, not mine. If he'd lived."

"Wrong is wrong, and if you believed they were doing something wrong then maybe you should have confronted them. At least then we'd know the truth."

He offered a smile that was altogether lacking any happiness. "Don't turn your anger on me, Arianne. I'm on your side."

Words like that followed a familiar path straight to her heart, but she'd gotten used to ignoring the danger in them. She'd made the fatal mistake of refusing to believe what he'd said about marriage. *Not for me.*

How could she protect her heart if he stayed in Cranbury much longer? Especially when he did what he was doing right now, leaning so close all she had to do was turn to him and she'd practically be in his arms.

"Arianne," he whispered, his tender tone another arrow straight inside, "truth has a way of surfacing sooner or later. That's why we shouldn't even try stopping the letter."

The burden doubled because his words were so opposite of what she thought best. Even if he was right, there was only one way to face such rumors. Not with Jonas at her side, reminding everyone of their parents' sin—but without him.

"Then I'll say it again, Jonas. I want you to leave. Not just the kitchen. I want you to leave Cranbury. Now."

CHAPTER FORTY-ONE

Jonas came around to face Arianne since she refused to turn to him. "I don't want to leave Cranbury," he said. This wasn't the way he'd planned to tell her that, but he obviously couldn't wait any longer.

She folded her arms as if she needed something to hold. He wished he had one ounce of confidence to take her into his arms without fearing she would push him away. But considering she'd just asked him to leave town didn't instill much courage.

"If the rumors are inevitable, it'll just be that much harder if you're here," she said. "Everyone will look at you and be reminded of Charlotte. It'll be worse if you stay."

"Because I'm still a stranger in this town? Even after I've proven I want what's best for you?"

"Charlotte will bear the worst of the blame. She wasn't from around here. Do you want to see that? Make it worse because you'll conjure her image every time someone passes you on the street?"

"You don't have much faith in your neighbors, do you? Or was Binny wrong to defend the town when Tummers said he was worried about me?"

Her only response was to shift—and likely tighten—the hold she had on herself.

He knew there was only one way to get all of this over with, and that was to do what he'd done in Philadelphia. Face the rumors head on. Leaving the city had only let them fester, only to ooze out when he'd returned. The same thing would happen here, every time either one of them came out of hiding.

So he grabbed her hand, pulling her toward the storeroom. The door to the shop was closed, which made him suspect there had been plenty of customers present when Arianne received Clarence. Jonas might be wrong; he might be about to do one more thing Arianne would have a hard time forgiving. But he had to give her a reason to let him stand by her side.

Bursting into the shop, he saw the audience was perfect for his purpose. Mrs. Jenkins was the one who'd held power over the town's reception of him before, and having her on their side now was exactly what they needed.

Now if only he could guarantee to Arianne—and to himself—that the woman really would be on their side.

"What are you doing?" Arianne demanded, attempting to free herself of his grip. But he held fast, never more convinced he was doing the right thing.

Holding up his free hand to draw those present near, he kept her wiggling hand firmly in his. "I wonder if you could spare us a moment of your attention, friends?" Oh, how he hoped they lived up to that endearment . . .

"No, Jonas! How could you do this?" Her free hand tried prying his away, but he held tight. "Let me go!"

"No, Arianne," he said gently. "There's only one way to get through this and that's to get it over with. Facing it." He turned to those who seemed all too eager to listen. He saw another older woman beside Mrs. Jenkins, along with Phoebe and Binny, and Leta Turner. He thought he could count on Miss Turner, at least, to give Arianne hope. Still, there was no real knowing until after he spoke. His experience in the city proved some people needed time to forgive, even if it wasn't their place to offer or withhold such a thing.

"Arianne needs your help. There are some folks from Philadelphia who started rumors about my mother and Arianne's father, and those rumors are on their way here. I guess I don't have to be too specific because your imagination will fill in what I won't say out of respect. You might guess it's about how well my mother knew Arianne's father before my own father died." He saw a few shocked faces and the tilt of one head toward another with a couple of premature whispers. "These are the kinds of rumors meant to hurt someone. Maybe get back at them for doing something they judged as wrong. I can't tell you what to think, but I can tell you to remember the people you'll all be talking about. Good people who loved God and even if they made a mistake it's not our place to say. Because we don't really know one way or another."

Sometime during the course of Jonas's speech, Arianne stopped struggling. She stood stiff at his side, her face turned away and looking at neither him nor her neighbors. Instead she stared at the nearest table, once filled with ample evidence of goods this town valued along with the finest paper produced right here by Cranbury's own.

"You all showed to me how much you care about each other here in Cranbury. It's not that way in Philadelphia—the city of brotherly love isn't so loving when people let rumors cloud memories. I guess they have an excuse, though. My mother never really called Philadelphia home, so they didn't care about her the way you cared about Mr. Casterton. Just remember, Arianne is the only one who'll be hurt when people start talking. So remind her that you're family here, flaws and all."

Finally he turned to Arianne again, whispering, "I'm sorry, Arianne. But getting ahead of the talk is the best way to make it go away that much faster."

Then he let go of her hand, though he did not move away. He stood back, ready to answer the questions, face any accusations, withstand the talk. He'd done it before; he could do it again.

Arianne wanted to flee to her room, bury her head under her pillow and never come out again. How could Jonas do such a thing? He hadn't even defended them!

Maybe it was her place to do so . . . But when she opened her mouth to speak, not a single word came to mind. Shame overcame her, and she was unsure whose shame it was: their parents, or hers for not believing in them, after all.

"Who is responsible for such talk?"

Arianne looked at Mrs. Jenkins, whose tone held all the umbrage she'd first been looking for in Jonas then tried summoning in herself.

"I think the rumors originally started with someone who worked with my family," Jonas said. "I'm not sure. What I do know is that my mother lived apart from me and my father for a while before my father died. I suppose that was why the rumors started. People like pointing to the faults of others, maybe to make them forget their own faults for a while."

"So you believe these rumors, young man?"

Every eye joined Arianne's in staring at him. Arianne didn't even breathe, waiting for his answer.

"I don't know what happened, and I don't care. I know my mother loved God, and if forgiveness is necessary Jesus covered it on the cross. She doesn't need my forgiveness."

"Very noble," Arianne said quietly, unconcerned if anyone else could hear her. "You might as well have admitted you believe them." Maybe she was too late, but she could defend her father now. She turned to the others. "I don't believe any of the rumors. Not a single one."

Then she finally did flee the room.

· · ·

A tap on her bedroom door robbed Arianne's breath. She sprang from her bed, convinced Jonas was on the other side. Would he add another scandal to the one he'd just unleashed downstairs?

But a moment later Leta stepped inside, and Arianne let her temporarily suspended tears flow again. Leta wrapped her in her arms.

"He—he had no right to do that," Arianne cried with a hiccup. "I'll never forgive him. Never."

Leta patted her back, then led her to the edge of the bed where they both sat down. Pulling a handkerchief from under her sleeve, she wiped at Arianne's tears. "He was only doing what he thought best."

"You came to defend him? When he doesn't even believe the best of either his mother or my father?"

Leta shrugged. "I think that's for each one of us to determine on our own. Maybe he has reasons to think the way he does."

"Oh, he's told me his reasons," she said, refusing to admit aloud that he had nearly convinced her as well. "But he should keep them to himself."

"It's my guess that he will, now that he's acknowledged the topic. Why are you so upset with him? He only wanted to let everyone know it's no secret, once the letter arrives. He tried taking the teeth out of it."

"I could have stopped it! Maybe . . ."

But Leta was shaking her head, and the somber look in her friend's eye warned Arianne there was more to Leta's visit than simply to comfort her.

"Arianne, there is something you should know. I didn't say anything because frankly it's none of my business. But maybe I was wrong to shelter you."

"From what?"

Leta twisted the handkerchief still in her hands. "I heard these rumors a long time ago. Williamsport has its own rumor mill, and you know I sew gowns for a number of women from there."

"What!"

"That's not all, Ari. Mrs. Jenkins just now told Jonas she'd heard the same rumors from the Williamsport carriers. She stuck by your father. So they exchanged a few letters when your mother was still married to Jonas's father? It never meant anything. She told everyone to mind their own business." Leta sighed. "I guess she can scold one of our own the way she often does, but she won't allow it from an outsider."

"Oh!" Arianne's tears replenished themselves anew and she threw herself on the mattress. "People have known before I did! And Jonas was right after all. I'm the idiot."

Leta pulled Arianne's hair away from Arianne's soggy eyes. "About what?"

She lifted her head. "He said I didn't have faith in my neighbors. He was right. But, Leta, he doesn't have faith in my father or his mother. Do you believe the rumors? About my father?"

Leta cocked her head to one side. "No, Ari. But then your father was so much like my own, I couldn't imagine him doing anything wrong. Does it make a difference anyway? Who am I to cast a stone? Any of us?"

Arianne lifted her brows. "Even me?"

Leta dabbed one of Arianne's tears. "Even you."

Arianne wasn't sure if she felt better or worse to learn there were those in her very own town who might have had doubts about her father's integrity long ago. But a shout from downstairs interrupted her wish to dwell on it all.

Leta opened the door to better hear the commotion.

"Fire in the mill!"

CHAPTER FORTY-TWO

Jonas was the first out the door after Gideon charged into the room with shouts of a fire. He slipped on the moss-covered pathway but it only hastened his descent.

At once he saw a foreign orange glow from the vat end of the mill. The door was already ajar; he rushed inside and saw the flames were too high to be fought with the one full bucket always kept near the door. He threw it at the flame anyway and it instantly disappeared, hungry flares reaching out in defiance. Kicking that and another bucket out the door, he turned to the items he knew Arianne would risk her own life to save: the moulds.

They were stacked neatly just as he'd left them not long ago— for now beyond the reach of the fire, but with flames in between them and Jonas. Grabbing a chair as a shield, he dashed forward hoping the flames would lick it instead of him.

The moulds, eight in all, took both hands to lift given the unwieldy size of the two largest. Throwing the chair to the side, he grabbed the moulds and jumped back, this time nearly within reach of the fire now concentrated on the fallen chair. He lost no time in going around it to get out of the building.

Tossing the moulds onto the grass, he saw others joining him. He pointed at the buckets already there, seeing Binny and Arianne carried two more. Then he dashed away, rounding the side of the building and scrambling down the wooden stairs leading to the water. Leo had once shown him a pump and hose, kept close to the water and well clear of the fire pit that warmed the macerated pulp.

He stopped short. Clarence was already there, ineffectively pumping with the hose barely attached.

"What are you doing here?" Jonas demanded.

Clarence mustn't have noticed his approach; he looked up with annoyance at the interruption. "Trying to get this thing to work."

"Get out of the way!"

Jonas shoved Clarence, and the man fell back on the rocks lining the bank. But he was on his feet in an instant, rushing to regain control of the pump. Jonas shoved him again. Clarence was better prepared this time and didn't fall back. He returned the push, and Jonas nearly lost his own footing before they exchanged swings. His fist connected to Clarence's jaw and Clarence fell once again.

When Clarence popped up to resume either the fight or another attempt at the pump, Jonas grabbed him by the lapels of his once pristine gray suit coat. "We can fight each other or the fire. Let me get the hose going then you can pump. Clear?"

Clarence threw up his hands with a mix of disgust and capitulation, but stood clear enough for Jonas to properly attach the long rubber hose coiled at the water pump's base. Then he twisted the knob Clarence must have ignored and started pumping. Water—not air—soon poured from the spigot.

"Pump!" Jonas commanded, then grabbed the copper tip at the other end of the hose and pulled it out and between the mill's foundation pillars. He was both irritated over lost time and frantic to put out the fire before it destroyed much of the mill.

The hose was meant to reach all the way into the vat room, the only area likely to catch fire because of the warmed pulp. At such a length it was heavy, and he thanked God Arianne wasn't the one trying to fight this fire on her own. With the hose looped over his shoulder, he made his way through the line of bucket brigadiers. Water was beginning to pour from the nozzle, making the hose heavier still.

"Arianne's in there!"

Jonas spun around at the words. "What!"

Phoebe and Binny, both with buckets, pointed in horror.

Jonas lost no time. He dropped all but the end of the hose and sprayed it forward as if it were a weapon—and so it was, the only one he had.

———

The vat room was engulfed in smoke, though Arianne saw flames coloring the corner. She covered her face in the crook of her arm then plunged through the cloud, knowing without her father's equipment she would never be able to create paper in the only way she knew how. She'd seen a few moulds already on the grass but wanted to save any felts she could carry.

Coughing through her tears, she saw the felts near the vat were already engulfed in the fire. Then she stumbled to the glazing room where smoke invaded as well, each breath slicing through her throat. There, she dragged the massive table to the open entryway and tipped it on its edge. There was no door between the rooms but perhaps the thick tabletop would stave off the fire and smoke until it could be doused. At the very least, it would buy some time to save the glazing rolls her father had made.

Then at the opposite end of the room she threw open the door to her watermarking closet, where she broke through the shutters and cast out her tools, finally crawling out to safety herself.

"Arianne!"

She heard Jonas's voice from inside the mill, through one of the windows at the saul. Frantic, she rounded the building, seeing the bucket brigade of her customers and neighbors in full swing, hoisting water from the river below. She thought of the pump, but when she rushed closer saw its shadow like a huge friendly snake, traveling right inside the building.

"Arianne!" This time the shout came from Phoebe, who nearly dropped the filled bucket before passing it on to Binny next to her. "How did you get out?"

"Through the window in watermark room. Let me help!"

"Jonas is in there—looking for you!"

"What!"

She tripped forward, but Binny grabbed her wrist. "Hold on there—you can't go back in now, not until it's safe."

"But if he's looking for me, he's not safe!"

"He's got the hose," called Leta from nearby.

Arianne went to the front of the bucket line, where Gideon was at the threshold. "Jonas! I'm here!"

But she could see nothing through the thick plume of smoke.

CHAPTER FORTY-THREE

Arianne's voice was like water on the worries flaring inside of Jonas. The sound hadn't come from the other side of the upended table he'd been about to crash through. It had come from the open doorway where Gideon was throwing bucket after bucketful of water.

"Stay out, Arianne!"

"She's fine," called Gideon, coughing. "I won't let her in."

Assured Gideon was close enough to see she was safe, Jonas rejoined the attack against the fire, aligning himself with Gideon and the buckets, aiming the hose where it was needed most. But the fire was winning this battle, at least on this end of the mill. The fire had eaten through the entire wall nearest the vat, and even in the saul the outside clapboards were visible, creaking and crackling as they were devoured. Gideon had done the right thing in coming for help so quickly but the fire already had a significant grip.

Before long they, too, were forced outside as the fire consumed the vat room. Jonas and Gideon retreated, and once outside he tested the length of the hose to learn it barely reached to the window at the saul. But he stuck the nozzle through the window and aimed it directly at the upended table, now fully afire. He tried dousing the glazing rolls in the feeble hope of saving them, but despite their best efforts they, too, fell victim to the flames.

Even after the fire was doused and the roof collapsed into the vat room, smoke poured from cracks and windows still somehow intact on the other end of the charred mill. Jonas continued to direct the water, which sputtered now and then, to the remains of the building. But he knew the damage was great. He saw Arianne, still part of the bucket brigade, staring into the remains of the vat room and knew already what she saw: the vat itself remained, tilted and broken, the crate of rags barely an outline in a heap of ash. The walls and floor were gone, abandoned by the flames after they'd taken whatever they had to offer.

Worst of all the felts were gone, even those in the press. The glazing rolls were destroyed, too. The loft on the farthest end of the mill was still intact, but he feared its roof, left behind without such a large portion that helped to hold it up, could cave in.

He thought of the special page Arianne had left hanging up there, how she'd said when they'd moved items up there under threat of water damage that only God could take down that single sheet of paper. Jonas wondered if it was still there.

He had been able to save the moulds, but everything else was nearly as valuable, particularly the felts. How could he replace them? How could he make this up to Arianne?

While the buckets continued to pour, Jonas kept the hose aimed at the remains to make sure it was well soaked, though the water flow began to ebb. Imagining Clarence still pumping madly —and tiring—gave Jonas a moment of satisfaction, but the image quickly banished Jonas's sorrow over the mill's destruction.

Rage took its place.

Dropping the hose, he marched forward. Arianne stepped out of the bucket line and threw her arms around him as if to make sure he was all right. At any other moment he'd have relished such a sign of her concern, particularly after the way she'd looked at him in the shop not long ago. She herself was dirtied from the smoke, her hair askew, but she was sound, he knew that from the energy of her embrace.

So he didn't take time to speak to her. He pulled himself free then strode on his way, jumping down the steep incline at the back of the mill since the stairs had succumbed to the flames.

When Clarence saw him, he stopped pumping. He was breathing heavily, and his brows rose hopefully.

"Is it out?"

Jonas stomped around the pump and grabbed Clarence by his familiar lapels. "Was it you? Did you start that fire?"

Clarence's eyes puffed wide as a child's balloon. "I—no! No! Not on purpose. Ask that boy. He'll tell you. It was an accident."

Jonas grabbed Clarence's arm and pushed him forward, propelling him up the bank. Arianne was already there so Jonas shouted for Gideon. He came away from what remained of the scorched threshold, with Binny, Phoebe and others suspending the bucket brigade at last. Mrs. Jenkins, who had gone for more help, stood near a team of townspeople who had brought their own variety of buckets.

"Gideon," Jonas said, "what happened? How did the fire start?"

He raised a finger at Clarence. "It wouldn't have happened except for him! He was prowlin' around, sticking his nose everywhere—"

"I was curious about the process, that's all," Clarence said.

"And he stuck that stupid fancy stick of his under the vat, and when a flame struck back he dropped the stick along with a rag in his hand—"

"A handkerchief! That was all . . ."

"A rag! It looked like a rag to me. When the flame took hold, the dolt sprang back so fast he lost his hat, and that went up next. He tried stomping it out and kicked the flaming hat right into the rag bin. It burst into flames, and that's when I ran for help."

Every eye went to Clarence who looked only at Arianne. He shifted his jacket, pulling it straight then adjusting his sleeves as he approached her. He was anything but the slightly dandified gentlemen he'd arrived as, with dirt on his backside and a singed cuff, gloves and hat missing. His attempt at perfect posture and prideful tilt of his chin was not only out of place, the image imprinted itself on Jonas's brain. He vowed never to wear such a suit again.

"It was an accident, Arianne," Clarence told her. Then at least he had the courage to look around, evidently seeing what Jonas did: the cool stares he himself had once suffered. "I assure all of you I did nothing intentionally wrong." His chin went up a notch. "And of course I'll pay for repairs."

Jonas grabbed Clarence's arm again, directing him through the collection of townspeople. "If this is the price to keep all of you Fitzwaters out of our town, away from our business, then it's worth the cost of repairs. I'll take care of it. Now get out of here, Clarence. And take your father's business tactics with you. If we see any one of you again, it'll end in a court of law. Now get going."

———

Arianne watched Clarence walk up the pathway, the one that led to town rather than to her home. He never looked back, and she hoped that was the last she would ever see of him. He may have been sincere about the accidental start to the fire, but she wasn't convinced. Perhaps she would never know the truth.

She walked away from the cluster of neighbors lingering for a closer look at the damage. The remains were too hot and unstable to go inside, so no one dared doing so. And though she knew her friends would readily offer their sympathy and comfort, she wasn't ready for it yet. She stood back alone, staring at the ruins, knowing everything inside was lost. Everything her father had built was gone.

Was this the payment for his sins? Even as the thought took shape, she rejected it. Christ had paid for her father's sins, whatever they were. And for hers as well. God didn't demand more than He'd already provided.

Her gaze traveled slowly, stopping at the surviving moulds. Her eyes moistened again, this time not from smoke but from gratitude.

A lone figure neared as Jonas emerged from among the crowd. He stopped in front of her.

As she stared at him, the horror of having lost the mill eased somewhat. She wasn't alone, at least . . . Not yet.

"We'll rebuild," he whispered. "You know that, don't you?"

We. Such a lovely word. A fresh set of tears rose, but she closed her eyes against them, only nodding.

"It looks like the loft is still intact, and so is your watermarking closet."

She looked again at what was left. "Except for the shutter I broke," she said. "But the tools are safe."

He grabbed one of her hands. "We'll start work as soon as we can—tomorrow, if it's cool and safe enough to start carting out the mess. My guess is Leo and his brothers will do everything they can to help."

"Leo's father helped my father build this one."

"Then he'll know how to build it again."

Side-by-side, they stared at what was left of the building. Arianne believed him; they would build again. A selfish thought pushed its way through the tumult and fatigue caused by fighting the fire. At least this would delay Jonas's return to Philadelphia.

"Did you mean it?" she asked.

He turned to her, closing the gap between them. They might have been alone for all the attention she paid anyone else.

"I was about to ask you the same thing."

"About what?"

He held her gaze steady. "Did you mean it when you said earlier that you wanted me to leave Cranbury?"

"Not if you meant it when you said you didn't want to go. You just called Cranbury 'our' town."

Gently, he placed a hand on each of her arms. "Oh, I meant it," he whispered. "This is home now, because I never want to leave your side."

Then he kissed her, and even though the residue of smoke doubled with his nearness, she vowed the scent would bring his kiss to mind, not the loss that had come before.

CHAPTER FORTY-FOUR

"Was it you who saved the moulds?" Arianne asked, with only the quickest glance into his ready gaze.

Perhaps it was his imagination, but she seemed suddenly shy. Surely she was unsettled over the loss of so much of the mill. Her father's mill. Perhaps he shouldn't have kissed her, knowing she was so vulnerable right now, but he couldn't help himself. Perhaps he ought to let go of her hand, let them join the others alternately watching them and in awe of what havoc fire could bring. Pastor McNichols was calling on the townsfolk to thank God for sparing the forest around them and even their entire town.

But Jonas didn't even loosen his hold on the fingers entwined with his, and he didn't want anyone else's company yet. No matter why, she'd returned that kiss just now, and all he wanted to do now was repeat it.

Reluctantly, he acknowledged they had to face a few matters first. He looked at the mill. It would take time, delaying once again —and for longer this time—the orders they were still trying to keep up with. But time was their only challenge; money he had, and he'd meant what he said about taking care of the price to rebuild.

He squeezed her hand. "I couldn't save the felts, though. I'm sorry about that. Your father brought them from England, didn't he?"

She nodded. "Yes, but they were made in Amsterdam. How did you know my father brought them instead of buying them here?"

"Leo told me." He looked around, half expecting to see the man. But he must have left already. "I have a confession to make. Leo has been helping me improve my skills at the vat."

To his astonishment, her face lacked any trace of surprise. "I know."

"You do?"

"I saw the light. I heard you one night."

He stroked her cheek where a streak of ash was left from the fire. "Yet you didn't say anything."

She looked away. "I thought . . ." Then she looked back, eye to eye. "I was afraid I wasn't teaching you properly. Maybe Leo was a better teacher."

Jonas laughed. "First, Leo is a fine teacher. Knowledgeable and thorough, though I hate to admit that because I still think of him as a rival. He's far more experienced than I. But his paper is a little too thick. I think he's too impatient. He doesn't shake the mould long enough."

Her brows rose. "You could be right."

"I know mine isn't much better—yet—but I have all the patience I need to keep trying. I *will* replace what I sold. That's why I've been working night and day, Arianne. So I can make something that might compare to what you and your father made. I suppose that's arrogant of me, isn't it? To think I could make paper as fine as your father's?"

She shook her head. "I think you can do it," she whispered.

His pulse quickened. She'd never so much as complimented him at the vat. "Do you?"

The smile along with her nod convinced him, making him more determined than ever to complete the task.

———

Arianne's heart beat so rapidly she thought he surely could feel it when Jonas embraced her. She ought to draw herself back; they weren't alone. Her neighbors would think he was just consoling her, but whether she was right or wrong, Jonas's attention felt far more than just sympathy.

Despite that the smoke had cleared, a new wave of dizziness came upon Arianne. She suspected this renewed lightheadedness was more from the kiss than any recent lack of oxygen.

If Jonas was as foggy as she was, he cleared his thinking much quicker than she could. He left her side and began shooing people away from the mill.

"We'll want to make sure it's safe before we can go inside," he said by way of an apology for telling them to go. Then, as they all filed off in various directions, Jonas called for Gideon.

Hearing Jonas taking care of safety matters reminded her again that she was no longer alone.

"I'm going to look at the damage from what's left underneath, by the bank," Jonas said, but he was looking around. "Do you know where Gideon went off to? I'd like him to get Leo."

She looked around. "He may have gone to the loft end, to see if the smoke did any damage."

"Make sure he doesn't go inside, Arianne," Jonas called over his shoulder.

Finding it easier than she expected to follow orders she knew were issued out of concern, she walked to the opposite end of the mill, toward the second story row of opened windows.

Gideon was there, on the ladder her father kept behind the mill that he used to climb up on the roof for repairs.

"Jonas and I were wondering if you might fetch Leo," Arianne called to him. "His family will want to help with rebuilding, and we wanted to talk to them right away."

"The loft looks fine inside," Gideon said with a smile. He climbed down the ladder. "And your papa's paper is still hanging there. Imagine that!"

"Is it?" Arianne was tempted to climb the ladder herself to see, and might have if Gideon's smile didn't fade quite as quickly as it did. He looked both ways, as if to see if anyone else was around.

"I'll go for Leo right now. Only there's something . . ."

"Yes, Gideon?"

"It's just—I saw you've become pretty close to Mr. Prestwich. Kissin' him and all."

Arianne felt the warmth of a blush, even though she'd so easily cast aside any modesty earlier while enjoying that kiss. "I think we were caught up in relief that no one was hurt in the fire. He was trying to help me face what was lost. I'm sorry if we embarrassed you."

"Is that all?" Gideon's relief surprised her. "Just a kiss because he was comforting you?"

"Well, not entirely, but that might explain why he kissed me when others could see."

"That's just it, Miss Ari. I heard him say something to that man who started the fire. Before. Before he came back and started the fire."

"Clarence was in the factory twice?"

Gideon nodded. "I was in the loft, and it sounded like that fella wanted to ask you to marry him or something."

Arianne looked away, annoyed and embarrassed. "If he did, the only answer I'd have given was no."

"I guess so," Gideon affirmed, and even though he sounded relieved he still had a furrow of worry on his brow. "It's just that I don't think you have to worry about that question from Mr. Jonas."

"Why do you say that, Gideon?"

"Because he said he'd be going back to Philadelphia. He said he didn't care if you married that other fella." He frowned. "I just thought you should know."

A lump formed in Arianne's throat. An instant defense came to mind, she was so eager to believe the best of Jonas. But she caught the words without giving them voice. She might at least chastise Gideon for listening in on conversations that didn't concern him, but she knew he'd only mentioned it now out of loyalty to her. She couldn't reproach him for that.

"Thank you, Gideon. Please go for Leo now."

He trotted off, but before he'd even left the yard Arianne made her way around the side of the mill to join Jonas down by the bank.

CHAPTER FORTY-FIVE

"I think we can still depend on the foundation pillars," Jonas greeted Arianne when she joined him at the river's edge. "But I'd like Leo and his father to check." Realizing they were too close to the unsteady debris from above, he pulled her to a safer spot.

A hint of sullenness in her face caught his attention. Maybe the loss of the mill was beginning to settle in. It was likely too unrealistic to hope she still felt some of the euphoria from their kiss.

"We'll be back at work before you know it, Arianne," he said, realizing he was still after her smile.

She nodded but didn't look at him, another troubling sign.

"Are you worried about it? The felts? The vat? We can replace all of that. In fact, the glazing rolls might only need repair instead of replacement. Maybe." Then he stepped closer, taking advantage of the few minutes they would have alone before Gideon returned with Leo. "Did you say your father bought the felts in Amsterdam?"

She nodded again.

Jonas pulled her close. "We can go there to replace them. While the mill is being rebuilt, we can go to Amsterdam."

He wasn't sure her gasp was a good reaction or bad. Hadn't she realized he'd done more than just kiss her earlier?

"I love you, Arianne." Even as he spoke he realized he'd just gone against his earlier resolve. Here she stood, farther than ever from independence, and all he could think of was to convince her he wanted nothing more than to take care of her. "Will you marry me?"

Her eyes widened. "I—I can't believe you just asked me that. What about what you said to Clarence? What about going back to Philadelphia? What about Julia Kitteridge?"

He held her at arm's length. "What's all this nonsense? What did I say to Clarence? I told you I want to stay in Cranbury. Why would either Philadelphia or Julia matter?"

When her eyes sparkled with tears, he was once again struck with uncertainty. Were those happy tears, or sad ones?

"Gideon just told me what you said to Clarence. He said Clarence came here twice, and the first time you told him you didn't care if I married him, that you were going back to Philadelphia once the factory was working again."

He'd known, hadn't he, to leave lying behind? Just now, though, he was never more relieved to straighten out the truth. "I told that to Clarence so I could keep my own element of surprise, in case I needed to attack. No sense Clarence realizing you are my biggest weakness and greatest concern. As it turned out, he did himself in with his own clumsiness."

He could afford to be generous and call the fire the result of Clarence's *clumsiness*, so long as Arianne believed he loved her.

"Then you didn't mean it? You really do want to stay here?"

He leaned so close he nearly pressed his nose to hers. "Arianne. I love you. I know what I said to Clarence, and not a word of it was true. I shouldn't have lied, and to be honest God reminded me of that already. But confound it, the man will use whatever he thinks necessary to get his own way, and I wanted him out of our lives. For good."

One of the tears spilled over onto her cheek. "So . . . You love me?"

He pulled her fully into his arms. "Yes, I love you! I've loved you nearly since the moment I walked into your shop. I will love you until the day I die. I admit this before I should, because I want you to love me in return of your own free will, not just because you might happen to need me. But I want to take care of you for the rest of your life, starting with rebuilding. Besides, if we're to go to Amsterdam together, we'll need to be married first."

"You—you love me?"

He laughed. "Arianne! Haven't you been listening? I will tell you that every day from now on, for the rest of our lives. I love you."

Then she threw her arms around him, her eyes shining without a trace of the somberness she'd arrived with a moment ago.

"How could you doubt me?" he asked. "You're responsible for getting me to search for the papermaker inside of me. And I'll find him, too, and replace every single sheet of that paper. Just watch."

"The paper," she said, and her enticing shyness was back in the demure look she used just now, "was to be used for a Bible for me. A wedding Bible."

"Yes, so Leo told me. Hearing that only made my regret worse, knowing I'm responsible for delaying the day I long for most."

She lifted one brow invitingly. "Perhaps we might make it an anniversary Bible. I'm not sure I can wait to marry you as long as it'll take us to replace that paper."

He smothered her laughter in a kiss.

"Tell me you'll marry me," he said, his lips still pressed to hers. "You haven't said yes. Yet."

"Yes, Jonas. The answer is yes."

"And why . . . Tell me why you'll marry me, Arianne."

She pulled away to stare into his eyes. "Because I love you, Jonas."

EPILOGUE

Seven months later

Arianne looked up when the shop's bell jingled. She'd finished another watermark yesterday, and stood at the counter packing the finished paper for shipment while filling in for Phoebe who had gone home for lunch. She never tired of working in the shop, and often encouraged Phoebe to take a day off now that the mill ran so smoothly since it had been rebuilt. Arianne loved to sell the paper she, Jonas and Gideon made, knowing it was as fine or finer than any of the other items they carried. It might not yet be the consistent quality of her father's, but they were working toward that lofty goal.

A man stood at the shop's threshold, someone Arianne didn't know. With the Christmas season well behind them, it was always a pleasant surprise to greet a new customer, but Williamsporters seldom ventured so far just for a book or stationery this time of year. And this man was definitely from Williamsport, with his top hat and impeccable suit. Perhaps he even came from as far as Philadelphia or Pittsburgh.

He looked around, as if he wasn't sure which area to explore first. But when his gaze landed in her direction, his search stopped altogether. He held a leather satchel in both of his gloved hands, close to his chest, as he approached her.

"This shop is owned by the Cranbury Paper Mill? Run by the Castertons?"

She nodded.

"And are you Miss Casterton? Miss Arianne Casterton?"

"Mrs. Prestwich now, but I used to be Miss Casterton." She loved making that correction since they'd returned from their European wedding trip last fall. After buying felts in Amsterdam, they had stopped in England long enough to visit the grave of Arianne's mother, and to meet several dozen cousins, aunts and uncles. That had been her favorite part of the trip, seeing how enthusiastically Jonas had spoken to them of the paper trade. He'd even asked for demonstrations with their own handmade vats, each and every one giving him tips on how to improve his own technique.

The man in front of her settled his bag on the counter between them, withdrawing something wrapped in tissue. "Then this is yours, if you are the Arianne Casterton who claimed the body of Charlotte Casterton. I'm afraid this has been missing for quite some time. Nearly a year, in fact. It was found in the debris from a train accident that occurred just outside of Williamsport."

Arianne sucked in a breath so quickly it sliced her throat. She'd reached for the packet when he'd first spoken, but now pulled back. Fear hadn't checked her action, but awe had. As if the article had been delivered from Heaven instead of from a cluttered pile of train debris.

He unwrapped the item, and her breathing grew shallow as her pulse quickened. She recognized it immediately as a satin purse once belonging to Charlotte. Little wonder they hadn't any trouble connecting it to the Casterton Paper Mill once it was found; Charlotte always carried a stack of calling cards, proudly ready to direct anyone to the finest paper in Pennsylvania.

A myriad of thoughts swirled inside of Arianne, a mix she instantly regretted. Love and loss were inevitable and familiar, cutting through her as fresh as if the accident had been only yesterday. But the other memory came to mind, about what might have happened between Charlotte and her father before they were married.

They'd put all of those unpleasant memories behind them, she and Jonas. The doubts, the possibility of embarrassment. Few people in Cranbury had ever talked about what might have happened, at least in front of either Arianne or Jonas. It had made it easier to let the past stay there. When Jonas had asked after Charlotte's maid one last time, Arianne hadn't even been disappointed to learn she was still in Europe with no set date for return. Nor had they discussed looking for her when they were there, even though finding the prominent American family she worked for might not have been too difficult. At the very least they might have sent her a letter. But like Jonas, Arianne had finally accepted whatever had happened was between their parents and God.

Perhaps, though, the troubling past wasn't as far behind Arianne as she thought. Not if this purse brought it all back rather than only, simply and purely, the love she still held for Charlotte and her father.

"Thank you," she whispered, letting the man place the purse on the counter rather than in her hands.

The man cleared his throat awkwardly, as if he sensed the great wave of emotion that came with his delivery. "I'm happy to leave it with you then, Miss . . . Mrs. Prestwich. But I wonder if you would mind signing this receipt of acceptance?" He pulled that from his satchel as well, and Arianne mindlessly signed her name. Befuddled, she wrote Arianne Casterton then added the name she was so proud of, Prestwich, at the end.

Then the man left, passing Phoebe on his way out and tipping his hat politely as she made her way in.

"Well, I have just two things to say after seeing a stranger in the shop," Phoebe said as she removed her coat and passed

Arianne to hang it in the storeroom. "One, I guess it's too cold for Mrs. Jenkins to have come out to see who the stranger was, and two, did he buy anything? He looked well-funded, at least—" She stopped herself, staring at Arianne's unresponsive face. "What is it? What's wrong?"

Arianne reached for the purse, seeing her hand trembling as she did so. "It's Charlotte's. They just found it."

"After all this time? My goodness!"

It felt warm in Arianne's hand, despite having just been brought inside. So like Charlotte, welcome to the touch.

Arianne turned without a word, grabbed her coat and left the shop for the mill.

They only worked limited hours in winter, but the mill was still operational even when the river sported a top layer of ice. Even so, wet hands and cold paper didn't function well in a chilly mill. Jonas had installed a coal heater to fight all of the inconveniences, and even a portable generator to macerate the pulp. Something her father had never afforded.

Still, they'd decided to use Gideon only sparingly during the slowest months, so today Arianne found Jonas alone. She was grateful for that; she wasn't sure how Jonas would feel about the delivery.

"Well!" he greeted her with a broad smile and then a confused frown. "An unexpected and definitely welcome visit, but no food?"

She, rather than Binny, always brought his lunch when she wasn't working in the mill and they shared it together even on the days Gideon was there. She held up the purse.

"I brought this instead. It was just delivered."

"What is it?"

"It's your mother's." She watched him carefully. "It was lost in the debris until recently."

"All this time?"

She nodded. His face was somber, but curious.

"Anything inside?"

She nodded again; she could feel its weight, but hadn't looked inside. She hadn't wanted to open it without him. "Will you open it?"

He smiled and received the small pouch, leading her to the table along the side of the wall where they kept the Vaseline. Everything had been rebuilt to exactly replace the old mill; Leo's father had made sure of that. The table was also closest to the new coal heater. She sat beside him, her eyes on Charlotte's bag.

Slowly, wordlessly, Jonas withdrew the contents. Pressed powder in a cloisonné case; an embroidered handkerchief; the expected calling cards, advertising the Cranbury Paper Mill. And a sealed envelope.

"What's that?" she asked.

He opened it, withdrawing a sheet of fine Casterton paper, although Arianne saw immediately it wasn't from the special stock Jonas was, even today, working to replace. "It's a letter. To me."

A small sigh escaped her, one of surprise, delight, and a little fear. Jonas had told Arianne his mother planned to see him that day of the accident. Perhaps she'd planned to give this letter to him then.

His hand shook, ever so slightly, and he handed it to her to read as if he couldn't.

My dear Jonas,

I'm writing this to you because I fear saying the words aloud will be too awkward—though whether for you or for me, I'm not quite sure.

I'll begin with what I know will be easily spoken, but these are words that warrant being repeated. I love you and am so very sorry for being a disappointment to you. I would understand if you thought my move to Williamsport a selfish one. I've certainly accused myself of that as well. But the truth was I thought you would prefer peace over the tension so common between your father and me. Please know that it was peace I sought for all of us as I left the tension, not you, behind. I never wanted to live so far from you.

I wanted very much for you to come with me, or at least to visit me for extended lengths of time. But your father needed you, and I couldn't take you from him, whether he allowed it or not. Although your father and I could not love each other properly, please always know that we both loved you. Never doubt that.

That, my son, is all so easy for me to say as you will see when we're together. But what won't be so easy for me to say, or for you to hear, is what I must address now, as Mrs. Samuel Casterton. I know my marriage came not only as a surprise to you, but at a price as well. The rumors you suffer in Philadelphia have visited Williamsport as well, though I pray they will not follow me to Cranbury.

Perhaps you will want to believe I married Sam because of the financial challenges brought on by your father's will. As loveless a match as that might have been, such an assumption would be more innocent than the rumors accompanying the haste of my marriage.

What I must say and cannot bring myself to have you look upon me as I do, is that I am both guilty and innocent of the charges contained in those rumors. Innocent of breaking the vow of fidelity I made to your father, and yet guilty of emotional loyalty given to another man. I saw in Samuel the kind of man I wanted to marry, the kind of father I would have chosen for you, had I only known what lay beyond the elegant wedding my family and I enjoyed when I married your father.

That is not to say your father failed you, or even failed me. Your father and I failed each other; I didn't blame him for not wanting me any more than I blamed myself for escaping. We chose the path of peace in the end, a peace known only apart.

But you have suffered the rumors, the unkind and uncharitable words spoken with spite and hurt. I do not blame your father for starting the rumors; he was stung by my emotional detachment from him, and perceived my attachment elsewhere, perhaps even before I did. He thought such talk would hurt me. I don't believe he realized you would be caught in the target instead of me. For that I am truly sorry, and I am convinced your father would have been just as sorry.

Each of us are flawed, my dear son, and in desperate need of Someone to forgive us of our mistakes, both intentional or misguided. Our flaws are greatest when they touch others we love. I grew to love a young girl named Arianne, who has matured into a charming young lady. Through her, I fell in love with her father, but only from afar while I was married to your father. Since knowing them, I have enjoyed my greatest happiness as part of their family. I hope one day you will want to join us.

I am forever your loving mother.

Arianne didn't realize she'd begun crying until a teardrop landed on the paper, small and sparkling but barely absorbed because of the glazing. She brushed it away before raising that same hand to skim others from her face.

Jonas took her in his arms and still more tears replaced those she'd scrubbed away. She could tell Jonas fought his own battle with tears.

"It doesn't make it any easier after all, does it?" he asked. "The loss, I mean. I'm sorry I believed the worst, even for a little while. But you never doubted them, did you, darling?"

"You're right that it doesn't make the loss any easier. Will it ever get easier, do you think? Missing them?"

He touched her damp cheek with a thumb, gently rubbing the remnant of tears away. "It will. I know it will. The closer we get to our own eternities. We'll all be together then."

She nodded, welcoming his kiss that never failed to bring all good things to her: comfort, love, hope . . . And joy, even in the midst of longing for a future not yet seen.

<<<<>>>>

Thank you for reading *The Cranbury Papermaker*! I hope you enjoyed the story. If so, please consider leaving a rating or review on Amazon. Thank you!

ALSO BY MAUREEN LANG:

Cranbury Novels

The Cranbury Papermaker

The Cranbury Toymaker

The Cranbury Picturemaker

The Cranbury Troublemaker

Americans in the First World War

Pieces of Silver

Remember Me

Europeans in the First World War

Look To The East

Whisper on the Wind

Springtime of the Spirit

Split Era/Contemporary/Victorian

The Oak Leaves

On Sparrow Hill

The Gilded Legacy

Bees in the Butterfly Garden

All in Good Time

The Matchmaker's Match

Contemporary

My Sister Dilly

Novellas

A Prairie Romance Novella Collection

ALSO BY MAUREEN LANG:

Cranbury Novels

The Cranbury Papermaker

The Cranbury Toymaker

The Cranbury Picturemaker

The Cranbury Troublemaker

Americans in the First World War

Pieces of Silver

Remember Me

Europeans in the First World War

Look To The East

Whisper on the Wind

Springtime of the Spirit

Split Era/Contemporary/Victorian

The Oak Leaves

On Sparrow Hill

The Gilded Legacy

Bees in the Butterfly Garden

All in Good Time

The Matchmaker's Match

Contemporary

My Sister Dilly

Novellas

A Prairie Romance Novella Collection

AFTERWORD

A Note from Author **Maureen Lang**

I've always loved paper, which made my research for *The Cranbury Papermaker* all the more fun. As with any tourist of a trade, however, I hope all true paper artists will accept my apologies if I mistakenly misrepresented any part of the ancient craft. My heart is certainly with all those who love papermaking!

The Cranbury Papermaker is my first venture into independent publishing, but I promise you it won't be my last. **If you enjoyed this story and would care to leave a review on Amazon, I would very much appreciate it.**

Please visit me on Facebook or GoodReads or sign up for my newsletter on my website at www.maureenlang.com.

I love hearing from readers!
    Email me at: maureen@maureenlang.com
    Or snail mail:
    P.O. Box 23
    Belvidere, IL 61008